A PACT OF SILENCE

A PACT OF SILENCE

A Kavanagh and Salt Mystery

David Armstrong

This first world edition published 2010
in Great Britain and in 2011 in the USA by
SEVERN HOUSE PUBLISHERS LTD of
9–15 High Street, Sutton, Surrey, England, SM1 1DF.
Trade paperback edition first published
in Great Britain and the USA 2011 by
SEVERN HOUSE PUBLISHERS LTD.

British Library Cataloguing in Publication Data

Armstrong, David, 1946–
 A pact of silence.
 1. Kavanagh, Frank (Fictitious character) – Fiction.
 2. Salt, Jane (Fictitious character) – Fiction. 3. Cold
 cases (Criminal investigation) – Fiction. 4. Murder –
 Investigation – England – Fiction. 5. Shropshire
 (England) – Fiction. 6. Detective and mystery stories.
 I. Title
 823.9'14-dc22

ISBN-13: 978-0-7278-6971-5   (cased)
ISBN-13: 978-1-84751-309-0   (trade paper)

All Severn House titles are printed on acid-free paper.

Severn House Publishers support The Forest Stewardship Council [FSC],
the leading international forest certification organisation. All our titles that
are printed on Greenpeace-approved FSC-certified paper carry the FSC logo.

Typeset by Palimpsest Book Production Ltd.,
Falkirk, Stirlingshire, Scotland.
Printed and bound in Great Britain by the
MPG Books Group, Bodmin, Cornwall.

Language most shows a man;
speak that I may see thee.

Ben Jonson

For my Mother

April 1913 – July 2010

PROLOGUE

Shropshire
Saturday morning, June 24th 1969

There are, of course, many ways to die, and some of them are very unpleasant indeed.

'Oy, get the hose . . .' called Gary.

'You what?' shouted Terry as he shovelled ballast into the throbbing cement mixer.

'*Get* the hose,' repeated Gary, grinning, and nodded his head in the direction of the trench twenty yards away.

Young Terry uncoiled the end of the thing and pulled it across the unmade ground.

Gary climbed up onto the battered yellow digger and started it up. It belched out clouds of black diesel smoke in the bright morning air.

'Lie it in there and turn her on,' he said as he lowered the bucket into the horizontal position.

The tinny sound of Radio One came out of the transistor radio perched on a rough scaffolding plank adjacent to the trench.

Terry laid the end of the water hose in the digger bucket and turned it full on. At first, the water splashed around and a good deal of it sprayed out, but it was soon a foot deep and, the end of the hose now submerged, the bucket silently filled with gallons of water.

Led Zeppelin played 'Whole Lotta Love'. The young men couldn't see him, but they could hear Joe, their twenty-five-year-old foreman, join in the odd few words of the frantic song as he heaved another spadeful of earth out of the soak-away he had almost finished digging.

Gary shoved the vehicle into gear, swung it round and trundled towards the deep trench, water spilling out as the digger rocked its way towards the oblivious foreman. A little nervously, Terry walked behind.

The bolder young man lurched the thing to a halt above the edge of the chasm.

Joe looked up and said, with all the authority vested in his superior position, 'Just you *fucking* dare . . .'

They were the last audible words he ever spoke.

Gary hit the lever and, in an instant, the bucket disgorged its watery load. But the sides of the trench were not supported in any way and as the huge grey tyres jarred on the earth there, the trench collapsed in on the man, immediately transforming it into a deep morass of red mud.

'Fucking hell!' screamed Terry at his mate, reaching down into the swamp and trying to grasp the foreman's slithering hands. 'Fucking hell, what have you done!'

Gary thrust the machine into reverse and scrambled it back from the edge of the fallen trench. 'Get the shovels, quick,' he yelled, jumping down, the engine of the JCB still throbbing.

Terry raced back over the rough ground and grabbed a shovel from the cabin. They dug at the sucking mud again and again, but their efforts were useless: the trench was deep, and their desperate attempts to reach the man made absolutely no impression on the swampy mess.

An hour later, they knelt there in silence, filthy and sweating, their tears of anguish mixed with looks of stunned incomprehension at what they had done.

'What are we going to do?' said Terry quietly. 'You've killed him.'

'We,' said Gary, looking up and meeting the other boy's eyes. '*We*.'

'You fucking said do it,' said Terry, again starting to weep. 'It wasn't me . . .'

'It was both of us,' said Gary calmly. 'You got the hose . . .'

'You told me to,' he began.

'It was both of us,' repeated Gary firmly. 'We've got to think,' he said. 'We've just got to think.'

By eleven thirty, they had filled in the trench to the level of the surrounding ground and silently started to gather their few things together. In the little wooden cabin that the site workers used to make tea and fry bacon and sausages, Terry pointed to the foreman's canvas snap bag and said, 'What about that?'

Gary opened the flap and looked at the flask of tea, Penguin chocolate biscuit and half-eaten sandwich still wrapped in its greaseproof paper.

'You gonna take it?' asked Terry.

'Be better if you do,' said Gary.

'Me?' said Terry. 'Why me?'

'You're going to football. You can dump it . . .'

'Don't be stupid,' said the younger man. 'I can't go and play football. Not now. Not after this.'

'You've got to,' said Gary. 'We've both got to do exactly what we normally do. You go and play, and I'm going to Jenny's house.'

'I'm not taking it,' said Terry. 'You get rid of it.'

'OK. Let me think,' said Gary. 'It's probably better if we leave it here. It's too late to put it in . . .' And his voice trailed off at the thought of the interred man, his mouth and throat full of the sandy earth that had killed him.

Gary looked out from the little wooden shed at the half-built housing estate with its array of detached houses and large bungalows. 'In the show house,' he said. 'It's nearly finished. No one'll be going up there now.'

The two young men entered the open front door of plot number 33, took off their caked and muddy boots and climbed the unpainted staircase to the top of the house. Terry watched as Gary mounted a trestle and, using his strong arms and elbows, levered himself up through the loft hatch and into the roof space.

He straddled across the joists until he was in the furthest corner of the eaves, pushed the little canvas bag down into the roof insulation and fully concealed it.

Ten minutes later, the young men stood outside the metal gates of the building site as Gary padlocked it shut. 'We all left together. OK?' he said. 'I'll chuck the key in the stream.'

'OK,' said Terry.

'It never happened,' said the other man. 'Just forget

everything,' he said. 'That's all we gotta do. And me and you, we never say anything. Not to anyone, ever. OK?'

Terry looked back through the gates, nodded his agreement and they began the walk down the deserted road towards the town.

ONE

Both Frank Kavanagh and Jane Salt were aware that they hadn't had sex for a month. And right now, each of them wished that it had been a month and one night.

They lay there, completely still, quiet and embarrassed by the silence that hung heavy between them.

Eventually he breathed a sigh of the kind she'd heard him exhale a thousand times before. But they both knew that this was not the genuine sound of sexual repletion, merely a false and hollow echo of a noise that was meant to express that feeling.

And now they lay there, welded together in the silence and grateful for the darkness of the bedroom blackout blinds.

After what seemed a decent interval, the kind of interregnum that she always liked, when he held her and, in happier times, they might have murmured a word or two of love, he pulled away from her.

He sighed once more, as if to deny anew the barren nature of what had taken place between them during the last ten minutes.

This was their elephant in the room, but an elephant with a skin a deal more sensitive than the mammal's impervious hide.

Without looking at him, she handed him the box of tissues from the bedside table.

The trouble with people who know too much is that they know too much. Stupid people, people who are less aware of what's going on, they have a much better chance of relationship success, thought Salt.

Detective Constable Jane Salt – and Detective Inspector Frank Kavanagh, for that matter – was not stupid and they were only too poignantly aware of what, somehow, they had

lost somewhere. And what had got lost between them was
not going to be easy to find, for it was not one thing. It
was simply but undeniably the fact of love having leached
away, unseen, from their relationship.

'We should get away,' he said.

Yes, from one another. was her first uncharitable thought
as she lay there, her eyes closed. She said nothing.

'A few days by the sea, maybe?' he continued gamely.

'Can you pass me the tissues?' she said.

'Sure,' he said, and passed her the box.

Whether or not there *is* a tide in the affairs of men, there's
certainly a tide in the course of relationships, even though
it might be as imperceptible as the waters that silently engulf
the sands of Morecambe Bay and lure the unwary to their
watery graves there.

He was filled with regret. He knew he'd started to value
her less and withdraw from her. And now that he'd finally
succeeded in driving her away, when she considered leaving
him – something which she did on a daily, sometimes hourly
basis – she was able to imagine it with no sense of loss, but
only relief.

'What do you think, then?' he said. 'We had talked about
going to Crete, you remember?' he offered hopelessly.

'Let's see,' she said. She turned back the duvet and stepped
away to the bathroom. 'And anyway,' she said, standing at the
bedroom door but not looking back at him, 'with your ankle,
I don't think you'll be walking the Samorian Gorge for a
while.'

It had been two days now since he had twisted his left ankle
playing five-a-side football with a bunch of mostly much
younger colleagues. It was sprained, strapped and heavily
swollen. He'd not been into work since the evening of the
injury and he wouldn't be going back for a few days yet, he
reckoned.

It was time to stop playing football. It had been time to
stop playing football a dozen years ago, probably, but he'd
carried on, and now this.

He lay there and listened as she closed the bathroom door.
He stared up at the ceiling and knew without any doubt that
it was going to be a future without the woman who was,

even now, washing him from her on the other side of that door.

Ten minutes later, she came back into the bedroom wrapped in a white bath-sheet and said only, 'Frank, I can't go on like this . . .'

TWO

Shropshire
Tuesday June 27th 1969

'So, what time do you say you left the site?' asked the police sergeant.

Gary glanced across at Terry. All of them were smoking. The sergeant a pipe, the two boys, Park Drive from the twenty packet that sat on the Formica-topped table in front of them.

Terry's look said to Gary: just tell him the truth. Let's admit it and go to jail, and that'll be that. We couldn't help it, but they're going to find out. There's no way that they can't. It's written on my face, it's there in my eyes. I've nearly blurted it out with every minute that's passed. I've *got* to tell someone.

Gary pursed his lips, and said to the policeman, 'Don't say anything to the boss, will you?'

'Why?' said the sergeant. 'What you been up to?'

''Cos we nipped off a bit early; it was a little bit before twelve,' said Gary. 'It must have been only about ten to.'

'And you say you were all together?' said the sergeant.

'Yes, of course,' he said.

'And you all nipped off a bit early?' He smiled and, in his diligent hand, scrawled the time down on the missing person report sheet.

'It was a Saturday morning,' added Gary, as the sergeant wrote. 'You know, we always get away a bit before. There was no one around. There never is.'

'And there was only you three on the site?' continued the sergeant, and this time he looked across at Terry.

Terry looked to Gary, seeking assurance. His mate gave him an imperceptible nod, as much as to say, Yes, go on, tell him.

'We'd a bit of a driveway we were finishing, so the boss, you know, Mr Penley, he said we could work if we fancied it. Overtime,' he added.

'Time and a half,' said Gary, sensing that Terry might begin to falter.

Again, the sergeant wrote, and then he picked up his shallow-bowled pipe and tapped out the ashes. 'And then what?' he asked Terry as he reached across to his tobacco pouch.

'How do you mean?' asked the lad.

'You all left together. What did you do then?'

'I'd got a game,' he said. 'So I went to the Cross Keys. It's where we meet—'

'How d'you get on?' the sergeant asked as he tamped fresh tobacco down into his pipe.

'Won,' he said. '3 – 1. We went top of the league.'

Everyone who followed local football knew Terry Morgan. He'd scored goals at every level since he'd been in the primary school team.

'You score?' asked the sergeant, leaning back and lighting his pipe. He held the box of Swan Vestas matches over the bowl as he puffed away.

'I got two,' said Terry with his usual modesty.

The sergeant exhaled long and contentedly. He gave the clear impression of a man who was comfortable in his skin, at ease with his work, and who wouldn't wish to be anywhere else right now.

'And where did you go, Gareth?' he asked the other young man, the youth's full name an indication of the formal nature of proceedings.

'To my girlfriend's,' he said.

The sergeant jotted down the answer. 'Right. And what about Joe?'

'I don't know,' said Gary, perhaps just a little more quickly than he'd meant to speak the words.

'Didn't he say anything?' asked the copper.

'Didn't need to, I suppose,' added Gary. 'You know, he always has a drink on a Saturday afternoon. Always.'

Oswestry was one of those towns whose ancient charter allowed the residents – on the strength of their livestock trading history – to be served alcohol throughout the day on Wednesdays and Saturdays, something which many of the folk who lived there took full advantage of, notwithstanding that few of them would have known an Aberdeen Angus from a Lincoln Red.

'So you went to the Keys,' repeated the policeman, glancing at Terry. 'Yes,' said Terry.

'And you went to your girlfriend's, Gareth?'

'Yes,' he said.

'Where she live?' he added, and wrote down Jennifer Stannard's address on the far side of town. 'And wandering Joe headed off for a drink?'

The 'wandering Joe' said it all. The sergeant had absolutely no doubt that Joe would turn up. And it had not crossed his or anyone else's mind that the foreman could possibly have come to harm at the hands of these two young men, or anyone else for that matter. It simply didn't occur to him. The days of hard-faced perpetrators of heinous crimes disporting themselves on television to initially credulous, but eventually increasingly sceptical, viewers was still many years away.

Joe lived in a village ten miles away over the border in Wales, and often stayed in town drinking until he staggered back to a mate's house where he would spend the night on the settee. Occasionally, he'd stay in the town on Sunday, too, only getting back to his parents' house when he could cadge a lift back there that evening. No one, therefore, had voiced any concern about the fact that the man might actually be missing until he failed to turn up for work at eight o'clock on the following Monday morning.

The clerk of the works had opened up and the police had eventually driven up to the site at the top of the town and called the boss, the big local builder, Phil Penley, over for a word. Penley directed them to the two young men who had opted to work with Joe on the previous Saturday morning.

The two cops, their white and turquoise Ford Anglia parked on one of the many unmade roads on the site, had a quick look around, exchanged a few words with the lads, and left.

On the following day, when there was still no word on Joe Tate's whereabouts, the town's police inspector ordered a local pond be checked and the canal that skirted the edge of the town was dredged for fifty yards either side of the lock gate where people sometimes crossed the still, murky water.

The hedges and verges that fringed the lanes and B roads

that left the town in the direction of the man's home village were also examined. But nothing was found and so now, in the middle of Tuesday afternoon, the three men sat in the smoke-filled room in the police station.

'So, what do you reckon's happened?' asked Gary boldly.

'No idea, son,' said the copper. 'If he'd had a scrap in town, we'd have heard. We've been round all the pubs, but no one saw him. He locked up and you three all parted at the top of Water Street. And that's the last anyone's seen of him. I suppose he's got pissed somewhere or other and then he's had an accident. He'll turn up, or at least we'll find him,' he added more seriously. He got up from his chair and opened the window in the painted room. 'Anyway, you two had better get back to work,' he said. 'If you hear anything, anything at all, let us know.'

''Course,' said Gary.

'Yes,' added Terry, and the men left the police station together.

THREE

Deciding to leave is the hard bit. Leaving itself is relatively easy. By the time you start packing your favourite things, stuffing the suitcase with the bits you need, that decision's already been made, and now, you're just going through the actuality of the thing you've imagined a hundred times before. And, like most things that we fear, the fear itself is invariably worse than the deed.

Salt had kept waiting for the dreadful feeling to descend upon her. But it didn't come, and she actually found herself humming some tune as she pushed tights and knickers and bras into the bag, along with this jumper, that skirt and jeans and those couple of tops.

But deciding *where* to go, how to perpetrate the escape itself, that had been the hardest thing of all.

At least she'd got a little time. She was going to take the two weeks' leave that was owing to her. But where to go? She'd had crazy ideas these last few weeks as she'd weighed the options. Mad, outlandish, absurd. She'd even walked into a travel agent one day, sat down amongst the brochures and found herself looking at the itinerary of a Mediterranean cruise ship.

She had close friends and even some family that, at a push, she could have stayed with. But, as she'd run the notions through her mind, this or that person ruled themselves out of her reckoning. Was she supposed to turn up on her increasingly frail parents' doorstep in north London and invite herself home for a few days? Hardly. Her fashion-wholesaling brother, Howard, was protective and had always been caring of his younger sister in his own brusque way. He'd certainly always 'be there for her', she knew that. But she couldn't bear his bossy wife, Esme, and the idea of sharing her present relationship plight with them was anathema. And anyway, right now, her brother's big house in Golders Green was nowhere near far enough away from Kavanagh's flat in Crouch End, the flat that they virtually shared these days.

There were friends that she had a drink with, friends from her book club, and a couple of close colleagues that she was always glad to have a glass of wine with after work, but no, they weren't right for this particular situation either. She even had friends with whom she shared little bits of lascivious talk – girly, giggly, tipsy times that now seemed ridiculous.

Oddly, the person that she thought most likely she might be comfortable with was three hours away, in distant Shropshire.

Salt and Carrie Prowse had met at police training college years ago. But the job hadn't suited Carrie and she'd stayed in the force for only two years. Handling drunks and trying to separate fighting youths on Saturday nights – without herself becoming a casualty – wasn't her idea of a good way of spending the next couple of decades and, instead, she'd done a further degree, retrained and eventually joined the probation service.

She'd done well, and she was now a senior case handler. But it wasn't her tough-love probation-officer skills that Salt was interested in just now. When things had been rocky for Carrie a year or so ago, the two women had had lots of late-night phone calls. They'd also got together a couple of times, once up in Shropshire, and once in London. But, what was most important to Salt right now if she escaped to Carrie, were the two-hundred miles that were going to separate her from Kavanagh.

Kavanagh wasn't humming any tunes. He glimpsed anew the abyss that lay ahead of him and he contemplated a life without his woman with dread.

This wasn't the fear he'd experienced a few weeks ago in a service station on the M6 when he was one of a dozen coppers confronting a gang of aggressive lorry hijackers, nor even the time he'd disarmed a bloke wielding a knife in a Camden siege ten years previously, an event which still occasionally woke him in a cold, four-in-the-morning sweat.

No, this wasn't macho, bravado-inspired fear, this was 'can't eat, can only smoke and drink and contemplate folly' brick-in-the-stomach fear. It was the fear of the loss of his woman and the prospect of loneliness.

'And Crete?' he said plaintively as she stood at the sitting-room door, her coat on; Kavanagh was standing at the window, looking out.

'You never liked flying anyway,' she responded.

'Why Carrie?' he asked like a petulant child.

'Carrie's a good friend . . .' she said quietly.

'You haven't seen her for a year,' he dissented.

'You don't have to be in touch with real friends all the time,' she said. 'They endure.' Then she added a little cruelly, 'Do you have any friends, Frank? Real ones?'

'Davey Whisker,' he said, 'we're always on the phone.'

'Davey Whisker didn't even send us a Christmas card. He phones you once a month. And only when Preston North End have won. He's always drunk, and then you both shout down the phone at one another, talk at the same time and neither of you remembers a word of the conversation the following day.'

'That's mates, I guess,' he said, turning.

'Not for me it isn't,' she said unassailably.

He tried one last throw. 'Why don't I come to Shropshire, too? We could make it a sort of healing trip?'

Salt almost smiled, for she knew how much saying such a ludicrous, new-age thing was costing him. 'You know . . . I do love you, Frank. But right now, I have to have some time alone . . .'

He did 'know'. She went to the bedroom to collect her bags and then came back into the room, holdall and suitcase discreetly out of sight near the front door.

They met halfway across the room. 'Give me a few days and then let's see,' she said and kissed him gently on the cheek. 'Maybe you could come up then . . .'

It was a nice thought, but they both knew it wasn't going to happen.

He stood at the bay window and watched as she got into the minicab. She didn't even look back.

FOUR

Shropshire, 1972

I f necessity *is* the mother of invention, then adversity can certainly be a useful spur.

Gareth Thomas worked hard. He had a quick brain and strong arms and, even more importantly, an iron will. These things might not have been much good for writing short stories or working out long multiplication in the classroom, but they served him well in other ways. As a fourteen-year-old, he'd had paper rounds in the morning and evening, and he worked Saturdays with a mate of his father's carrying hods of bricks up scaffolding and mixing barrow-loads of cement down below.

By the time he was employed as a young bricklayer on Phil Penley's building site at the top of the town as a nineteen-year-old, he was declaring no more of his earnings to the Inland Revenue than any of the other blokes subcontracted there. And although almost every other man on the site was also inclined to have a bit of this, that and the other away, Gary was quicker off the mark than any of the others to spot a decent bit of skirting board, the odd stair rail, post or newel, a few feet of copper pipe lying around or even half a bag of roofing nails.

If there wasn't any overtime to be had at the weekend, he'd do some tree felling with a mate, charging the owner to bring down the rotten oak or ash in his back garden, and then flogging the sawn logs to some other householder from the back of his battered old pick-up truck.

A year after the accidental killing of the foreman, Gary married nineteen-year-old Jennifer, the girl he'd grown close to throughout their last couple of terms at school together. He was a strong, well-built, good-looking young man who could have had more or less any of the local teenagers – well, at least the ones who were not academics and planning to head off to university after they'd done their A levels – and, in brutal truth, Jenny Stannard was a plain sort of girl.

But Gary had his own agenda, and he knew instinctively that it was better to have an undemanding young woman at home, someone who would make supper and clean his clothes and eventually bear him children, rather than a flighty girl who would always be wanting this and that and who would make it more difficult to achieve the very thing that was to be the real work of his life.

He worked hard and put in long hours and even now he thought little of the summer morning twelve months earlier when a bit of innocent high spirits had led to a man dying. It was regrettable, of course, but it had happened and there was absolutely nothing that he could now do about it. In a curious sense, if he felt anything at all, it was that he owed it to the deceased man to work hard and do well. He certainly didn't lose any sleep about it. He'd wake to the very occasional nightmare, covered in sweat and barely able to breathe, his mouth full of sandy earth, but in his rational moments, during the day-long, waking, working hours, he knew very well that there was little chance of the innocent killing of the foreman now being discovered.

A year or so into their marriage, the van he drove now was only a couple of years old and it had his name nicely painted on the side. He'd been able to buy it because he'd a growing reputation as a young man who was reliable: if he said he'd turn up on Saturday morning, or even on Sunday afternoon, to fix a slate or seal a leaking gutter, he'd be there.

In a small town, your reputation's everything. In London and Manchester, of course, your client's never going to see you again and 'tradesmen' can get away with anything: overcharging, shoddy workmanship or downright theft. In this little town, though, you had to keep the people you worked for sweet, and Gary did exactly that.

But he was also aware that even if he worked – as he often did – twelve or fourteen hours a day, and for six days a week; if he did decent work and charged fair rates, even then, the only thing he would end up with in five years' time was a bigger van and a good few quid in the bank.

He could see only too well that buttering bricks with sloppy mortar was fine so far as it went, but securing the land and paying someone else to build houses on it was where the real money lay: it was the man who *owned* the fields and paid the contractors who was really coining it. But how to make the leap? That was the question. For that, you needed either a backer, or a decent bit of luck. And Gareth Thomas was about to get both.

Jennifer's father had run a small haulage business in the town for as long as anyone could remember, his three blue and red articulated lorries hauling nothing but pit props, his sole contract with the National Coal Board, the work guaranteed and as regular as clockwork.

Truth to tell, her father, Jack Stannard, had never been that keen on Gary: there was something that, in spite of his hard work and the young man's quiet, determined nature, he just didn't warm to. But, on the other hand, it was clear to him that the man was going to do alright. He was going to make a living and it'd be a decent living unless he was very much mistaken. More to the point, his only daughter clearly loved the young man and they'd be making him a grandfather one of these days, so what was the point of making an enemy of the boy?

And then, in January of 1972, two things happened: the National Union of Mine Workers put in for a forty-three per cent pay rise and, not surprisingly, the National Coal Board declined to pay it. A strike was called and Jenny's father, who'd always been something of a closet Tory, took on the haulage work that many of his competitors were either too afraid, or too conscience-stricken, to undertake.

Those three trucks had, until recently, hauled timber pit props up and down the mid-Wales roads from the dark forests where the conifers grew in their millions. Now, he immediately switched to transporting electric fires, portable gas heaters and paraffin stoves as the media stoked fears of the arctic gloom that was about to descend upon the country, and every household stockpiled candles, lamps, blankets and hot-water bottles against the cold, dark winter that was certainly about to come.

In only a few weeks, Jack Stannard's fleet grew from three lorries to a dozen.

He paid his men a premium for driving the things and, although they didn't much care for having the occasional rock hurled at their cabs and even less for being spat at as they swung their trucks through picketed factory gates, bulging pay packets took care of any feelings of guilt or solidarity with the striking miners that they might have otherwise felt.

The strike was settled in only a few weeks and things soon returned to normal but, by that time, Stannard had cash coming out of his ears and he'd have had no more idea what to do with it than anyone else had his son-in-law not spoken to him about a 'bit of business' he'd got wind of.

A building contractor from over Wrexham way, just a few miles over the border into Wales, had overreached himself on a speculative land purchase. He'd bought twenty acres of prime land on the understanding – with a quiet word from a golfing friend on the planning committee – that housing development planning permission for the land would go through on his nod, and was therefore more or less guaranteed.

But it wasn't. A local property owner, a friend of the chair of the same planning committee, was very much less sanguine about the prospect of seeing an estate of a hundred executive houses obstruct his sylvan view.

The planning application came up for discussion at the council and was declined. When the decision was appealed against, it was thrown out again. The Wrexham contractor was now saddled with twenty acres of land that he couldn't build on, and for which he'd paid nearly twice the market price.

He laid off a few of his workers as he tendered to secure a couple of other contracts, just to keep the firm going through this difficult time. But he was undercut by other builders who weren't carrying his overheads, and soon the word was out in the trade that he was in trouble. It might not have been completely true, but this kind of thing is the kiss of death for any building firm: no one's going to sign a contract with a builder who might run out of cash for supplies, or to pay his men's wages halfway through a job.

Two months later, the depot was locked and creditors were angrily massing outside the owner's home.

Gary confided to his father-in-law that he'd heard that the man was keen to get rid of his plant before the bankruptcy administrators got their hands on it. If they came and flogged it off to the highest bidder, the man would get nothing whatsoever and even his creditors would be paid only some paltry percentage of what they were owed. 'If we get in quick,' said Gary, 'I can get it at a snip.'

'How much?' asked the older man.

'About twenty grand for the lot. Trucks and bulldozers, diggers and ramps, lifters and scaffold, right down to the generators and jackhammers. Everything. He wants more than that, but he's not in a good position. I reckon I can get it for twenty grand if I've got the cash. I'll pay you back within two years, I guarantee it.'

In nine months' time, and now aged only twenty-three, Gary had a good deal of decent knock-down plant, and had accumulated a workforce of fifteen blokes to use it as he built a couple of houses here, did a barn conversion there, and still worked harder and longer than any of the men whose wages he was paying. And the posts, newels and bits of copper pipe didn't walk off Gary's sites. Ever. When he caught a chippie with a few quids' worth of electrical cable in his tool bag, the man got a broken nose and a split lip for his trouble and didn't even come back for his wages.

Yes, hard work will get you some way, but to really get moving, to make serious money, there was nothing like a bit of luck, and for Gary Thomas, that luck was especially sweet if it came to you on the back of another man's misfortune.

FIVE

Shropshire, 2010

S alt was emotionally exhausted and slept on the Virgin train up from Euston to Birmingham, dropping off before it had even passed through Watford, only ten minutes out of London.

Midday was a good time to travel and the platform at New Street station in the second city was almost deserted as she waited for the Arriva local train up to Shropshire. The four-carriage thing rolled in on time and she sat, curled up in her window seat, feeling vulnerable and a little raw, but also relieved to be away from the cloying atmosphere of the last few months that had engulfed her and Kavanagh.

At Wolverhampton, the train filled up a bit and a young boy sat opposite her and played some game on a hand-held machine. At Telford, a couple of youths got on and swaggered down the aisle, cans of Stella in their hands. One of them glanced at Salt, and she immediately looked away.

She breathed more easily when they moved through to the next carriage. Most people's experience of crime has nothing to do with jewel heists at the Millennium Dome or daring motorcycle raids on Bond Street diamond merchants. It's the high street mugging, the snatched bag theft and the unprovoked assault that most people see, and are very distressed by.

The automatic doors opened and the two hooded youths stepped back into Salt's carriage. She looked out of the window, avoiding any eye contact and put her magazine on the seat beside her. The youngster opposite her was oblivious to the youths' presence and exercised his thumbs in rapt concentration. The young men came down the aisle and took the seats across from Salt. She watched them in the reflection of the window glass.

One of them put his music on loudspeaker and the noise blared out down the carriage. She felt herself tensing but remained steadfast in her resolve not to intervene. The boy at last looked up from his Nintendo.

One of the youths leaned across and said to him, 'What?'

'Nothing,' he said nervously. Salt looked at the open landscape. Where was the guard? He'd already checked tickets several times, but what about these people who had boarded at Telford? And how far were they going? Just one stop, maybe? Only up the line to Wellington?

She watched as one of the track-suited young men took a long drink from his can, crushed it in his hand and kicked it down the aisle.

'What you got on there?' said the taller of the youths as he came across and sat next to the boy. 'Let's have a go,' he said and put out his hand. The boy looked across to the policewoman. She felt wretched as she looked steadfastly out of the window and willed the train to get to the station at Wellington.

She turned slightly, not looking at either youth and took her phone from her bag. The yob opposite her kept his eyes on Salt. His steely look said, 'Don't think about using your phone to report this.'

She dropped it back in her handbag.

The tall young man took the console from the boy and returned to the other side of the gangway. The boy looked both helpless and embarrassed at his humiliation. The only other passengers, an elderly couple sitting further down the carriage, silently got up and went through to the next car.

The train pulled into Wellington but the youths remained seated. No one joined the train.

As soon as it pulled away, the other one took a ready-rolled joint from the inside pocket of his tracksuit top and lit it.

Salt made to get up, but the boy put his feet right across the aisle up on the gangway seat, blocking her way. 'Excuse me,' she said.

'You're alright for a bit,' he said. 'Soon be at Shrewsbury.'

He inhaled deeply and blew the smoke of the spliff directly at her face.

Ten minutes later, the train pulled into Shrewsbury and they got up, taking the boy's console with them. 'We get off first,' said one of them, indicating that Salt and the boy should remain in their seats.

As soon as they had left, Salt said to the boy, 'I'm sorry.' 'It's alright,' he said. 'It's not your fault.'

As the youths smirked past the window, low down, below the ledge, Salt clicked her camera phone. 'Sorry,' she said again, and the boy opposite her now got off. She remained seated as the train pulled away and the guard now appeared with a refrain of, 'Tickets, please.'

SIX

It had been a horrible last part of the journey, all the more so as intimidation and a daylight petty theft felt somehow more of an affront up here in the countryside than in the city where such things happened all the time. Maybe she'd report the incident to the local police when she had a minute.

For now, though, she felt a huge sense of relief to be at Carrie's house. It was in a hamlet a couple of miles south of the market town, the middle one in a row of three former miners' cottages with tiny front gardens and random stone walls that fronted a single-track lane. She'd left the flat in Crouch End at eleven that morning and got here at just after four o'clock that afternoon.

She said little about the unpleasantness on the train, just skated over it, and the two women had a couple of gin and tonics, then supper and drank a bottle and a half of wine. They talked until two in the morning and there was mostly laughter even as they swirled and eddied around Salt's travails as she unpacked her relationship woes.

Women are resilient. They cope. They look to one another for support, and they generally get it. Blokes: blokes are useless. They do the drink thing pretty good, but they are useless when it comes to the talk, and so they just go round in circles on their own and eventually top themselves in some quiet spot, or drink even more. Kavanagh had never known a single relationship breakdown in which, six months down the line, the woman wasn't coping, but the bloke was.

The following morning, the cottage was quiet and not a little fusty. Salt telephoned a local garage and arranged to collect a car later that morning. She then checked her emails at her laptop on the table and Carrie lay on the sofa, swathed in a duvet and drank tea and smoked her first cigarette as she watched TV with a throbbing head.

With the back door open, by ten o'clock the spring sunshine had started to dispel the mist in the valley outside and defeat Carrie's cigarette smoke within.

Salt expected there to be a message from Kavanagh and was surprised and not a little disappointed when there was nothing from him. 'Let's clear up,' she said, closing the machine and picking up bottles and glasses and an ashtray from the hearth.

'Let's not,' said Carrie. 'Put on your trainers. We're going round the block,' and she stubbed out her cigarette and nipped into her bedroom to dress.

'Round the block' was some three or four miles on the quiet lanes. There was birdsong on the air, bright green hawthorn in the hedges and open pasture carpeted in buttercups and dandelions on either side of them. They could have walked in jeans, not jogging pants for all the effort that was involved in the leisurely hike. They dawdled along, stopped when they felt like it and sipped water as they took in the view of the next valley and the local landmark of Admiral Rodney's Pillar.

'So, I think I had my turn last night,' said Salt. 'I'm sorry if I went on a bit.'

'Not at all,' said Carrie. 'You were fine,' she added reassuringly.

'Well, it must be your turn now,' she said. 'How's things for you?'

'We're OK,' said Carrie. 'Quiet period, I think. Things are just tootling along, no drama. In fact, just the way I like it.'

'It won't last,' said Salt. 'It never does, not if there's a man involved.'

'Maybe,' said Carrie. 'We'll see.'

'And is Buster still on probation?' Salt asked as they began the climb up a steep hill.

'Buster?' replied Carrie.

'Keep up,' said the cop. 'Buster Edwards. Great train robber from the early 'Sixties. He ended up selling flowers, too, outside some railway station in London.'

'Oh, right,' said Carrie. 'Well, Ben isn't a train robber. In fact, he's not any kind of robber at all. He just grew a bit of dope, Jane,' she said defensively, the use of her friend's name suggesting that she was not entirely comfortable with the woman's implied criticism of her boyfriend.

'A bit?' said Salt. 'He had two massive greenhouses under cultivation as I recall, and an electricity bill that would have lit up the Isle of Wight.'

'You exaggerate,' said Carrie, 'as usual. Anyway, the only thing he's growing these days are tulips.'

'What, he grows them himself?' said Salt.

'No. Of course not, they come in a truck from Holland; he just sells them.'

Like every other motorist in the city, Salt had often had to squeeze past those huge white juggernauts that blocked the Islington and Crouch End pavements as they delivered their blooms and plants to the capital's florists.

'But it's going alright?' asked Salt. 'The flower business? *And* the relationship?'

'Yes to both. Everything's fine between us,' said Carrie, foreclosing the conversation, and clearly a little peeved.

'Sorry,' said Salt. 'We nearly there?' she asked as she leaned down and put her hands on her thighs.

'Yes,' said Carrie. 'Nearly – just to the top of the hill.'

Salt straightened up, said, 'Sorry,' once more and the two women ploughed on up the incline in reflective silence.

SEVEN

Shropshire, 1972

In the three years since they had killed the foreman, Gary Thomas had prospered. Terry Morgan, his reluctant accomplice in the accidental crime, had done so too. At least for a while.

The building trade has always been a precarious place to work. After the fishing industry and digging for coal a mile beneath the ground, it's the place you're most likely to go to work in the morning, but not come home that night. But even the dangers associated with the building trade are as nothing compared with the business of being a footballer: playing professional football makes building site work look like the very height of probity.

The thing about football is that, whereas there's only one Pelé and Puskás, and one Diego Maradona and Cristiano Ronaldo, just about any third-division, former tyre-fitter can end a talented player's career with one horrible tackle.

Gary might have set his mind on achieving his aim of financial success, but Terry had no need of such application. The young man was naturally gifted and didn't have to apply himself because, like all truly gifted people, he simply didn't need to. Scott-Fitzgerald and D.H. Lawrence wouldn't have benefited from attending creative writing courses, and Terry wasn't going to learn control and passing and shooting from any coach on the touchline.

Yes, at some point in his career, if he was going to be a good professional, he'd have to learn how to slot into a team, how to read the abilities of the (less good than himself) players around him – what they could and couldn't do, where and when to thread a pass or chip a lob for them – but in his own talents and skills, he was entirely (and justifiably) confident.

It wasn't long before he left the muddy pitches and local

pub teams behind, being chased by wheezing right backs on Saturday afternoons, a couple of pints of lager swilling in their bellies as he feinted past them down the wing.

He was still playing pub football for the Cross Keys when he was spotted by a touchline scout. Gresford, a North Wales team, who were playing the likes of Ruthin and Llangollen, signed him up and paid him 'expenses' to train with them one evening a week, and to play before crowds of a couple of hundred on Saturday afternoons.

A season later and the manager of Wrexham, then in the third division, came to have a look at him. He didn't have his best ever game, but the man could see that whatever he didn't have, he could get, and what he did have, you just couldn't teach. He signed him the following week and, within a month, he turned out at Wrexham's Racecourse ground for his league debut.

There were no foreign managers at work in any of the leagues at that time and very few foreign players, either. The notion of the game attracting thoughtful, cultured men like austere Arsene Wenger, or even media hustlers like José Mourinho, were still decades away.

These were the days when diet played no part in any footballer's life and if he fancied a fry-up an hour before a game, then a centre forward would have it. No one had heard of pasta, and the only spaghetti most players knew came in a yellow and red tin and was eaten on a couple of slices of buttered toast.

Just like everyone else, most players smoked cigarettes, sometimes having one in the changing room at half-time as the manager puffed away and explained his tactics for the second half. It sounds absurd and it looks as absurd as that old newsreel footage of cabinet meetings and press conferences, even press conferences where health and medical matters were the subject under discussion, where everyone had a fag in their hands or at their lips, but it was just the way it was.

As well as the cigarette smoking there was a deeply-embedded drinking culture attached to the game at every level and Wrexham was no exception. After every Saturday afternoon game (the idea of a Sunday kick-off was unthinkable) every player and all of the coaching and management staff went to the bar, everyone drank lots, and many players then got straight into their Ford Capris or MGBs and drove themselves home. The only reason no one gave any thought to the likely effects this might have on any player's game was that the opposition were certainly, at that very moment, doing exactly the same thing.

From Wrexham, Terry went to Bolton Wanderers in the second division where he flourished as a pacy left-winger. On his twenty-second birthday, he married Abbie, a nice-looking Manchester-based Scots girl he'd met in a club a few months previously, and six months later, she gave birth to their daughter, Kate.

Morgan now had not only the 3.8 Jaguar, a wife and lovely little child, but a house in a desirable Lancashire suburb, too. And whilst as a player, Terry was never George Best, and his pretty young wife, no Miss Glasgow – apart from the one terrible memory that cast a dark shadow over his life – things looked very good indeed for the young man.

But, just when it couldn't get any better, at an away game in the Midlands one November Saturday afternoon, late into the second half, as the rain fell under the glowing floodlights, Terry was a fraction of a second too slow in avoiding a scything centre back's leg. In that moment, he bought one of those terrible knee-high tackles that make even some of the callous crowd on the terraces wince. As he writhed in agony on the bright green floodlit turf, he knew that this was a very bad one indeed.

Stretchered off to heartless jeers from the home supporters, Morgan's fibula was snapped. He never played football again.

Yes, he got a very decent insurance pay out and the club treated him well enough, but Terry had got the best part of his life still to come, and this was a young man who didn't have an O level or GCSE to his name: the longest thing he had written since he had left school was his name on a contract or a cheque, and his future now looked to him an unfamiliar and very frightening road.

EIGHT

Julian Betts had been working for the top national Sunday broadsheet for the last thirty years. He'd seen leader writers and investigative reporters come and go. He'd seen TV critics pen their stuff, get tired or bored and be replaced by others as they went off to write memoirs or esoteric poetry, penance and payback for the years of drivel they'd had to watch on the small screen throughout long daylight hours. Cineastes had watched a thousand films, written their columns and died of drink or drugs or left the office to write the novel they felt that they had to pen before their own credits finally rolled.

Betts had outlasted no fewer than three obituarists and countless columnists, those thirty- and forty-year-old women who were hired by every newspaper these days to write a thousand words on some encounter with a New York taxi driver, the dating habits of their Lithuanian au pair, or the particular shade of green they simply had to paint the kitchen of their new apartment in Chelsea or Tribeca.

Betts' restaurant column had begun life as a serious piece of journalism (or, at least as serious as writing about mangetout and crème brûlée way back in the Eighties ever could be) but had for several years now become, in keeping with the zeitgeist, a tongue-in-cheek, faintly ironic and knowing pastiche of itself. No one took either his back page column or the writer himself seriously any more, and he was just as likely to turn up on an early evening chat show and utter entirely fatuous things about the culinary arts, as he was to eulogize the cooking of some emerging chef and his hidden-away, coterie establishment.

It wasn't, though, merely on account of his own increasingly jaundiced view of his own 'work' that he had decided to leave the job (he could just as easily have penned his two thousand words from anywhere in the country – or even the world, frankly). No, the fact was, Julian Betts had finally had enough of living in London, elegant though his west London home was. At the end of the day – to use the sort of phrase of which he despaired, but which he occasionally employed anyway – at the end of the day, London was London. Yes, his own spacious flat was chic enough, and the nicely-groomed concierge who was to be found in the marble foyer at every hour of the day and night was a reassuring presence, but the city itself, the stuff beyond that marble floor and those solid glass and brass doors was dirty and seemed to get dirtier and busier and noisier with every passing day.

Betts was going to move out. And the place that he was going to move to was the little Shropshire market town on the Welsh border where, as a child in the early 1950s, every summer holiday from the age of ten, he had visited a favourite aunt and uncle who kept a sweet shop on the Cross in the centre of the town.

Perhaps, like his literary hero, Marcel Proust, for whom the very taste of a madeleine steeped in an infusion of tea, had fuelled the French writer's four-hundred page novel some thirty years after the events at Combray, it was his own indelible memory of a Sherbert Fountain or a dark chocolate Fry's Cream that had subconsciously drawn him back. Maybe it was the clear recollection of the broad, almost deserted High Street at any time of the day? Or just the sound of the church bells on a Sunday morning, followed by their customary walk around the park before lunch with his uncle that did it.

In any event, after a couple of recent trips to the town and short stays in the town's only hotel (from where, to defray his personal expenses he penned a future column about its 'terrible' Courtyard restaurant with its 'amusingly naïve rustic offerings' and the 'even worse' Balcony trattoria and its 'truly execrable' menu), he decided that, yes, this was the place to which he was going to relocate and retire.

His current editor never particularly liked either effete Julian Betts or his fey column, but the postbag and emails that accompanied the man's droll annihilation of this restaurant or that chef or novelty eatery each week was testimony to the – to his mind, mystifying – popularity of the page.

'Have you thought about filing a piece from up there, Julian?' he asked the immaculately-dressed, slightly-built man.

'I don't want to do the travelling any more,' said Betts. 'I've absolutely no wish to spend half the day stuck on the M6 looking for some dreadful restaurant outside Birmingham or a barn of a place down a country lane in Wales . . .'

'Yes,' agreed Tom, the editor. 'Can't say I blame you. More coffee?'

'I did wonder about one thing, though,' began Betts.

'Yes?' said the young man, pouring them each another Americano. 'Go on.'

'This little town I'm going to, it really is the back of beyond . . .'

'Yes,' said Tom. 'So I believe.'

'I'm wondering whether readers might find it amusing if I did an occasional piece on, you know, a sort of London-critic-relocates-to-the-sticks kind of thing.'

'Sounds interesting,' said the editor, passing him the large white cup.

'The house I've bought, it's the very last place I would have imagined I'd ever even consider. I'm not entirely sure why I have. It's in the suburbs in the quietest part of a very quiet town.'

'Yes?' said the editor, thinking how appalling the whole thing sounded, and wondering whether there wasn't some unknown, ulterior motive for his popular columnist's change of life. It was widely assumed that Betts was gay, but he wasn't 'out'. Maybe that was just a generational thing? He never mentioned a partner, either male or female, and he sometimes referred in his pieces to being accompanied by a woman dining companion, sometimes a man.

'I've stood in the front room there, you know,' he went on, in something of a reverie, 'for half an hour and just looked out of the window and, do you know what?'

'What?' said the editor, thinking that it was all very well that Betts had already effectively begun *his* sojourn, but that he himself had an editorial meeting to chair and a newspaper to get out in only forty-eight hours' time.

'*Absolutely* nothing moves. Not a thing. Eventually, you might just see a cat or a squirrel, perhaps, but that's it. If a car trundles down the road, it's the highlight of the hour, if not the entire morning,' he said, smiling at the arch notion.

'Umm,' said Tom, not a little concerned as to just what the man might find to write about once he'd identified the neighbourhood's cat, to say nothing of the occasional Ford Focus driving by. But that wasn't his problem. 'So, what were you thinking, exactly, Julian?' he said.

'I thought a weekly column: "In Praise of the Suburbs",' said Betts.

The allusion to Auden's poem of a similar name was lost on the editor, whose background was City rather than arts, but he could see that the faintly ludicrous, essentially whimsical idea might have some resonance with his readers, readers with very short attention spans and an apparently insatiable taste for the frivolous.

'Sure,' he said. 'Why not? Let's give it a go. What say we try it for a few editions and see how it goes, eh?'

'Fine,' said Betts replacing his coffee cup on the desk, and Tom walked him to the door where he held the older man's hand in his own for a fraction of a second before they parted.

NINE

T he last little bit, to the crest of the hill, was a steep climb up the lane for the two women; most cars had to pause and slip into first as their vehicles laboured in second gear. But the view was worth it. You could see fifty miles into Wales, past Breidden Hill and the winding River Severn, along Long Mountain and down past Welshpool towards Newtown and beyond.

'Wow,' said Jane Salt, impressed. London was full of good things, and she liked living there, in spite of the light pollution that meant no one saw the stars these days, and the furthest you could see from most bits of Crouch End was the tall clock on the Broadway.

OK, on a Sunday afternoon, you could take a walk up Primrose Hill if you fancied jostling with a dozen other families and, invariably, a film crew or two, shooting the scene for local 'colour' for a low-budget romcom. And from that place you'd get a decent view past Regent's Park and across to Westminster and down to the river beyond. But this was something else again. These were truly open spaces: gently rolling Shropshire hills and valleys, with a plume of cottage smoke here and there, a farmyard in the far distance, a few houses dotted in the landscape if you really looked hard, and one huge black-and-white timbered house just a couple of miles away, nestling in woodland with a sweeping view to the front; yes, this was exactly as those weekend break TV ads said it should be: it was plain lovely.

'Good, eh?' said Carrie, feeling slightly proprietary about her county.

The two women stood there in silence for several minutes, breathing in the air and savouring the place.

'And whose is the Elizabethan pile?' asked Salt mockingly, pointing to the huge timbered mansion way down the valley, a house with dozens of multipane, leaded windows glinting in the sunshine and a dozen enormous corkscrew brick chimneys.

'Gareth Thomas,' said Carrie. 'He's our local Roman Abramovich.'

'Yes?' said Salt. 'And that's his Stamford Bridge?'

'Sort of,' said Carrie. 'He did well in the building trade at first, but now he also owns a couple of big car dealerships, as well as lots of property, and a few other things I don't suppose we know about,' she added.

'Yes?' said Salt. 'So?'

'So what?' said Carrie.

'I can hear there's more. I'm waiting for the "but", the "however". It's in your voice.'

'They should promote you to inspector,' said Carrie, acknowledging Salt's perception.

'Yes? Drop the commissioner a line, will you,' she said, and drank from her water bottle as a lone buzzard wheeled above them in the blue, hazy valley. 'So, what else? Go on,' prompted Salt.

'It's a beautiful place, right,' Carrie began, 'and a local family had it on the market for ages, but they couldn't sell it.'

'No?' asked the police woman.

'Blot on the proverbial landscape,' said Carrie. 'There's a fantastic view from what can be a fantastic house, but right across the road there's a farm that's got very rundown over the years . . .'

'Where?' said Salt, almost doing that thing that actors are supposed to do, but never in fact do, where they put their hand to their brow and peer into the distance.

'Try this,' said Carrie, and took from her pocket a monocular and handed it to Salt. 'Look right across the lane from the place,' and she pointed as Salt held the device to her eye. 'See?'

'See what?' said Salt.

'Exactly,' said her friend. 'Those few blackened stumps from what was the barn, and that pile of rubble near the hedge, is all that's left. He's got himself a nice view now, eh?'

'Blimey,' said Salt. 'Your local magnate did that?'

'So they say,' agreed Carrie. 'Gary Thomas bought it for

next to nothing, and the next thing, six months later, there's a huge fire and the place opposite burns right down to the ground.'

'"Unexplained",' said Salt, and passed the monocular back to Carrie.

'Unexplained,' agreed Carrie. 'But now our Mr Thomas has got the best view in Shropshire.'

'And no one charged?' asked the cop.

''Course not,' agreed Carrie. 'Everyone knows, or at least assumes, it was him, but there's not a shred of evidence. He was actually out of town on the night of the fire. But this is a man with a reputation for getting what he wants. Always,' she added darkly.

'Who lived there?' asked Salt.

'Billy Hughes. He had half-a-dozen cattle, a few bantams scratching around and grazed his dozen acres around the place with sheep. He's been there since he was a child, and the place has been in his family for generations, but he was on his own there since his wife died several years ago. The word was that Thomas thought a decent sum would buy him out. Who wants to be milking and shearing and running a smoky tractor round the fields in all weathers? Better get a bungalow on the estate down in town and put your feet up.'

'Sounds alright to me,' agreed Salt.

'Yes, me too. But not to Bill, apparently. It seems he didn't mind having no central heating and the mud around the yard. He was used to it and even at his age, he wasn't interested in a comfortable life in the suburbs.'

'How old is he?' asked Salt.

'Seventy-five, perhaps,' said Carrie. 'Thomas, so the word is, offered him stacks of money. Whatever it was worth – a hundred and fifty, maybe two hundred – the man offers him twice that, but Billy doesn't want it. What's he going to do? Go and live in Dubai? He's got all he wants and all he wants is his heifers and ewes and to fall asleep by the Aga in the kitchen.'

'Sure,' said Salt.

'Next thing, the house is on fire . . .'

'And what happened to the old boy?'

'He got out alive. Just. But he's still in hospital. He was unconscious when the paramedics got to him and he'd inhaled a lot of smoke.'

'So, he won't be coming back?' said Salt.

'No,' she said. 'He'll never come back – he's much too old and sick now to think about rebuilding the place.'

Salt tucked her water bottle back in the little rucksack the women were sharing.

'Not much of a way to end your life, eh?' said Carrie.

'Horrible,' said Salt with feeling. 'What kind of person does that?'

'And the land's due to be sold at auction. Thomas will buy it and will have got what he wants.'

'But there's no evidence?' asked Salt.

'Not a scrap,' agreed Carrie.

'Maybe he didn't do it?' said Salt, playing devil's advocate. In her experience, the person most likely to benefit from a crime invariably perpetrated that crime, no matter how much they managed to muddy the trail.

'Maybe he didn't,' said Carrie without conviction.

'When you're back at work, I'm going to take a walk down there and have a look around,' said Salt.

'I think it's a bit late for that,' said Carrie, kneeling down to tie her lace, 'and anyway, you're on holiday.'

'Well, I wouldn't exactly call it that,' said Salt as she discreetly opened her phone. There were no messages from Kavanagh. She may have come up here to escape their moribund relationship, but that didn't mean she didn't want him to at least *try* and be in touch with her. But her innate sense was that he was playing hardball: he was doing that male pride macho thing whereby he'd hold out for a few days and see if she started to miss him. Some hope. No, unless she was very much mistaken, he was missing her. He might even be playing fast and loose. So be it. If that was the case, let him trawl the bars with his dodgy mates, or even sign up to an on-line agency and find some divorcee to get laid with. Good luck to him, she thought as her resentment grew.

'Shall we get back?' said Carrie, getting to her feet. 'I fancy a coffee, and the good news is that it's downhill all the way.'

'Sure,' said Salt. 'Let's.'

TEN

'So,' said Salt, as the two women lounged on the sofa with coffee back at Carrie's home. 'You and Ben?'

'Yes?' said Carrie.

'Where is he now?' she said gauchely gesturing to the cottage sitting room.

'We keep separate places. He's got a little flat, well, a couple of rooms, really, above his warehouse, and he has to go to the flower market in Birmingham very early, so it's better that way. I'm used to my own space and he likes to be able to do his own thing too, but we stay together when it suits.'

'Sure,' said Salt.

'And anyway, I told him you were coming up, and that we needed time to chat.'

'Did you say anything to him about me and Frank?'

'Only a bit. That there was some stuff going on for you two, and that you and I would need to hunker down. One of the good things about Ben is that he's been around a bit and he knows when to make himself scarce.'

'Thanks,' said Salt.

'But he wants to meet you, and he's made me promise that we can all get together sometime.'

'That'd be nice,' said Salt politely.

'There's a band plays in the pub up the road. A few old hippies get together and play. I think he's got to know some of them a bit. To be honest, the music's pretty terrible, but it'll be OK after a couple of glasses of wine.'

'It sounds fun,' said Salt. 'And are you two still "under cover"?'

'Yes,' said Carrie. 'Professionally, I don't deal with Ben directly, of course, but I know everything that's going on. You know as well as I do, there's no such thing as client or patient confidentiality: cops, doctors, social workers, and certainly probation officers. It simply isn't going to happen.'

'Of course not,' said Salt.

'Is there anyone who really thinks that when medics get together for a drink they don't discuss Mr Smith's tumour, or the way someone in another practice messed up by not diagnosing his condition early enough to have saved him, or at least given him another year to live?

'Doctors, probation officers, cops, we're all the same,' she concluded.

Ben Williams had been so late for that first appointment with Carrie's junior colleague, probation officer Sandra Twomey, that the woman had already left the office to go to her next meeting at a client's maisonette down on the worst part of the local council estate. Twenty minutes later, Carrie had answered the intercom and, looking at the man on the TV monitor there, notwithstanding that she was now alone in the office, had allowed Williams up to the first floor of their building just off the main street of the little town.

He was tall and very muscularly-built with just one little oriental tattoo on his forearm; he'd got a small, deep scar above his left eye and he wouldn't have been anyone's patsy in prison, she guessed. He hadn't shaved for a couple of days and was wearing jeans and a white T-shirt with a Bench jacket. The only danger in him, she reckoned, resided in his self-assured good looks: reassuringly, he looked neither mad, psychotic nor violent. Half the criminals she dealt with, and invariably those whose offences involved violence, were distinctly unpleasant looking people. She'd rarely met a violent offender who didn't look anything but eminently capable of such behaviour.

She'd already seen the man's case file and knew, anyway, that Williams had just completed half of his two-year sentence inside a category B prison. He'd been paroled on licence, an early release conditional on his fulfilling his probation requirements. No, unprovoked, he wasn't going to hit any-one, and certainly not her, of that Carrie Prowse was quite sure.

They sat down in the little ante room adjacent to the main office and she gave him a glass of chilled water from the foun-tain and poured one for herself. 'Sandra's had to leave, I'm afraid,' she began. 'But why are you so late, Mr Williams?'

'Am I?' he asked, flipping open his phone and checking the time there.

'I think so,' she said, gently reprehending him. 'Your appointment was for two thirty? Sandra waited until nearly three, but then she had to go to meet another client.'

'I'm sorry,' he said. 'I thought it was for *three* thirty. I'm useless without my diary.'

'You have a diary?' she asked, with the flicker of a smile parting her lips. The idea was almost unheard of amongst the people she generally saw, even though she'd often recommended it to clients as one of the – surely not particularly difficult – steps in organizing their (invariably chaotic) lives.

'Yes, but I seem to have left it somewhere,' he said, patting his jacket pocket. 'Maybe it's in the van?' he added reasonably.

'You do know, keeping your appointments is part of the contract you've signed up to?' she said, but felt stupid saying such a thing to the man who was obviously assessing her every bit as thoroughly, but rather more coolly, as she was him.

'Sure,' he said. 'I'm sorry,' and he now smiled a little, too.

'It's OK,' she said, overcompensating. 'Give me a minute. I'll get Sandra's desk diary and let's make you another appointment. Are you working at the moment?' she added as she got to her feet and straightened her back.

He paused as he looked her up and down. 'I only got out a few weeks ago,' he said. 'But I have got something I'm lining up.'

'Yes?' she said.

'Yes. I'm going into the flower business,' he asserted.

'Really?' she said.

'I'm in the middle of negotiating for some premises right now.'

'That's great,' she said. 'It's not everyone . . . you know . . .?'

'What?' he said.

'Well, it's not everyone who'll give someone who's just got out of prison a break.'

'Sure,' he agreed, and without elaborating went on, 'There's a couple of shops in the town I reckon I can supply, and

I'm also going to do a bit of retailing from a stall myself. The council have given me the OK for a pitch on the square.'

Carrie liked the idea of real flowers being sold on the street. She abhorred cellophane-wrapped supermarket sprays, a notion of flowers about as far from a clutch of bluebells – her own favourite flowers, with their watery stems and delicate scent – as could be. The only thing worse, to her way of thinking, was the would-be lover's late purchase of a garage-bought bouquet, blooms whose only fragrance was forecourt fumes, and which cost about twice as much as a gallon of top-dollar petrol.

'I wish you luck,' she said sincerely. 'Really, I do.'

'Thanks,' he grinned.

She was aware of him watching her movements, as she left the room and went through to the adjoining office.

'How about next Tuesday? At 11.00?' she said, returning and taking her seat, the office diary on her lap.

'It should be OK,' he said, glancing surreptitiously at her bosom as she wrote the appointment in her colleague's book. 'So? All done?' he asked, getting to his feet and taking a step towards her.

'I think so,' she said.

She, too, got up and he extended his hand and gave a further little grin as they touched fingers for a second.

'I'll see you,' he said, and was gone.

She immediately opened his file anew. There were several gaps in the chronology, but he'd been in jail for growing skunk. Before that, he'd spent time abroad and he'd worked for what the file described in vague terms as a 'charity fund-raiser' in the Midlands. And, on the side, for heaven knows how long, he'd been cultivating high-grade skunk which, according to the trial judge's summing up, he'd then been wholesaling in Birmingham at five grand a time per kilo. As part of the authorities' powers under the Proceeds of Crime Act, the judge had ordered the appropriation of his bank account savings, car and city-centre flat.

There was a tap at the door and Williams stepped back into the room without waiting to be invited. Carrie closed the folder as he stood there. 'Sorry,' he said. 'Did I leave my keys?' He looked around the place and picked up his key fob from the table. He glanced at the buff folder in the woman's hands, his name on the top, his life and background laid out there in her slender fingers. 'Anything interesting?' he said, grinning, and turned and left the room without waiting for her answer.

ELEVEN

'**D**o you want to put this in your window?' asked the young woman assertively.

'Sorry?' said journalist and food writer, Julian Betts, looking up from where he was wholly involved turning over the soil and forking a little compost into the deep hole he had dug. He'd bought a Victoria plum tree, a James Grieve apple sapling and a grafted pear at the local garden centre five miles away that very morning.

'What is it?' he said, looking up at the gamine girl who was holding out a coloured sheet to him. He sank the tines of his fork into the earth and sat down on the rockery wall. He'd never had a garden before and knew absolutely nothing about horticulture, but he'd bought a couple of books in the local shop and was now enjoying pottering about in the sunshine as he planted stuff out and sowed odd-looking seeds in trays and pots.

It was still a very remarkable idea to the former London writer that you could put something in the ground, often shrivelled, unpropitious-looking items and, if you were lucky, these seeds might actually grow into plants of beauty, just like the pictures on the packets suggested they might. And heavens, some of them you could actually then eat.

He took the sheet from her as she stood beside him. A man of thirty-five in a nicely-tailored hacking jacket and blue jeans was leafleting the opposite side of the road.

In spite of a little backache, Betts was feeling benign; the sort of mood that these last few sunny days fiddling about in the garden tended to induce in him.

'"Keep It Local" poster,' she replied, as he stretched out his legs and read the sheet. 'You know?'

'I'm afraid I don't,' he said. 'I'm new in the area,' and gestured to the garden as if its state went some way to explaining his newly-arrived status.

'It's the campaign,' she said. 'To stop the supermarket.'

'Oh, I see,' he said, glancing at the lurid text on the flyer. Betts liked supermarkets; he liked just about everything about them: their anonymity, the fact that you could rummage about on the shelves, picking up this and that, compare products and examine ingredients, and buy any amount of stuff without interference from anyone at all. If you were lucky, even the person on the till said little or nothing to you beyond volunteering the barest of civilities about your need of a bag or help with the packing. And two-for-ones? Who didn't like those? There was no one in the entire world who didn't like a bargain, and you certainly never saw offers like that in your local wholefood or farm shop.

'We've got to "Keep it Local",' the twenty-year-old with the pink hair and tiny bosom repeated, and inclined her head slightly as she sought some acknowledgement from him.

Betts was drawn to look at her nose stud, even though the things always made him wince. 'Yes, I'm sure,' he acquiesced.

'It's the only way to keep the town centre alive,' she said, 'and to keep the local shops in business.'

'Of course,' he agreed. He could see the logic of this, but he still liked Sainsbury's well enough.

'So, stick it in your window?' she said again peremptorily and with a nod of the head, as if speaking to a slow, possibly slightly deranged person.

'Sure,' he said.

'There's a march on Saturday, too. It's on there,' she added, and pointed to a footnote on the sheet.

'A march?' he said. 'I'll do my best. But I might have to be away,' he added weakly.

'Umm,' she said, recognizing the untruth and identifying him as no likely fellow traveller to the cause. 'Bye,' she said. She turned away back down the drive and joined her male friend who was standing idly by before they made their way down the road, his arm around her waist.

Ten minutes later, inside the house to make his mid-morning cup of coffee, Betts screwed up the poster and dropped it in the bin. In the rear sitting room, the place that he'd designated his study, he sat down at the word processor and resumed work on the article he was writing for the following week's column.

There was little enough to write about, in one sense, since he'd moved in a few weeks ago, but that, in a way, was the whole point of his column.

He'd filed a couple of pieces already, one about his actual move into the place, and the contrast between that and the difficulties that accompanied any London relocation, with its likelihood of incurring parking fines even as the removal men bundled your stuff up the steps into your new flat, and the constant vigilance required to make sure that some villain didn't spirit away your espresso machine whilst your back was turned. All this he'd compared with the harmony of his arriving here, and the estate agent's turning up with not only the keys to the house, but a bunch of flowers, too, and then the removal men's orderly depositing of his furniture and books and crockery throughout the forty-year-old house with its spacious drive and parking for three cars.

His second column had written itself as he had gently ribbed the speech and mores of the couple of local odd-job men who had begun to get to grips with the overgrown back garden and eventually removed the tons of gravel from the front that the previous owner had laid down, and which had made the plot look like a barren garden of remembrance.

And he'd started to collect a list of topics that might serve for future pieces in his columns. He knew without doubt that at sometime he'd be writing about that staple of any local press: the youngsters' car crashes that seemed to occur with depressing regularity and which appeared to remain a topic of grotesque fascination for the paper's readers.

Only a week after his arrival, he had stood on the town's main street and watched as a hearse drove slowly past, an Everton football shirt draped over the coffin, a profusion of blue and white iris covering the pine box in the long wheel-base Volvo. But he'd also been struck by how the local bus still rumbled by and picked up pensioners from outside the post office and, round the corner, how the man with the flower stall continued to wrap roses, possibly for the very mourners who were on their way to the church. Yes, life really did have to go on.

After he had poured his coffee, he jotted down a reminder to use the 'Keep it Local' activists in some future column.

Their doubtless unintentionally absurd acronym KIL would certainly make a good start.

Perhaps he *should* join their march on Saturday? He would at least be able to observe them more closely. He went back to the kitchen bin, picked out the poster and flattened it out with the palm of his hand.

TWELVE

London, 2010

Kavanagh kept in touch with the office by phone but he knew that, with his swollen ankle, there was no way that he could be back amongst the all-consuming distractions of his daily work for at least a week. No, he was stuck here in the flat, spending most of the day lying on the sofa with a bag of frozen peas held to his throbbing ankle. He muttered profanities at the daytime TV chat shows and wished that at least the Crucible snooker, the Augusta golf or the test match series had been on.

Locally, a Somali boy had been killed in a drive-by shooting as he stood outside a Hackney kebab shop the previous night with a group of friends. It was almost certainly a case of mistaken identity or, just possibly – and at least this conjecture would allow some sort of twisted logic, some screwed up 'reason' for the killing – an act motivated by the kind of kudos that would accrue to the perpetrator as he avenged some insignificant or even wholly imagined slight.

The boy was only fifteen years old and, had it been worth the thought, Kavanagh and his ilk might have wondered just why he had been out on the street at all at one o'clock on a Wednesday morning, but not anymore.

Kavanagh's office colleague, the aptly-named cadaverous DI Adrian Skinner filled him in on the details and briefly explained the well-worn procedure that was already under way. They were going through the motions of assigning officers to house-to-house enquiries – where they would be met with frightened silence, if the doors on the tower-block flats and two-storey maisonettes surrounding them were opened at all – and specialist teams were already out in the area searching for the gun. They were, even now, lifting drain covers, scouring gardens and refuse bins, and wading through filthy local streams and dried-up culverts. Shopkeepers were giving three- and four-word witness 'statements'; other officers were collecting security CCTV footage and posting crime-scene placards and boards. Neither man even took the time to comment on what fruitless tasks these would be: it was the procedure, and it had to be done. But when, exactly, was the last time anyone in these parts had paused to read a yellow and black 'serious incident occurred here' street placard, and then public-spiritedly walked into his local police station to report what he had seen of the violent crime?

Unfortunately, even the teenager's slaying did not occupy Kavanagh's thoughts for very long, and he limped through to the kitchen, emptied the half-full ashtray and poured himself the first of the day's gin and tonics.

By late that evening, he was desperate to phone Salt but couldn't bring himself to for fear that it might be the 'wrong' moment, he abject, and she having a glass of wine or chatting happily to Carrie.

In fact, Salt *was* in the pub up the road from her friend's cottage with Carrie, her boyfriend, Ben, and the few old hippies who got together there every so often to play banjo, flute and fiddles, and she was certainly more drunk than she knew was good for her.

The next morning, the swelling had gone down a little and Kavanagh gingerly felt around the puffy skin of his twisted ankle before making slow progress to the shower without the use of his walking stick for the first time since he had sustained the injury. He checked his messages again, but there was nothing from Salt.

He phoned the office only to learn that the Somali boy had been staying with an aunt, and even now, his parents, still at home in a prosperous suburb of Addis Ababa, were being sought by Foreign Office officials so that they could arrange to be flown to England, the place they had chosen for him to live so that he might have the chance of a better life.

Later in the day, rat-like DI Skinner phoned with an update on the East African boy's killing. A girl on the local housing estate might be prepared to talk 'if the money was right'. Naturally – it was a given – she would also want protection, anonymity and a new identity. It was a big ask, but it was almost certainly the only way that the boy's murder would ever be solved. 'Is she reliable?' Kavanagh asked.

'Are you alright, Frank? asked Skinner. 'You sound a bit . . .?'

'What?' said the half-drunk DI.

'A bit slurred,' said Skinner.

'It's just the pills,' he lied. 'The doc's got me on these strong painkillers.'

'Sure,' said Skinner.

'Would the witness, this girl, stand up in court under scrutiny?' Kavanagh asked his colleague. 'And anyway, is she even kosher? You know as well as I do, it's usually just some rival boyfriend bollocks or a vendetta of some sort.'

'You telling me, Frank?' said Skinner. 'I know, mate, have no fear, but right now, she's all we've got.'

Kavanagh was astute enough to be sceptical, even if he was drunk. Relocations and identity changes cost hundreds of thousands of pounds and had to be sanctioned at the highest level: he was glad that it was not his decision to make.

Late that afternoon he spent a good five minutes brushing his teeth, rinsing with mouthwash and then chewing gum before taking a taxi to the doctor's surgery. His brisk Irish GP proclaimed the ankle to be healing remarkably well 'for a man of your age', and told him in no uncertain terms that he should have stopped playing football years ago. 'You'll be back at work in a week,' she said, and then added cheerfully, 'Get rid of your football trainers, Mr Kavanagh, and spare a thought for our limited NHS resources.'

He called in at the local convenience store and, as soon as he got home, poured himself three-quarters of a glass of Bombay Sapphire with just a splash of tonic.

He wanted Salt to come back to him, but the longer that she declined to be in touch, the clearer was his belief that she never would. He'd removed her moisturizer and spare toothbrush from the bathroom on the day that she had left, but even destroying those clothes of hers that still hung in the wardrobe was not going to deliver to him the peace of mind that he sought.

He gulped another mouthful of gin and tonic, put his foot up on the cushion, lay full-length on the sofa and switched on the TV.

THIRTEEN

Shropshire, 2010

'Terry? Fuck me, Terry, how you doing, mate?' said the man.

Terry sat there, his eyes with their perennial glaze, his carrier bag of drink close beside him on the bench.

'Alright,' said the drunk, and he extended his hand, with no idea who the man was.

'You don't remember me, do you?' said the park keeper.

Morgan looked at the man and smiled as he moved his head slowly from side to side. 'No,' he said.

'We were at school together, mate. You must remember Willy the science teacher. We called him that cos he wore tight trousers and you could always see his cock down one side . . .'

'Yes?' said Morgan, but it was impossible to tell whether he had any recollection of the teacher.

'You and me, Terry,' said the parkie, as if he were speaking to a stroke-afflicted friend, 'we used to play in the school team. Football, you know? You were in the year below me, but you were such a talent, even then, you played with the older lads in the under fifteens, remember? You were only fourteen. You might not have even been that?'

'Yes, that's right,' said Morgan. 'I was good,' and he mimicked heading the ball, almost falling from the bench as he did so.

'I heard about your injury,' said the park man.

'Yes, it was a bad 'un,' he offered. 'Finished me, the cunt did.'

'Everybody heard about it round here,' the man went on.

'Yes?' said Terry, and took another bottle from the bag.

'Thing is, Terry, I'm sorry mate, but if you're thinking of bedding down here,' and he gestured to the nearby bushes, 'you'll have to find somewhere else to kip. I'd let you stay,

of course, but I can't, you know, kids around and all. They'd
sack me. Have you got anyone you can stay with?'

'It's alright,' said Morgan. 'I'll get somewhere. I thought
I'd come back for a while, you know.'

'I know,' said the keeper, and he reached into his pocket.
'Here,' he said and handed Terry all the change he had. 'Get
yourself a pie or something, eh, mate?'

'Thanks,' said Morgan, pocketing the coins. 'Good on yer.'

'You set me up for a sitter once,' said the keeper, taking
up his litter picker. 'Only goal I ever fuckin' scored.'

'Cheers, mate,' said Morgan. 'Thanks.'

'I'll see you around,' said the man. 'Better move them on,
too,' he said, pointing to the increasingly rowdy group of
teenagers clambering around the bandstand.

'Yes,' said Morgan as he got up from the bench. 'Cheers,'
he said again and stood there unsteadily for a moment before
heading away towards the off-licence on the high street.

People do generally go home, eventually, and being back here
in Oswestry was pretty much home for Terry Morgan.

It is a cliché in both police and criminal circles, an absolute
one hundred percent certain given, that if you want to remain
undetected, if you're on the run or in hiding, you do *not* go
to the countryside. What you do, is get yourself lost in the
most populous part of one of the busiest of cities.

Morgan wasn't on the run and he'd committed no crime.
Well, OK, he had purloined the occasional bottle of spirits
as he'd picked up his wine or cider from the supermarket
shelves but, on the rare occasions that he'd done this, and
on the even rarer occasions when he'd been caught or
detected on the shop's CCTV security cameras, no one had
ever called the police, they'd simply required that the man
hand over the bottle of spirits and be on his way.

He was a swaying, emaciated alcoholic whose trousers
had hung loose on his hips long before such a sight was any
kind of fashion statement, simply on account of his diet being
ninety percent liquid. And it was clear to the most callow
of youths, charged at only twenty years old with running a
Co-op or corner shop booze outlet, that the man was no
troublemaker or professional thief. As his life had fallen

apart, since that career-ending tackle decades previously, everything about him had gradually unravelled. The drinking that had accompanied his time as a professional footballer soon became a problem for those close to him, and only eighteen months after they'd married, his young wife Abbie returned to her parents' home in the Scottish Borders, taking their infant daughter, Kate, with her. She promised him that if he sought the help that was, surely, his only salvation, she would then try and rebuild their broken marriage. There were a couple of token attempts to do exactly that. Morgan's GP referred him to a treatment centre and he stayed sober for a week before walking out and going on a bender that left him destitute and beaten up by his newly-found drinking cohorts, who then stole everything he owned.

A year later, he had made no serious attempt to contact his wife and child, and to his growing daughter, her father was no more than a man in a wide-lapelled suit in the wedding photograph that sat on her mother's bedside cabinet.

Occasionally, when she was a little older, her mother showed the girl photographs in a family scrapbook of her footballing father, a serious-looking man in a pre-season team photo in one; in another, an action newspaper shot that the girl treasured the sight of, her father's left leg fully extended, eyes focussed on the ball as he volleyed the thing into the net in some now long-forgotten game.

For himself, Morgan was living in a near-empty house, a place that was eventually repossessed by the building society as the mortgage repayments on it went even further into arrears. And then the spiral ran down very quickly indeed. No house, no job; no wife or child; his father infirm and his mother deceased, Morgan was adrift in the world and there followed a decade or more of Salvation Army hostels, soup kitchens from the back of do-gooders' vans, underpasses, shop doorways, grubby sleeping bags and cardboard boxes for beds; fights and scrapes and seamless twenty-four-hour drinking. 'Friends' who drank together for weeks on end and then disappeared, never to be seen again. A stumbling, listing, mumbling presence, Morgan progressed from one city to another with no end in sight, with no aim but to have a bottle in his hand and, on the good days, yet another one in his carrier bag.

His daily, hourly thought, was for the next numbing drink but, if there was one thing in his mind besides the liquor and the scything tackle that had done for his burgeoning football career, it was a haunting recollection that never left him. Morgan never shrugged off the torment of his accidental involvement in the death of an innocent man on a summer's morning many years ago, a man just a few years older than himself who had been engulfed in a swamp of sodden, killing clay.

After yet another short spell in jail for being drunk and disorderly, Morgan had used his release money to buy a couple of big bottles of strong cider and a ticket on a National Express bus from the north-west back to his Shropshire home town.

There was an immediate trip to Bargain Booze and a walk in the park to find a quiet bench to drink another of the several bottles now in his bag.

He'd watched through milky eyes as the kids played football on the grass, and had been vaguely aware of a couple playing tennis on the tarmac courts. He almost smiled as the bunch of youngsters – the girls wearing short skirts, some of them with leggings, others with bare legs, the boys in tight jeans and basketball boots – hung around the bandstand drinking coloured bottles of booze, smoking joints and acting up.

Terry was no more sure of what he was doing here than he had been of almost anything else during the last few years, but he had some notion, some vague disquieting sense, that this was the place that he now needed to be if he was ever to face his deeply troubling daily thoughts.

FOURTEEN

'Hi, how you doing?' asked Salt breezily.

The youth was sitting on the backrest of a wooden bench in the little town square, his feet on the seat. He was expectorating every few seconds, almost as if he was afflicted with some sort of uncontrollable phlegm tic. Some of his spit was forming a mini-lake on the pavement as it dripped through the wooden slats of the bench. But plenty missed and was collecting on the timbers of the thing. The two heavily made-up girls sitting to one side of him were wholly untroubled by his unsavoury behaviour.

He looked up at Salt. 'What?' he said, threateningly.

'How you doing?' said Salt once more. The girls ignored the woman. One flipped open her phone and checked for messages.

'What's your problem?' said the youth aggressively.

'Don't remember me, do you?' said Salt.

'No,' he replied immediately.

'On the train. The other day. You stole that boy's console.'

'Bollocks,' he said, and swung down from the bench.

'I don't think bollocks,' she said.

'Anyway, what the fuck's anything to do with you?' he said, spitting again, but this time with some force, the horrible mess landing close to Salt's walking boots.

She pulled out her warrant card from her jeans' pocket. 'I'm a police officer,' she said, 'that's what.'

He sneered.

'You're a bit out of your zone, aren't you?' she said to the youth. 'You got off at Shrewsbury the other day.'

'So what if I did?' he said. 'What's it to you?'

'Nothing,' said Salt. 'Just mentioning it. You two,' she said to the girls. 'I think you'd best be on your way, your friend's coming along with me.'

'Am I, fuck?' he said.

The girls looked at one another and sullenly sloped off.

'Before you think about doing anything stupid,' said Salt

quietly, 'you'd better think about your options. It's Friday lunchtime. Lots of people around. You're not on a train now with a guard hiding down the carriage.' And then she opened her phone and showed him his hazy picture there. But he wasn't stupid.

'So what?' he said.

'So, nothing,' agreed Salt, 'just to show that you and your mate were there,' and she punched the buttons for 999.

'It's not priority,' she explained to the operator, 'but I'm an officer and I've detained a person who you need to speak to about a theft I reported a day or two ago,' and she gave her details. 'Yes, we're on the town square,' she said. 'No, he's not going anywhere,' she added, looking directly at the boy. 'Five minutes? That'll be fine.'

'Cunt,' said the youth to Salt, and pushed his hands deep into his tracksuit bottom pockets.

Why did flower sellers always look, if not exactly like criminals, then certainly as if there was something just a little underhand about them, Salt wondered? Does the resettlement officer, the probation guy or woman, say to blokes about to get out of jail, 'Get yourself a pitch in some little market town and sell tulips, John. It's a decent living, with little outlay. You need no training, and where better to meet any number of women?'

According to Ben Williams, his new-found career was something he'd come up with himself but, based on Jane Salt's non-scientific observations, there seemed to be a hell of a lot of guys with similar backgrounds to his own out there on the high streets punting blooms for their ubiquitous presence to be *quite* such a coincidence.

An hour after the yob had been questioned down at the police station, and subsequently released, Salt took a seat in a little retro café on the opposite side of the town square, adjacent to the stone-arched mediaeval butter market. OK, the kid would only get a few hours' community service or a police caution, but she felt not a little pleased that she'd spotted him and played some part in his being humiliated in front of his young female admirers.

Maybe the cafe wasn't retro, she thought. Maybe it had

always been like this and was just stuck in a time warp? She sat at the rocking, uneven table on an uncomfortable hard-wood chair and a woman brought her a cup of milky coffee, a little of it spilled in the saucer.

She opened her *Guardian*, but didn't get beyond the head-line. What was the point in coming two hundred miles to a town in Shropshire and then reading a newspaper that you could read on the tube every day of the week?

She put the paper down, stirred her coffee and watched the man. Carrie had had to go back to work this morning so, after a lie-in and a shower, Salt had walked the mile or two into town just to hang out there for an hour or so. Just because her own life was listing and awry and she'd taken the bit of the leave that was owing to her, it didn't mean that the rest of the world wasn't going about its business in much the same way as always.

She looked across at him as the man shifted his weight from foot to foot, took a call on his phone, and then punched the buttons to text someone. But really, she wondered uncom-fortably, what *exactly* was she doing here?

The previous evening, the three of them had driven to the pub where the old hippies got together every so often to jam. OK, these guys weren't quite ready for the Roundhouse or the Jazz Café, maybe, but after a few drinks, the atmosphere had been loud and boozy and by eleven o'clock people were doing that crazy, swaying, arms-in-the-air dancing – including Ben and the two women.

Jane Salt was ten years younger than her erstwhile lover, Frank Kavanagh, and she also worked out at the local gym three times a week and swam a dozen lengths of the pool a couple of early mornings a week. She looked better than half the women she worked with, many of whom were a good bit younger than herself. She was aware that this was something that was not going unnoticed by Ben. He was a man whose physical presence next to her as they danced forced her to acknowledge just how Kavanagh really had become the older man that they had once merely joked about him being.

She could feel the heat of Williams and his sexuality and was flattered that it was being directed entirely at her. Whilst Carrie was getting yet another round of drinks, there was a moment as Salt and Ben swirled around one another and brushed close together that was accompanied by a quick look between them which they both knew said: What do you think? What if?

She'd immediately felt very ashamed of herself. Carrie was a good friend, and Salt was staying with her, and yet here she was thinking wildly inappropriate thoughts about this man. And he was looking back at her with only one thought in his mind and only one look in his eyes, a look that had nothing to do with the wailing harmonica and the man with a swaying ponytail who was sawing a frantic violin.

Maybe she'd imagined the whole thing? But if so, what was she doing here now, feeling traitorous towards her friend?

Before Carrie had left for work this morning, Salt had ventured an open-ended: 'What a night . . . I haven't been drunk like that for ages. I hope I didn't . . .'

'What?' said Carrie innocently. 'You needed to let your hair down, Jane. It was good for you.'

'Good,' replied Salt. 'I just hope I wasn't too . . . embarrassing.'

'Who's to know, anyway?' said her friend, smiling.

'Yes, I suppose so,' said Salt.

'Right,' said Carrie, picking up her bag and briefcase, 'I'm away to the office. I'll see you about five to half past. OK?'

'Sure,' said Salt.

'You got anything planned?' asked her friend as she stood at the open cottage door.

'No,' said Salt, colouring and feeling treacherous. 'Nothing much, just going to mooch about, maybe take a walk.'

'Well, take care,' said Carrie, and she was gone.

Salt watched from the café as the flower seller scrolled down his message before sending it. Maybe he was texting Carrie right now? Salt checked her own phone. Nothing. Kavanagh was either alright, or he was pretending to be. She dropped her Nokia back down into her bag.

Williams wrapped some anemones for a woman and they exchanged a few words before she left with a smile.

Those Great Train robbers, recalled Salt, they knew they were after a lot of cash and postal orders, but even they were surprised when they found they'd got sacks full of the stuff: a couple of million quid it turned out to be, if her memory served, which was a lot of money back then. It wouldn't pay a Chelsea striker's wages for a month these days, but in 1963 it was enough to buy you a bar on the Costa *and* have enough left over to send the kids to private school back in the UK.

She sipped her coffee as the man rearranged the flowers in his galvanized buckets. He gathered a few bunches together, chucked the water from the two empty vessels down the gutter and took a few steps back to look at the rearranged display.

Those blaggers had achieved almost mythical status, a bit like Lady Di and the public's hysterical reaction to her tragic death, behaving as if they'd actually *known* the woman. The train caper was much the same, as if these London crims with records that went way, way back, were just a bunch of plucky geezers having a bit of a laugh.

After they'd done their time, most of them went back to their old thieving ways, but Edwards had a mid-career change of heart and, unless Jane Salt was mistaken he, too, took to flogging roses outside Waterloo or King's Cross.

This man, standing beside his striped awning with its racks and metal buckets on Oswestry's Mill Street was no train robber, and the worst that happened here were Saturday night scraps and the occasional window being put in just for the sound of falling plate.

Salt finished her coffee. Was she supposed to ask for the bill, or go up and pay? She looked to the woman behind the counter and gathered her few things together.

Williams was serving two youngsters. They had one of those fierce-looking dogs with them on a very short lead. Can't judge a book and all that, she thought. You can have something that looks like what the tabloids were calling a 'weapon dog', and also be a decent enough kid to be buying your mother or your girlfriend a nice bunch of flowers, she reasoned.

The flower seller tucked his phone into his collar and wrapped a bunch of roses at the same time, but then he didn't give the boys the yellow flowers, he held them towards them, glanced surreptitiously up and down the street and then slipped something under the wrapping as they passed him money. They immediately walked away. Salt smiled to herself and felt relieved on at least two counts. 'Right,' she murmured. 'Old habits.'

'Sorry, love?' said the café owner who was now standing beside her table.

'Oh, sorry, it's nothing,' said Salt. 'Lovely cup of coffee,' she added. 'Just like my mum used to make.'

FIFTEEN

Older people usually have a sense that they are being observed. If they're walking down a dark lane at night, they'll be wary, think that there might just be someone the other side of the hedge or fence or behind that tree, ready to jump out and kill them or whatever. It never happens, of course, because, if they were to think about it, just what kind of criminal, hijacker, blagger or plain bad man is going to spend days, weeks, months, maybe, hiding down this very isolated dark country lane waiting for someone to come along whom they can mug? All the real robbers are hanging out in dark alleys and underpasses in the city, not amongst the hedges and trees with the stoats and weasels and badgers. No matter. Maybe it's because older folk have seen too many movies where this is precisely what *does* happen that they are a little wary and afraid.

But young folk, kids, what do they know? They're never on their guard – maybe they've not seen enough movies yet – especially when they've drunk a couple of vodka Red Bulls or bottles of strong cider.

Gary Thomas's daughter, Lauren, wasn't drunk this Saturday afternoon. Not exactly, but the sixteen-year-old was a slight girl and it only took two or three shots to put her into that hazy, slightly disconnected, faintly happy mood that she liked very much indeed. It was the kind of feeling, after all, that kids sought and why they even had a drink in the first place for God's sake. When the politicians and drugs' counsellors talked about the terrible harm that heroin and cocaine and the like did to people, how it blighted their lives and ruined them – which of course it did – very few of them ever mentioned the fact that the reason people took drugs at all was, before they *did* ruin your life, taking them felt pretty good. For most people, it was the best feeling they'd ever had: it was better than good sex and much better than money in the bank. It made you feel *terrific*.

So, Lauren was sixteen and if she didn't drink so much that she got ill and threw up and felt awful, she liked hanging around in the park near the bandstand and playing about a bit with the other kids of her age.

Her boyfriend, seventeen-year-old Daniel, walked her to the traffic lights at the edge of town. They stood on the pavement, swaying slightly in one another's arms, and had a long kiss goodbye as he held her to him and she slipped her hand down the back of his jeans. A couple of painters went past in their van and hooted good-naturedly at the loving young couple.

A few minutes later, Daniel disappeared round the corner and Lauren began the rest of her walk home. She was feeling pretty wasted and pretty good and she wandered about from side to side and, once or twice, missed her footing and stumbled from the pavement into the road.

These days, even in places more remote than this, on mountainsides and high passes, there were drinks' cans, cigarette ends and sweet wrappers to be found, and when Lauren stepped back onto the pavement she aimed a girlish kick at a pizza box along the footway until it, too, tumbled into the road.

She walked close to the high stone wall now, trailing her fingers along its rough stones for a few moments. The wall that bordered the woodland of her father's estate extended from the very outskirts of the town, south, right up to the security gates at the imposing front drive of their house.

Headphones in her ears, she was unaware of the occasional car that laboured up the hill and then passed by, or the late afternoon birdsong on the air.

From a gap in the wall on the other side of the road, a place where a coping stone had, over many years eventually been forced out by the thick ivy there, an unseen man watched her halting, swaying progress.

A maroon Vauxhall approached the girl from behind and slowed to a crawl. The man on the other side of the wall, a bottle of Buckfast Abbey wine clutched in his hand, looked on.

The car drew away from the youngster, and carried on up the hill. The watching man took a long draught from the bottle.

The girl's phone, which she clutched in her hand, beeped and vibrated and she stopped, read an incoming message and immediately tapped the keys in reply.

The man leaned on the other side of the wall and wiped his lips with the back of his hand as the Vauxhall came back, passed the girl on the opposite side of the road and then reversed into a turning place a hundred yards further on.

The driver turned the car round and this time, as he drew level with the girl, he leaned across the passenger seat and wound down the window.

'Er, do you know . . .?' he began hesitantly. She moved towards the car and bent down to the window. At that moment, a Range Rover appeared at the crest of the hill and came speeding down the road. The Vauxhall driver glanced up, saw the vehicle, engaged first gear and accelerated away.

As the Range Rover pulled up opposite her, the girl crossed the road, opened the passenger door and stepped up into the huge vehicle.

In a voice that combined in that one, three-letter word surprise, affront and just a hint of reluctant gratitude for the lift, she said, 'Dad?'

As he pulled away, and she fastened her seat belt, she turned her face away from him, the cigarette tobacco and alcohol of an hour ago still on her breath, the packet of chewing gum that she always kept with her on these occasions, still unopened in her pocket.

'You alright then, Lauren?' asked her father brightly, glancing at his daughter from the armchair comfort of his seat.

''Course,' she said, looking out of the side window, and careful to breathe only through her nose.

'Was that one of your friends in that car?' he asked.

'No,' she said. 'I don't know who it was. I think he was lost, he was just going to ask me something, and then he drove off.'

'You know what we've told you,' he said seriously, looking across at her. 'Don't speak to strangers, and don't ever, *ever* get into anyone's car, no matter what they tell you, even if they are lost. OK?'

'Dad, you've told me a million times. Alright? I *am* sixteen you know.'

'Yes,' he said. 'I *do* know.'

Almost every father loves his daughter more than his own life. But Gary Thomas had been forty-two years old before his wife, on her third IVF cycle of treatment, had finally conceived their first child, and it was therefore possible that he loved his only child even more than most other men.

'Anyway, what made you come down?' Lauren asked her father.

'Just fancied getting out for a bit of air,' he said as they sat in the climate-controlled vehicle. 'There's nothing on the tele, anyway. You know what Saturday afternoon's like . . .'

The man behind the wall watched as, a little further down the road her father did a three-point turn and roared back up the hill until they disappeared from sight. He sucked the last drop of wine from the bottle and dropped it onto the pile with the others that lay in a heap there.

SIXTEEN

London, 2010

Maybe it was on account of her inappropriate and ill-judged behaviour with Carrie's boyfriend but when, later that evening, Kavanagh did finally call her number and she saw his name against the incoming call, Jane Salt was glad to open her phone and punch the 'receive' button.

For his part, when she said 'Hello,' he found himself at a loss as to how to begin. He recalled all too clearly the way that, only a few days previously, she had come back from the bathroom into the half-lit bedroom and said: 'Frank, I can't go on like this . . .' and he had seen their life together lurch to an end.

'How are you?' he asked solicitously, as if speaking courteously to a complete stranger.

'I'm OK,' she said, neither of them speaking any kind of truth.

'How's Carrie?' he asked absurdly.

'She's OK,' said Salt. 'Carrie's fine.'

'Jane, look,' he said boldly, 'I was thinking of coming up.'

There was a long pause.

'I don't think that's a good idea,' she said.

'No?' he ventured.

'I need a little bit of time . . . you know?'

'More time?' he said, and there was a further long silence between them.

'I think so, yes,' she said. 'How's your ankle?'

'On the mend. It's getting a bit better,' he said.

'And things at work?' she asked. 'Anything special?'

'The boy in north London, the one who was shot . . .'

'Yes, I heard it on the news,' she said. What a relief it was to speak of third-party things, notwithstanding the tragic nature of that event, rather than their own travails.

'How's it going?' she asked. 'Any leads?'

'Skinner's on it,' he said. 'But it's the usual. Everyone clammed up, afraid. There might be some kid prepared to stand up . . . you know? If the deal's right.'

'Sure. I'm sorry,' she added.

'What are you doing up there, Jane?' he asked her directly.

'Not much,' she said, seeking to reassure him. 'We go for a walk, and we talk a lot. We went to the pub the other night. I'm just trying to get some thinking time,' she said.

'About us?' he asked plaintively.

'Yes, about us. About everything, really,' she added.

Another long silence.

'I think maybe I'd better go now, Frank. Is that alright?'

'Sure,' he said. 'If that's what you want.'

'Just now, I think it's best.'

'Jane, you're not seeing someone else are you?' he blurted out. He was deeply embarrassed to ask such a thing, but his need to ask the question was even greater than the humiliation that he felt in posing it.

'Of course not,' she said emphatically.

'Take care,' he murmured, a little reassured.

'Goodnight,' she said, and closed her phone.

SEVENTEEN

Shropshire, 2010

Writer Julian Betts was like a man who had found a new church in which to worship, but he was a man who was singing the praises not of the Lord, but of Linden Lane and Whispering Oaks, and his very own little piece of suburban heaven at 33 Low Brook Road on Meadow Rise.

However, it wasn't all Eden: Betts had lived in his west London mansion block for the previous twenty years. The flat was spacious and, surrounded by other apartments, more often than not, he'd had to open windows and turn down the central heating to keep the place cool. Up here in Shropshire, not only was his new suburban house detached, but the town was hundreds of miles further north than balmy London.

The previous owner of Betts's home had lived there for nearly forty years and manifestly had little interest in matters domestic. According to the estate agent, the somewhat shabby condition of the place – a fact reflected in the price, of course – was on account of this man having spent much of his time away from the house.

Retiring early from the local tax office on 'health grounds' – Derek Hayes had recurring migraine problems that necessitated his lying in a darkened room for hours on end when he was thus afflicted – the civil servant spent months at a time in places as far away as southern Africa and the Americas researching nineteenth-century railways for the book he was one day going to write.

Once retired, the man's migraines became much less frequent and he died from a heart attack at seventy-eight, leaving behind a dozen notebooks filled with the information that was his book in embryo. His nephew threw them all away one Wednesday afternoon – along with all of the other bits and pieces of which the grateful young man had no need

– as he and his girlfriend cleared out the house, prior to its being sold in probate.

If the bad news was that, even now, in the early springtime, it was pretty cold at night, the good news was that, rooting around for an idea for his next newspaper column, Betts was pretty sure that there'd be enough of a story in his having insulation contractors in the house for him to tease a few hundred words out of the experience.

Writers could always turn a phrase. And if you could turn a phrase, you could write about anything. What was it one of the writers on the *Superman* movie said? 'Some people can read *War and Peace* and come away thinking it's a simple adventure story. Others can read the ingredients on a chewing gum wrapper and unlock the secrets of the universe.'

Betts was no Tolstoy, but he knew very well that he could write. After all, he'd made a good living out of penning inconsequential nonsense about soufflés and scallops for over thirty years. So what that now, one week he knocked out a few paragraphs on having his furniture hauled up to Shropshire; the next, a thousand words on the uncanny quiet of the road he lived on? Up here, the very flap of a pigeon's wings at noon could be as startling as a thunderclap, and the next-door neighbours conducted their domestic affairs so quietly that to hear two plates colliding on their way to the washing-up bowl was often the only signal in an entire day that anyone lived there at all.

He'd wrapped it all up a bit, of course, and been careful not to identify anyone directly as, given that even up here in the cultural permafrost of the Shropshire borders, someone might just stumble upon his piece in the Sunday broadsheet or – less likely this, surely – the local rag pick up something from his column and comment on it, and he had no wish to make enemies of any of these people.

So, the sound of birds and the sight of lots of lovely (unidentifiable) trees one week; a wry pop at the 'Keep It Local' campaign and their proselytizing against supermarkets the next. And now, here he was jotting down a few words of nonchalant, witty observation about Shropshire tradesmen and their idiosyncratic ways. No matter that he hadn't even yet hired the company who were going to insulate his house against the permeating weather: he'd already met enough local workmen to feel quite sure that whoever turned up would generate a little dross for him to fashion into columnist gold.

And he did have to write with a certain panache to ensure that his column was read at all these days. His own Sunday broadsheet had as many words in it as a decent-sized novel. After he had collected it from the front doorstep, he always stood at the kitchen table and ruthlessly filleted its twelve or fifteen sections – sections that included such things as the prospects for economic growth in the Cayman Islands and the state of Malaysian ecology.

Betts was someone with a vested interest in the pile of newsprint that remained but, as day followed day throughout the week, he felt reproached as most of it sat there unread.

On Saturday evenings, he invariably put the whole thing in the recycling box and felt a sense of relief that lasted only until he heard the ominous thud of the following morning's delivery, something which felt like finding a fresh corpse lying on the doorstep every single Sunday morning.

He opened the *Yellow Pages* and called the first company that he came to. 'Shropshire Insulation. Dawn speaking,' chirped the girl. 'How can I help you?' she said.

'Hello, this is Julian Betts. I'd like someone to come over and see me about double glazing, or possibly having the roof insulated? Yes, I'm in Oswestry. A detached house in Low Brook Road. 33. Do you know it?'

Replacing the phone, the diminutive man stood at the study window and looked out on the garden. He was delighted to see the first tiny green spikes of the sweet peas that he had recently planted there breaking the surface of the earth.

EIGHTEEN

Jane Salt was faced with a dilemma. Relationship break-ups, relationship fall-outs, they were always difficult. She knew it very well, was right in the middle of one herself. But right now, more to the point, and much more pressing, was exactly what she should share with Carrie about her drug-dealing boyfriend's behaviour.

It would have been bad enough if he'd simply been an early-release prisoner who'd compromised the terms of his parole supervision. Half the lags that were let out on licence did that. No surprise there. After all, most of them had no education to speak of and had been in trouble with the law since they were kids. They didn't know anything else and they didn't know anyone else. If anyone at all met them at the prison gates it was their mates and scallywags and they went straight to the pub or some crack house or scored some skunk, spent their get-out-of-jail dosh in a day or two and were out robbing again within a week. It was understandable, and it was tragic and it was very, very difficult indeed to break that cycle, of course. Precisely where were they going to find some new mates who went to bed at a reasonable time and got up and went to work in the morning? They weren't. At least most of them weren't.

But Ben had somehow got involved with Carrie, or she with him, and this was much more high stakes. She would prob-ably lose her job if her relationship with him were revealed at all, and she would certainly lose it if it were found that he was not only bedding her but, instead of wrapping tulips, was dealing ten-pound wraps of coke or skunk on the streets of the very town where she lived.

However, as with all relationship issues, there were dif-ficulties; people broke up and people took sides, and there were boundaries to be observed. It was a very delicate area, and one which, in overstepping those boundaries, you immediately put your own relationship and friendship with one or other – or usually both – at risk.

'Carrie?' said Salt, lifting the saucepan lid and checking the rice on the hob.

'Yep,' she said.

'You and Ben . . .?'

'Yes?'

'How's it going? Really?'

'Still pretty good, detective,' her friend replied.

'Honest?' pursued Salt.

'Honest,' said Carrie. 'I wouldn't necessarily give him a kidney just yet . . .'

'A kidney?' queried Salt.

'You know, like those stories in the TV regional news they're always doing, where a brother or a lover gives up an organ for a child or their sister or something.'

'Oh, right, yes, I see,' said Salt.

'Anyway, why do you ask?' said her friend.

'Is he . . . behaving?' queried the policewoman.

'He behaves for me,' she replied with a smile. 'He's very good actually in that department . . .'

'Yes?' said Salt. 'I didn't actually mean that.'

'Is he behaving?' repeated Carrie. 'Ben runs a flower stall, Jane. He goes to the market in Brum at five o'clock most mornings and is in bed by ten every night except Saturday, when, if we're lucky, we get a curry from the local Indian and then he falls asleep in front of the football. Yes, I think you could say he's behaving.'

'Does he make any money?' asked Salt, pursuing another angle and hoping to lead her friend gently to the place that she needed her to be.

'He does alright. He doesn't make as much as I do, and he doesn't make as much as when he was growing dope. But he's legal now. He pays his rent on the flat and the ware-house and he usually offers to pay if we go to the flicks.'

'Right,' said Salt, leaving the door for further enquiry open.

Carrie opened a bottle of Shiraz and said, 'Why do you ask, Jane? I don't think you like him, do you?'

'I like him fine,' said Salt. 'I'm just concerned, you know . . .'

'Concerned?' echoed Carrie. 'How do you mean?'

'It's high stakes, Carrie, your job and all that? Can you

imagine if he were to step out of line, or something? The local press would get it and then you'd have the *Daily Mail* knocking down your door. You'd lose your job, and everything that goes with it—'

'Hey, hey,' she interrupted. 'Jane, I know what's at stake. We are very discreet. He's given me his word. He's not some low-life robber or something. He was growing dope as a business; there was nothing impetuous about it. He virtually had a business plan, and in a way, who can blame him. Here, have a glass of wine,' and she passed Salt her drink.

'Thanks,' said Salt and the two women clinked glasses and exchanged an awkward smile. 'I just think you should be careful,' said the policewoman.

The lid on the rice pan started wobbling and Carrie lifted it to stir the basmati. 'So, has Frank been in touch?' she asked pointedly.

'Yes,' said Salt. 'But let's not go there either, eh?'

'Sure,' said Carrie. 'Why don't we leave both of the men out of it?'

'Deal,' said Salt, and they touched glasses once more. 'Why not?'

NINETEEN

The last march that sixty-five-year-old Julian Betts had been on was to protest about the war in Vietnam in 1968 as a rather late-developing twenty-three-year-old. He had suspected that the war was almost certainly wrong, but in truth, not only did he know very little about it, but he was slightly worried by the vast numbers of people as young, and sometimes a good deal younger than himself, who seemed absolutely certain about the rights and wrongs of the conflict, and spoke about it as if they were on first-name terms with all sorts of people in that faraway country.

Notwithstanding the little he knew about the Vietnam war, he went on the march to the American embassy in Grosvenor Square on that Saturday, but he made sure that he stayed well to the back when the running amok, fighting with the police and the throwing of missiles began.

He was only there, really, because his girlfriend, dark-haired beauty, Barbara, four years younger than himself, did appear to feel passionately about it, and if she were to continue to feel passionate about him, he felt that the least that was required of him was to feign something like commensurate commitment to the cause.

Truth to tell, even had he felt entirely sanguine about his opposition to the war, he would not have felt comfortable chanting puerile refrains as some young man with a megaphone repeatedly bellowed, 'America; America' to which the crowd responded rather predictably with, 'Out; out; out,' and urged them into battle against the embassy, the cops, and almost certain destruction beneath the hooves of those – even at a hundred yards away – terrifyingly large horses.

So, Betts didn't like chanting crowds, and he wasn't even sure that he'd have been able to place Vietnam on a blank map back in 1968, and he certainly felt distinctly ill at ease when it came to calling out the name of Ho Chi Minh, the North Vietnamese leader, as if he actually *knew* the man.

However, Barbara was a beautiful young woman and, even though a full acknowledgement of his true sexual orientation was several years away, at this heady time, a couple of hours tramping through west London streets and calling out a stranger's name had seemed a very small price to pay for enjoying the pleasures of her dark and mysterious being.

This Saturday morning, Betts stood in the doorway of the newsagents, a *Daily Telegraph* tucked discreetly under his arm, and watched as the crowd milled about and prepared to march around the town's main streets. People fixed placards and balloons to pushchair and bicycle handles, and even now, someone was starting to mumble inaudibly into a whining microphone.

A few minutes later, the first of several speakers mounted the little platform. It was not unlike the anti-American chanting in Grosvenor Square all those years ago, but here, today, the watchword was 'local'. The audience was apparently receptive to any speaker, just so long as every other sentence that they uttered employed that word: local politics, local campaigns, local issues and local food. In an impressively rambling speech, one young man managed to excoriate motor cars, Spanish strawberries and Kenyan green beans in a seamless diatribe.

Another speaker began a tirade against the only franchise coffee house in the town with its comfortable sofas, free newspapers and good coffee and insisted the place should be boycotted until it was forced out of the town.

Under one of the sagging banners, suspended between eight-feet-high poles, the boyish-looking girl with pink hair who had delivered Betts's leaflet was in conversation with the man in the expensively tailored hacking jacket with whom she had walked away that day. He eventually mounted the dais and was introduced as the vice chair of Keep It Local. He shifted uneasily from foot to foot and delivered his 'speech' in a diffident manner, eschewing rant or excess.

His reasoned arguments against the proposed supermarket – it would be too close to the town centre and there were other much more suitable alternatives – and his quiet delivery, impressed Betts. The little crowd, however, was by now quite boisterous with whistles and horns and bells and appeared to want something more animated and impassioned from their speakers. There was only a ripple of applause as the sandy-haired man handed the microphone over to the chairperson of the group, Carol Reddy, who delivered her punchy points in staccato lines with pointed emphasis that even a babe in arms – of which there were several – could not fail to appreciate.

A girl of eight or nine approached the writer as he huddled in the doorway reading the headlines of his newspaper. Her stern-faced mother held out a petition to him. He took the piece of paper from her and signed it immediately. 'You on the march?' she enquired glancing at the newspaper under his arm.

'I'd have loved to,' he asserted, 'but I have to get home. I've some workmen due in an hour.'

'Umm,' she replied, unconvinced. She took the sheet from him without thanks or acknowledgement and walked away. That was the trouble with people who advocated radical change, he had often found: they were such miseries that, no matter how worthy the cause, they were invariably people in whose world you would choose not to live.

TWENTY

Regrettably, on a regular basis, youngsters used the twisting road out of town towards Welshpool, past Gareth Thomas's estate, as their Friday night race-track. And, not infrequently, their hatchbacks with their big exhausts and shiny alloy wheels would leave the road, mount the pavement and smash into the high stone wall on one of the many fast bends there. Remarkably, many of the drivers, and some of their passengers, survived with little more than broken bones, whiplash, concussion, cuts and bruises. Some didn't, of course, and left their bereaved parents to mourn their loss for the rest of their lives. Wilted flowers, even faded plastic ones, marked the spot for months after the tragedy, annual tributes to this or that teenage son or daughter appearing every year in the local press, a photograph of their child, frozen in time, maudlin rhyming couplets accompanying the piece. So what? Just because the authors of these mawkish sentiments weren't Tennyson or Larkin didn't mean that their feelings were any less heartfelt.

This Friday evening's crash had not involved a death, and the three youngsters in the souped-up Fiat had been taken to the local hospital, but were all back home with their grateful families the following day.

The car, though, was a write-off and the teenagers had had a lucky escape. The wall itself had lost quite a few stones and, by the following mid-morning, two of Thomas's men stood there and for a few moments looked down at the million fragments of windscreen glass, the tarmac stained with oil and now covered with sand, before they began to rebuild the wall.

The sun shone as they stacked stones and mixed cement on the pavement just above the place where the car had hit the gutter and left the road before glancing off the wall. At noon, after a cup of tea, Sean, the younger man said, 'I'm off for a piss.'

'Sure,' said his mate, Dennis, as he sat down on a cement bag and rolled a cigarette.

With the aid of an overhanging branch to help him, Sean clambered over the wall at a place where a coping stone was missing.

A few minutes later he returned. 'Some bugger's sleeping rough down there,' he said.

'Yes?' said Dennis.

'Must be an alky. There's a ton of bottles there, along with a couple of black plastic sacks and a sleeping bag.'

'Rather him than me,' said Dennis. 'You wouldn't get much sleep with kids driving into the wall half the night,' and they laughed at the bitter joke.

'We'd better tell the boss later,' said Sean.

'Yes,' agreed the other man as he chucked another shovelful of sand into the mixer. 'He'll have him moved on, that's for sure.'

TWENTY-ONE

Following a lengthy consultation with a man from the insulating company, Betts had eschewed the notion of replacing the fluted-glass front door with a new, aesthetically-distressed double-glazed one – no matter what the claimed energy-saving benefits – and had opted instead for the best part of a foot of fibreglass wool to be laid in the loft.

He was meant to remove the existing material himself before the men arrived to install the new stuff but, as the surveyor had made clear to him with the Shropshire equivalent of a nod and a wink, if he 'sorted' the contractors out a 'drink', they'd be prepared to remove it and dispose of it for him.

It didn't even cross Betts' mind that he might do the job himself: having once peered through the hatch when he'd originally bought the house, he knew that he wouldn't have been able to clamber into the loft, let alone straddle the joists there and remove what looked like acres of moth-eaten, tatty fibreglass, to say nothing of the possible effects of the horrible stuff on his lungs.

As arranged, Darren and his big, lumpen mate, Tony, arrived on Saturday, just after noon. Slim Darren ascended the ladder into the roof space. Five minutes later he stepped back down onto the landing and went through a hands-on-hips, blimey-that's-a-big-dirty-job routine that secured bargaining rights with their clearly prosperous client.

'So, how much do you think you'll charge me, then?' asked Betts. 'To remove all the old stuff?'

'What do you reckon, Tony?' asked Darren, milking the theatre of the moment.

'How long'll it take?' asked his doltish-looking mate.

'Three hours, at least,' he said, looking at Betts, 'and we've got to bag it all and then pay for it to be disposed,' he added, a little ungrammatically. 'About two hundred?' said Darren. 'It's a good price, really, Mr Betts. Alright?'

'Alright,' said the writer. They could have said five hundred

for all he knew or cared. He was still on London rates and
his column earned him twice that, took him about forty minutes
to write, and he didn't have to wear a breathing mask, knee
pads and overalls when he wrote it. And anyway, it was clear
to anyone at all who looked around his house that Betts wasn't
short of a grand or two: he had his newspaper stipend, a couple
of hundred thousand pounds in savings that had effortlessly
accrued over the years, to say nothing of the huge premium
he had taken out of the sale of his London flat, a mere forty
percent of which he had needed to buy his new house in
Shropshire.

Tony, a naturally distrustful man, and also a man who had
an innate talent for misreading almost any situation, said
bluntly, 'We get paid upfront, you know? Before we do the
job.'

'Really?' said Betts. 'I don't think I've two hundred in cash,
but I can pop down to the cashpoint right now if you like?'

'It's OK,' said Darren. 'Later'll be fine. You couldn't put
the kettle on, though, could you? A cuppa would be great.'

'Certainly,' said Betts, and left them to their work.

It was odd hearing other people in his house. He was not
yet fully acquainted with all the little creaks and jolts and
noises that any house makes as the central heating warms
through the place in the evenings, the cistern in the loo refills
and the odd floorboard creaks as you tread about the hall.

But there was something almost companionable about having
even these strangers working here, and he liked hearing them
call to one another as they went about the job and he himself
sat contentedly at the word processor tapping out paragraphs
for the following week's column.

When Darren had filled the plastic bags, he shoved them
down through the loft hatch to his mate below who then
trailed in and out of the back door and stuffed them in the
van.

Betts made the men tea and washed up his breakfast things.
'I'll just nip into town,' he said, and left them to it as he
drove his smart Audi away to the bank.

Half an hour later, when he returned, Darren was sitting in
the driver's seat of the van, the door open, his feet sticking out

between it and the front pillar. Tony was on the doorstep. Both men were eating and reading newspapers.

A little unwisely, perhaps, Betts couldn't entirely resist a pointed look at his watch, suggesting very clearly to the lunching men that their three-hour task of stripping the loft had been something of an overestimate.

This bit of theatre didn't go unnoticed by Tony, who immediately got up from the doorstep. 'Problem?' he asked as he towered over the writer.

'No, I don't think so,' said Betts. 'Excuse me, please,' he said, and made to enter his home.

'We've got something for you, Mr Betts,' said Darren seeking to defuse the tension.

'Yes?' he said.

'We found this up there,' said the roofing man, and handed the writer an old brown canvas bag from beside him on the passenger seat.

'What is it?' asked Betts, taking it from the young man.

'Somebody's lunch bag,' he said. 'It was tucked right down in the eaves. Probably been there since the house was built. Someone must have left it there,' he added.

'Did you open it?' asked Betts.

'Course,' he said, 'but there's no gold in there.'

'The tea's gone cold, too,' said Tony, sitting down again and picking up his newspaper.

It took Betts a moment to realize that the man was making a joke and was talking about the flask that was sticking out of the bag, not the grubby mug on the step beside him.

'Yes, I bet it has,' said Betts in his own awkward attempt to negotiate a sort of peace with a man to whom he had taken something of a dislike.

Betts lifted the flap very gingerly. Its brass clasp was completely green. Grimacing slightly, he peeled apart a piece of Sunblest greaseproof paper that had the residue of some sort of green mould on it. A chocolate wrapper had the melt and stain of brown on it. The man in the van watched him as he then took out a yellowed Daily Mirror, the newspaper folded open to the horse-racing pages.

'Amazing,' said Betts, and he knew what next week's column would now be about. This was much more interesting than run-of-the-mill stuff about the town's profusion of Chinese herbalists and Bach flower therapy practitioners. Who knows, if he found the time, he might even check out the history of the housing estate and come up with some whimsy about just who this thing might once have belonged to. 'Shall I make some more tea? I quite fancy a cup myself,' he said brightly.

'Never say no,' said Darren, getting down from the van and arching his back. 'We've only got to lay the new stuff now. We shouldn't be long.'

'Good,' said Betts. 'Excellent,' and he carried the bag with him into the kitchen.

Later that afternoon, the roof insulators were down at the council tip where, having agreed a backhander with the supervisor, they dumped the old insulating material into one of the skips there. 'We left the best bit behind,' said Darren to the man as they unloaded sacks from the van.

'Yes?' said the supervisor.

'You never guess what we found up in the roof.'

'A body?' said the man, downbeat.

'Yes, you bet. No, we found a bag. It'd been there for years. Had an old paper in it and all . . . 196 . . . What year was it, Tony?'

'Fuck knows, but it had a rotten fuckin' sandwich in it, I know that,' he said. 'And you wouldn't want to eat that fucker,' he added in his most expansive comment of the day.

'I bet,' said the man, little interested and wholly unimpressed. Ten minutes later, he took the twenty pounds from Darren, and the men were gone.

It wasn't the most interesting story that the council tip supervisor had ever heard, but he did mention it to a friend that evening in the pub in between discussing that day's premier league results. His mate mentioned it to his wife the next day and, within a couple of days, Betts himself got a call from Brian Dalton, the long-time editor of the local paper.

'How on earth did you hear about that?' asked Betts, a little discomfited and not a little put out at the prospect of having the subject for his own column pre-empted by the provincial rag.

'Oh, it came in from one of our "sources",' said Dalton rather grandly.

'Really,' said Betts.

'You're making quite a name for yourself,' said the editor, with just a hint of disapproval.

'Yes?' said Betts, both a little alarmed and intrigued.

'You know, the piece you did recently, about the Keep It Local campaigners?'

'Yes?' said Betts. 'What about them?'

'Oh, nothing,' said Dalton, 'but people round here, you know, they can get quite worked up about local issues.'

'It was only a light-hearted piece,' said Betts, feeling a little chastised.

'Of course it was,' said the editor, dismissing the man's concerns. 'Anyway, about the bag that was found at your house . . .'

'Yes, what about it?' said Betts defensively.

'Well, I was thinking we might do a bit of a piece on it. You know, kind of mystery of the last lunch, and how did it get there sort of thing.'

There was silence down the telephone line.

'Hello, Julian?' said Dalton. 'Are you still there?'

'Well, I'm not sure,' said Betts, feeling rather protective of his little story as he felt it begin to slip from his grasp.

'I wonder if you'd mind if I came up and took a look at it?' said the newspaper man, ignoring the columnist's reservations.

'Well, I suppose you could,' said Betts reluctantly, 'but do you mind if we leave it just for now. I have to be away for a day or two. I've an appointment in London,' he lied, as if the very name of the capital vouchsafed the importance of his fictitious trip.

'I'll only take a few minutes of your time,' pursued the editor.

'Let me check my diary, and I'll give you a ring back,' said Betts, doing his best to close the door on the conversation but without being too abrupt.

'I really would be very grateful,' insisted the man. 'You know, with it being a local interest story and all. Our readers love anything like that. They'd be dead chuffed.'

'Yes, I'm sure,' said Betts. 'Look, can I give you a call back later?'

'Thanks a lot, Julian,' said Dalton, fully resolved that whether Betts liked it or not, the local paper would be running the story. 'It'd be much appreciated.'

TWENTY-TWO

'Great!' thought Salt. 'I come up here to get away from the stress of my own rubbish relationship, and what happens? My bloke doesn't even contact me for days and now, here I am, stuck in a rented car in the middle of nowhere on some pathetic surveillance operation on my friend's dodgy boyfriend. Bugger! What *am* I doing?'

She hunkered down low in her car, one of several in the potholed car park on the mini industrial estate, down a track off some B road in a Godforsaken place called Morda. A joiner had his workshop there, Ben Williams had his flower wholesaling warehouse, there was a car paint-spraying outfit and another company which, according to the sign above their unit, was a furniture upholsterer.

At the same time as Salt was scrunched down in her car watching Williams's warehouse, writer Julian Betts, was putting the finishing touches to his customary one o'clock, lunchtime salad.

He didn't receive a lot of calls these days. People say they'll be in touch, but they're not, of course. He was up here, those very few friends that he had – and all of his former colleagues – were 'down there'.

Since his long-term partner had passed away two years previously after a long struggle with an AIDS-related illness, Betts had lost touch with even more of their mutual acquaintance, for it was with his companion, Robert, that most of them had maintained their friendship, rather than Julian himself.

His former work associates – his editor and subs and a photographer or two – were not the kind of folk who were going to call him and invite themselves up for a weekend in the country. Thank God. He'd never had that kind of relationship with anyone in the office, and he no longer had those kinds of friendships.

He didn't mind. He was having the house improved, he

was penning his column, he'd even begun growing a few things in the formerly barren and neglected garden. He'd already bought a couple of books and found himself listening in to *Gardeners Question Time* on the radio, along with all the other folk who were presumably too stupid or too idle to take down a book from the shelf in the library, or buy one in W.H. Smith's. Oh, well.

No, he didn't receive a lot of telephone calls these days. And he certainly didn't welcome any just as the lunchtime weather forecast was ending and *The World at One* was about to begin. 'Bugger,' he muttered as he walked towards the telephone.

'Hello?' The line was open, but there was no sound from the caller. 'Hello?' said Betts more peremptorily. 'Hello?' he said again.

Silence.

'I think you must have the wrong number,' he said and was about to replace the receiver when a voice said, 'Betts.' The use of his name left him in no doubt whatsoever that this was no wrong number.

'Sorry?' said the writer. 'Who is this, please?'

'Just shut up,' said the man's voice. 'You've got to learn when to keep quiet.'

'What . . .? What on earth do you mean?' Betts stuttered out. He looked to the window, and then the kitchen door, afraid that this horrible intrusion into his quiet, ordered life might suddenly metamorphose into someone's actual arrival in his house.

'Do you understand?'

'W-why?' he stammered. 'What have I done? I haven't done anything . . .'

'Just keep all of your stupid thoughts to yourself,' said the man. 'Do you understand? And don't say anything to anyone about this call. Then everything'll be alright.' And suddenly the line was dead.

Salt must have been watching the warehouse for more than an hour when Williams finally sauntered out and climbed the fire escape's iron staircase to his flat above the premises.

What was she looking for, anyway? She'd no idea, but

she didn't want to jump in and cause what was certain to become a huge problem between this man and Carrie. At least not without having some more stand-up evidence of his wrongdoing than seeing him slip something to a couple of dodgy-looking young lads on the high street.

And anyway, although 'intelligence' was vital to police work, operations based on it often went wrong and it was just as often proven to be well wide of the mark. Salt had been involved in any number of surveillance tasks where the stake-out had been undertaken on little more than a hunch, the outcome entirely unpredictable.

And it was so *boring*. Of course, in the flicks, it was over in a few minutes, people joshed and broke wind, and folk went for coffees (always just as the action was about to kick off) and if you were lucky there were all sorts of sophisticated listening devices and even mini-cameras, that not only conveniently framed the suspects, but were always in focus and of improbably good picture quality.

The operations Salt had been on were more like her present sojourn in the driver's seat of her Volvo S40, with intercoms and walkie-talkies that didn't work properly, no back-up, and officers who simply fell asleep with the sheer ennui of the interminable business.

She held an old *Observer* crossword in front of her as someone drove up in a Toyota saloon with a damaged passenger's-side door. He disappeared into the vehicle workshop and, a few minutes later emerged with a man in overalls. The guy stood back and took in the damage with a professional's eye. He then ran his hand along the car door and made some notes on his pad. The two men exchanged a few further words and the owner drove off.

Salt yawned. What was Ben, bloody flowerpot man, doing up there? Having lunch? Watching TV? Or had he gone for a kip if, as Carrie had said, he'd been up and down to the flower market in Birmingham at five o'clock this morning? The guy must be knackered. She certainly was. The newspaper slipped from her hand and she let it fall and gave in to the overwhelming temptation to close her eyes just for a few seconds.

Her phone had rung so little since she'd been up here in

the sticks the last few days that she'd forgotten to turn it off, and she jerked awake when she heard its ringtone from somewhere deep in her bag. She immediately scrabbled about to locate it in the capacious thing.

A familiar voice said, 'Salt?'

'Frank,' she replied very quietly.

'How are you, Jane?' he said.

'I'm on a job,' she whispered, hunkering even further down between the steering wheel and the fully-reclined driver's seat.

'On a job?' he said. 'What do you mean? I thought you were . . . you know . . .'

'Yes, I am,' she said in a whisper. 'Or I was. It's complicated . . . I can't really talk now, Frank.'

'About us?' he said.

'About anything,' she said inconclusively. 'But yes, about us, too.'

'Good,' he whispered, glad to be included in the picture, no matter what that picture was.

'Can you call me later?' she murmured.

'Of course,' he replied.

'Frank?'

'Yes?' he said quickly.

'It's good to hear . . .'

'It's good to hear you, too,' he said.

'Sure,' she said. 'Later?'

But he didn't let her go. 'Are you alright?' he said, concerned at the subterfuge.

''Course,' she said.

'So, where are you?'

'Middle of nowhere,' she said unhelpfully.

'Yes, but *where* in the middle of nowhere?' he persisted. 'I want to know.'

'Some little industrial estate outside the town.'

'Why?' he said. 'What are you doing there?'

'I don't know,' she said. 'I shouldn't be here. It's to do with Carrie's bloke. He's in the flower business, and I probably shouldn't be getting involved. I feel very awkward about the whole thing.'

'You take care,' he said and she heard what sounded like

a train station announcement in the background. She snapped her phone shut as the driver's door of her car suddenly opened. 'Hello, Jane. What can I do for you, then?'

'Bloody hell! Ben,' she said. 'You frightened me. What are you doing?'

'What am *I* doing? What are *you* doing?' he said. 'Visitors usually come to the door. And they knock. They don't lie down in their cars to watch my place. Anyway, I thought you were supposed to be a cop. Didn't you see the CCTV up there?' And he gestured to a 360-degree camera attached to the end of a roof opposite his warehouse.

'Yes, sure,' she lied. 'I was—'

'Wanting some flowers?' he said and then, with a smile, 'You'd better come on up.'

In truth, she felt just a little uneasy about the prospect of following the man. It was a no-go for any officer, and certainly a woman, to follow anyone into their premises without back-up and without communicating their intentions to other officers and the station.

But this was different: she was solo, and she was not even at work. And anyway, although she wasn't exactly on buddy terms with Ben Williams, notwithstanding a moment's lasciviousness during some drunken dancing a couple of nights previously, her good friend had been dating the man for several months.

She also felt compromised and disadvantaged in their exchange, having been observed clearly behaving so under-handedly. It was almost a question of etiquette that led her to say after a moment's hesitation, 'OK, then.'

TWENTY-THREE

Brian Dalton might have been only an editor of a weekly local paper with a circulation of twenty thousand, but he was still as dogged in his pursuit of what he thought might be a half-decent little story as any *News of the World* reporter with a salacious scoop on a footballer's illicit night spent with another player's girlfriend.

When Betts had declined to phone him back 'later', as he had suggested he would – or indeed the following day – Dalton had called him himself and left a message on his phone. He got hold of his email address and also posted there his request once more.

For his part, since the deeply upsetting threatening phone call, Betts had absolutely no wish to discuss his find with anyone, and wasn't even sure that he was going to use the story of the bag himself. And anyway, he thought, did the call even relate *to* the bag? But apart from its find, and a little playful mockery at the expense of the KIL campaigners, what else could the menacing caller have been referring to?

The next morning, cowering and not a little frightened, Betts stood at his sitting-room window, the phone in his hand and dialled the *Oswestry Gazette*. He fully intended to tell the editor that he'd decided to let the story lie for a while and wanted him, Dalton, to as well. But, before the switchboard operator could answer, the timorous writer saw that there was something very wrong in his garden: the three fruit tree saplings that he had only recently planted had been uprooted, their branches torn away and broken from their slim trunks.

He put the phone down and went outside shaking and afraid.

The flower borders were trampled, the marks of big footsteps deeply embedded there, the plants trashed and kicked all over the drive, and his seed trays of lupins, nasturtiums and sweet peas had been scattered about the garden. Of course, Betts had seen plenty of very unpleasant things during the many years that he had lived in the city, but there was something about this scene of wanton destruction in such a quiet spot that was particularly brutal and heartless.

He turned back towards the kitchen door feeling more than ever alone and vulnerable, even as the birds continued to sing on the quiet suburban road.

One of the things that Detective Inspector Frank Kavanagh had learned was that, just as the police detection handbook said – or would have done if there had been such a thing – the cardinal rule for gathering evidence after any crime was that people were invariably creatures of habit. He felt pretty sure, therefore, that the people gathered on the platform around him on New Street's gloomy subterranean railway station were almost certainly the same people who would be making this exact journey at precisely this time next week and, in all likelihood, the week after that, too.

Maybe he should have told Salt that he was here, right now, and en route to see her? And yes, it had felt underhand not to have told her, but his need to see her had been greater than any sense of decorum, and he had also feared her telling him, yet again, that his visit would not be welcome.

The tall girl in a beret and green, three-quarter length coat on his right had a big bag over her shoulder but, unusually these days, wasn't clutching a phone and had neither iPod nor laptop with her. She carried no shopping, either – no Primark or Selfridge's carriers this early Wednesday afternoon – only her big shoulder bag. I wonder what she does for a living, considered the distracted cop. He glanced up again at the train timetable display: 13.30 for Chester, calling at Shrewsbury and Gobowen, expected 13.41. 'Bollocks!' he murmured.

The man to his left looked straight ahead, he was a big man and he stood unnaturally erect in his serge blue overcoat, the top three buttons fastened tight over his chest and belly, the lowest one, open. He looked too old to be at work, thought Kavanagh, and yet every indication was that he was, wearing dark, striped trousers and a sober tie. His lined face and white hair were apt, but his stance would have been odd in any man – in a person of his age it was extraordinary.

Kavanagh moved from foot to foot to relieve the aching

in his heavily-strapped ankle and glanced up at the display board yet again.

When the train did eventually rumble into the station, it was clear that the erect man knew precisely where it stopped as he positioned himself at the far door of the second carriage.

Kavanagh followed and sat across the aisle from him. As soon as the man had settled into his window seat he opened his ticket wallet on the table in front of him and closed his eyes, and in that act of repose all his former 'presence' slipped away. But he looked no more at peace than the agitated policeman was.

The Glasgow train on the adjacent platform pulled away and began its journey north. Kavanagh closed his eyes, too. But his mind still raced and his thoughts leapt and darted about. It had been bad being estranged from Salt. If he hadn't finally phoned, and she chosen to take his call, how would she know he wasn't dead? How would he know that *she* wasn't?

When he opened his eyes, the big man's mouth had fallen open and his rasping breath was audible even as the train jolted away at last.

The guard stepped into the carriage and Kavanagh swallowed two more pain killers as the train headed north-west towards her.

TWENTY-FOUR

Jane Salt followed Williams up the exterior iron staircase. 'Come in,' he said as he unlocked the heavy door and pushed it open. 'Make yourself at home,' and he gestured to the sofa. He went through to the kitchen as she stood there awkwardly. The flat was barren. There was little in the way of creature comforts, personal effects and the like, and what was there was old and tatty and, more to the point, thought Salt, the place wasn't very clean. Salt couldn't imagine her friend Carrie spending a lot of time here on the two-seater sofa that looked as if it might have come from one of those charity furniture places that councils set up these days for folk on benefits.

But the man had only been out of prison for a few months, and in that time he had set up a business as well as having started to date his probation officer's boss. Yes, she thought, be charitable, find the Buddhist in you, Jane, and give the man a break. There remained, however, the unresolved question of the man dealing dope to youngsters when he should have been retailing roses and the like.

'What were you doing, then?' he said from the kitchen doorway, his fingers inside a couple of glass tumblers and a bottle of Jack Daniel's in his hand.

'Sorry?' said Salt.

'You wanted to see me?' he said with a smile.

'Well, sort of,' she said warily. 'Just in a manner of speaking.'

'What manner's that, then?' he said, bringing in the glasses and bourbon and setting them on the table between them.

'I . . .' she began, but felt embarrassed. What was she supposed to say sitting here on the sofa as he stood over her: Yes, I came to spy on you? She didn't think so. 'It's Carrie,' she began, like an awkward schoolgirl, explaining away a friend's gauche behaviour.

'Carrie?' he asked, genuinely surprised. 'What about her?'

'I was concerned, I suppose,' said Salt.

'Yes?' he said, his voice changing just a little.

'She's my friend,' she went on. 'A *good* friend.'

'Yes?' he said. 'So?'

'Yes,' she asserted. 'She's—'

'Jane,' he interrupted, and he sat down close beside her. She didn't like the way he said her name. It signalled something she didn't want to hear. 'Jane, you've come here because you wanted to see me, yes? Nothing to do with Carrie? The other night at the pub, when we were dancing . . . you know . . .'

'I was drunk,' she said hastily. 'I didn't mean to—'

'Yes, me too,' he said. 'It was a good night. But I'm not stupid, Jane. I've been around a bit. I guessed you'd show up here some time.'

She made to stand up. But he put a hand on her shoulder, and in that touch she knew that she was in real trouble.

'I have to go, Ben,' she said firmly.

'Yes?' he said. 'Sit down, eh. Just sit down, Jane.'

Of all the stupid, stupid, completely irresponsible, against the rules, idiot behaviour, this was the worst. What had she thought she was doing? Yes, this man was her friend's boyfriend. But he was a con and a liar, that much she'd already known, and yet she'd walked up those iron fire-escape stairs with him. 'OK,' she said, and sat down.

He poured bourbon into their glasses and drank a good measure. 'Cheers,' he said. 'I could see the difficulty,' he began. 'You're staying with Carrie. What are we going to do? Wait until she's gone to work and then you call me and I pop round? I don't think so. Better here . . .' He took another gulp of his drink.

'It's not like that,' said Salt, keen to forestall the words that he seemed about to utter and which would then be only a fraction away from becoming the deed itself. 'Look, Ben, everything's alright. You've . . . I was just concerned about what I—'

'What?' he asked, intrigued. 'Concerned about what? What is it, Jane?'

The man had no idea that she had observed his drug dealing and she was now about to give him a reason for her being seen as a threat to his well-being. 'Concerned about Carrie,' she said hopelessly.

'Don't mess me about,' he said. 'You weren't going to say that. What was it? Tell me.'

Her phone rang. 'I have to get that,' she said. 'It's important.'

'I don't think so,' he said firmly. 'Not now.'

'The person who's phoning, they know where I am. I spoke to them from the car, just before you . . .' How on earth had he got down to her car without her seeing him, she wondered.

'Yes, I bet you did,' he said. 'Leave the phone alone, eh.'

It stopped ringing.

'So, what was it you were so "concerned" about?' he said again. 'Let's sort that out, and then we can move on.' He emptied his glass.

Jesus wept, she thought. *Move on.* A quarter of an hour ago, she couldn't keep her eyes open, now she felt terror as she looked at the scruffy unmade bed in the adjacent room.

'Drink your Jack,' he said.

'I don't want it,' she replied. If she was going to be raped or attacked or killed, he was going to have to fight her, and she wasn't going to be drugged with a spiked glass of bourbon.

'Suit yourself,' he said, and he got up and walked to the window.

'I saw you on the high street the other day with a couple of lads,' she began. 'They weren't buying flowers.'

'So what?' he said, turning, but totally unfazed.

'That's all,' she said, relieved to see he thought as little of his dope dealing as he apparently did.

'Flowers, you know, they're alright, but you gotta sell a lot of tulips to make just a few quid. A couple of deals of this and that, it helps the world go round. It'll be legal in a few years' time anyway. I'm just ahead of the game. I always have been.'

'Of course,' said Salt. 'Look, Ben, Carrie, you know, she's a very good friend, we go back a long time.'

'Carrie needn't ever know about us,' he said, as if to reassure her.

'I couldn't do that,' she said and then immediately blurted out, 'I don't mean that. What I mean is, I would *never* betray a friend, no matter what the situation. And I don't want to have anything to do with you. I'm having a crap time with my partner. That's why I'm up here with Carrie.'

He smirked and sat down next to her again. 'You know what they say the best thing for getting over a bad relationship is?'

'No. Yes,' she said. 'But it's not true. Not for me, anyway.'

'I'm good,' he said. 'And I'm not just saying that. Carrie doesn't have to know anything, and it'll help you forget whatever his name is. It'll be alright, really.'

'It won't be alright,' she said firmly. 'I'm telling you, it won't.'

Her phone rang again.

'Leave it,' he said as she made to reach down to her bag.

'Ben, look, you haven't gone too far, and I swear I won't tell anyone what's happened here. Ever. You can stop. You're out on licence, and this would be enough to put you back inside for a very long time.'

Her phone continued to ring. 'Can I get it, *please*?' she asked.

'No,' he said. 'You came here on your own; no one brought you and no one told you to come. You came up here on your own. It'll be on the cameras. It'd be your word against mine. Two adults in my flat? You know that ain't gonna stand up.'

The phone stopped ringing.

He walked to the door, turned the key and calmly asked, 'Do you need the bathroom at all?'

TWENTY-FIVE

n the couple of months of Betts' sojourn in his new house in the suburbs he had not been slow to acquire knowledge of the prevailing etiquette.

He rarely saw neighbours, but always felt that their watching eyes were not far away. The curtains didn't exactly twitch, and there was little net these days at the windows, the fashion now seemed to be for those vertical blinds from which everything could be observed and monitored just as discreetly, but without any actual twitching.

As he sensed their presence, it often gave his most desultory activities a slight air of performance, whether he was unloading the shopping from his car or meeting the postman on the threshold.

When his immediate neighbours were working in their garden, an immaculately tended place with manicured lawns, ordered flower beds and severely tonsured herbaceous borders, they did so in silence, but for the occasional sotto voce exchange, a few terse words spoken between them, as if arcane knowledge about their dahlias or chrysanthemums being eavesdropped by Julian Betts next door might jeopardize the enterprise in some unfathomable way.

They were in their mid-thirties and, he imagined, both worked in IT or some-such. They left the house each morning in their Mini Coopers – identical but for the fact that hers was white and black, his a more sober slate grey – and they drove up the hill in similar fashion, each of them changing gear in exactly the same spot before the engines of their highly-polished cars showed any signs of strain on the little incline.

Of course, in Betts's former mansion block home, people had been just as inclined to keep their – doubtless much more interesting and cosmopolitan – lives to themselves, but there, urban and urbane civility required that they show interest in one another that manifested itself in excessive displays of emotion when meeting in the lift or foyer. They'd express

inordinate interest in where a neighbour had just returned
from, or was leaving for whether it be on holiday, on business, to visit offspring in Switzerland or Australia, perhaps,
and they invariably parted with promises that they must get
together for dinner just as soon as they could, a promise that
was never kept, something which was obviously a relief to
both parties.

But here in the suburbs there was no such patina of civility
or expressions of fabricated emotion. On the first occasion
that they had actually met, Betts's neighbour, wearing a top
that flattered her trim figure, informed the man that she and
her husband – who continued to tend the conifer hedge that
separated their properties, even as she spoke – 'kept themselves to themselves', but added the proviso that, if he, Betts,
were ever to 'fall ill during the night', he was not to hesit-
ate to call on them for help. Quite how he was going to do
this, following a four a.m. stroke was not discussed.

This opening exchange, with nary a word of where he had
hailed from or, indeed, just why he had chosen to come to live
here at all, struck Betts as strange and he was a little put out
at the implied suggestion that even had he *wanted* these people
as friends, they would not be making themselves available to
him. On the other hand, maybe it was simply that they had in
some way been made aware of his sexual orientation, and that
emancipation in these matters was still to make it all the way
up the M6, along the M54 and down the A5 to this part of
Shropshire.

Whatever the reason, the young business woman and her
taciturn husband avoided any contact with their new neighbour. If he, Betts, was about to haul his bin down the drive at
the same time as the man next door was doing, his neighbour
would scurry back to his burrow and cease any further activity
rather than exchange a single word of greeting.

On this occasion, however, Betts was so upset at the sight
of his destroyed plants and uprooted saplings that he felt,
notwithstanding that he had not yet actually suffered a stroke,
he had little alternative but to call on them.

'Hello,' he said as he stood at the front door. 'I am sorry
to trouble you,' he began, but the woman didn't ask him in,
merely invited him to complete the sentence.

'Someone's done something awful to my garden. I wondered whether you'd heard anything?'

'Heard anything?' she repeated, without enquiring further what the nature of the awfulness was. Her husband padded silently along the parquet-floored hall and joined her at the front door. The woman repeated Betts's words to her husband. 'Someone's done something awful to our neighbour's garden.'

'Can I show you?' enquired Betts.

'I'll get my shoes,' said the man, and the three of them trooped next door.

'Blimey,' the neighbour said.

Notwithstanding his considerable distress, Betts felt almost gratified at having elicited from the man what passed for a tidal wave of emotion.

'Who would *do* this?' asked Betts. 'And *why*?'

'It's not the sort of thing we get round here,' said the woman, almost suggesting that the writer must have been responsible for bringing the outrage upon himself in some unspecified way.

'No? Perhaps it's children?' he said, thinking this was the least troubling hypothesis. Of course, it wasn't nice, but then again, children weren't nice sometimes, either. And at least, as far as he understood them, there was little logic in their behaviour, and an illogical act was a less uncomfortable notion for Betts than a calculated one.

His neighbour ignored the hypothesis and put his size nine-and-a-half brown slip-on shoe inside one of the deep footmarks in the garden border. 'It's at least a size twelve,' he offered, scotching the notion of any child's high spirits.

His neighbours stood there in silence for another thirty seconds before muttering slightly embarrassed goodbyes and leaving. The exchange over, they returned to their quiet home next door, but Julian Betts was every bit as troubled as before.

TWENTY-SIX

At Shrewsbury, several people discreetly spread their belongings on the seats beside them, or on the tables in front of them. Others looked stonily out of the window, so apparently distracted by the scene there that they couldn't possibly be aware of the throng jostling down the aisle looking for seats.

Kavanagh had long since dispensed with these charades, bits of hammy theatre that would not fool any traveller who was no longer actually wearing diapers. And anyway, there were plenty of *Guardian*-carrying rail travellers who saw such obstructive behaviour as nothing short of a challenge and were only too pleased to stand there, hovering above the window-gazer, and declaring with an air of patrician authority, '*Excuse* me, is this seat taken?'

No, these days, Kavanagh simply displayed on the table in front of him some explicit novel with a gratuitously offensive cover in an attempt to deter any would-be fellow-traveller from sitting next to him. Of course, it often failed, many readers having a taste for this kind of thing anyway, but for a deal of the population the author of *The Bone Collector* could just as well have been Jane Austen as Jeffrey Deaver, the difference meaning nothing whatsoever.

These folk were marginally more desirable close travelling companions than the ones who spent their time listening to iPods, the noise from the headphones of which always sounding identical, no matter what the music playing. Others did word puzzles in fat books that were produced on pages that looked like the blotting paper Kavanagh hadn't seen since his own miserable schooldays decades previously.

His mate Presley had no truck with these niceties and had told the inspector that the only way to guarantee himself peace and quiet on a train was to display prominently a copy of *Hot Babes*, or some-such publication, magazines little read by most rail users and even fewer *Guardian* readers.

The near-naked women on the cover invariably guaranteed Presley the solitude that he sought, except on the very rare occasions that its enticements actually *attracted* other like-minded individuals to his proximity.

This morning, the inspector had found time only to collect a copy of the *Daily Telegraph* at Euston station, and when he left it on his seat later that day, even the crossword on the back page was wholly untouched.

When the train pulled into Gobowen, the little railway station that served the town of Oswestry three miles away, Kavanagh hurried from it just as quickly as his strapped ankle would allow to the solitary taxi parked there.

'Where to?' asked the driver and turned to look at his passenger as he clambered into the back seat.

'Do you know an industrial estate, just outside the town?' asked Kavanagh.

'There's a few. The big one's down on Maesbury Road, but there's a couple of others. Depends which one you want.'

'I'm not sure,' he said. 'It's got a florist on it I think,' he added hurriedly.

'A florist?' repeated the cabbie, as if he was not entirely familiar with the word.

'Well, not a florist, maybe. You know, a wholesaler? Flowers and stuff.'

'It could be the one outside Morda,' he said. 'I think a bloke does flowers there. Hasn't been there long, just a few months? The bloke with the stall on the square?'

'Could be,' said Kavanagh. 'And can you shift it, mate. I'm in a hurry . . .'

'You're not from round here, are you?' said the man, and pulled the gleaming Rover away from the station in a sedate and stately manner.

In the grubby bathroom, there was only a sliding bolt to secure the door from the sitting room, something that a child would have easily been able to break open. Salt pressed her face to the dirty window with its iron bars that had been fixed securely inside the frame. There was also a substantial locked door with wired glass in its top half, giving access to an old wooden staircase that the man must have descended just half an hour ago to reach her unseen. She stood trembling as images of the next hour of her life assailed her.

'Can you go a bit faster, mate,' said Kavanagh leaning forward. 'I'll sort you out a decent tip. It's important.'

'It's a forty limit,' said the cabbie phlegmatically. 'I don't know about where you come from, but round here, the police like nothing more than giving out points. I think they're on commission.'

Kavanagh hit the buttons on his phone again, and listened to the unanswered ring tone.

'Nearly there, anyway,' said the man as they left the main road and pulled down a bumpy, unmade lane.

Salt stood in the bathroom with her back pressed against the far wall.

'Jane,' said the man through the door. 'Jane, I think you've been in there long enough.' She watched in horror as the doorknob slowly turned and the door pushed slightly in the frame against the secured bolt.

'You know I can push this open, so why don't you just come on out . . .'

The cab passed through a five-bar iron gate hanging open on one hinge, and into the yard with half-a-dozen sheds and several one-storey brick-built premises dotted around. A Volvo was parked there. Kavanagh threw a twenty-pound note onto the passenger front seat as he stumbled from the still-moving taxi.

'Do you want a receipt?' called the man, but the inspector was gone. The car was deserted and he winced in pain as he ran across to the warehouse and rapped hard with both fists on the solid double doors beneath the sign, 'Bloomin' Fantastic'.

He banged again and again and stood back, looked up to the first floor and called out, 'Jane? Jane, are you in there?'

A man came out from the furniture upholsterer's unit and said tentatively, 'Are you alright, mate?' Kavanagh ignored him and yelled again, 'Jane. Jane Salt. Are you there?'

A few seconds later, Williams opened the window at the front of the building. 'What do *you* want?' he said.

'I want Jane Salt,' said Kavanagh. 'Is she in there?'

'What's it to you?' said the man.

'I'm a police officer. Where is she?' he said.

Williams started to close the window when a voice from behind him called out, 'Frank! Frank! Thank God you're here.'

TWENTY-SEVEN

'And explain to me again, exactly how did you know I was there?' Salt said as they lay in bed at a guest house in a narrow lane just off Water Street.

'Inspired guess?' he said.

'You were already on your way?' she said. 'But how did you know?'

'I had to see you,' he said. 'I just knew something wasn't right.'

'And how did you find the place?' she asked.

'The cabbie knew there was a flower seller out there. Luck?'

'He was going to rape me, Frank. I must have been mad to have gone in there with him,' she said.

Kavanagh took her closer in his arms and she laid her head on his chest. 'I'm just glad you're safe, Jane,' he said, and she sobbed as he held her to him and kissed her forehead.

'So,' he whispered, half an hour later.

'Yes?' she said.

'Shall we get back down to town?'

'Town?' she said.

'London town, you know, where we live,' he replied. 'Not this metropolis.'

'Yes, I suppose so,' she said.

'"Suppose so"?' he asked, holding her to him.

She wrapped her leg around his. 'Ouch,' he said.

'Oh, Frank, I'm so sorry. Your ankle. I forgot.'

'It's OK,' he grimaced. 'I'd have thought you couldn't wait to leave here.'

'You're right. It's just that there's one thing,' she said.

His heart sank a little. He'd learned to fear this phrase almost as much as the patient dreads the consultant's, 'I'm afraid I have some bad news . . .'

'Go on,' he said.

'It's just something that Carrie told me . . . about a horrible arson attack on an old man's home.'

'Carrie?' he said. 'I was sort of imagining she might be out of the equation now.'

'Yes, she is, of course,' she said.

That lunchtime, they'd gone straight from Ben Williams's warehouse to Carrie's office in the centre of town.

Salt had pressed the intercom whilst Kavanagh sat in her car on the yellow line across the road and read the local paper.

'Jane?' said Carrie, surprised to see her friend standing outside the reinforced door of the probation office on the CCTV monitor. 'Come on up,' and she pressed the automatic door-latch button.

'Carrie, just a sec.,' said Salt hesitantly. 'It's probably better if you come down. Do you have a minute?'

'I'm with a client,' she said. 'What is it?'

'I can't talk about it now, not like this,' said Salt. 'But it's important. Please.'

'Give me five minutes, and I'll be down.'

'This is awkward, Carrie,' said Salt to her friend as she emerged from the building. 'Very awkward.'

'What on earth's the matter?' said Carrie as they sauntered along the street, neither of them quite sure where they were heading.

'It's about Ben,' said Salt, barely able to say the man's name.

'Ben?' said Carrie, surprised. 'What about him?'

'I was over at the warehouse. . . .'

'Why?' she said, immediately sensing that this really was something that was going to threaten their relationship.

'Look, Carrie,' she began, more stridently than she had intended, 'I saw Ben dealing dope to some youngsters the other day.'

'Really?' said Carrie, immediately prepared to be defensive about her partner. 'And how come you saw that?'

'I was watching him.'

'Why?' asked Carrie coolly.

'I felt I needed to apologize for the way I'd behaved in the pub the previous night,' said Salt.

'How *had* you behaved?' queried Carrie.

'There was a moment when we were dancing when we

got a bit closer than we should have done. It was nothing, really. We were all drunk. You were at the bar. But I just felt I had to tell him it was a misunderstanding, so that he didn't get the wrong idea.'

'Is that so?' she said. 'I'm amazed, Jane. You came up here to stay with me. I thought we were friends, you know.'

'We *are*,' said Salt. 'We really are, Carrie. It was just the drink and a misunderstanding. I went to tell him, and I sat in the café across from his pitch . . .'

'Watching him,' she said. 'Are you sure that's what you were doing there, Jane?'

'Of course,' said Salt. 'What else?'

'You tell me,' she said.

'You've got to believe me, Carrie. You really must.'

'Must I?' she said. 'So, what happened?'

'I saw him deal a bit of stuff to a couple of kids.'

'But you didn't tell me?' she asked, sceptical.

'I felt I needed to know more. It was awkward. What was I supposed to do? I knew it would make trouble between you two.'

'I bet you did,' she mocked.

'I know, it sounds ridiculous.'

'It certainly does,' agreed Carrie, 'especially with you and Frank being apart.' The two women had stopped and now faced one another, right there on the high street outside a busy charity shop. 'So, you went to the warehouse. Why? What then?'

'That's the whole point. I was watching him from my car, to see if there was anything going on, and he came down. He caught me there.'

'Oh, yes?' said Carrie with a bitter laugh.

'He invited me up, and I felt I had to. I mean, I do know him, even if it's only through you,' she said defensively.

'This is crazy,' said Carrie. 'I know what you're going to say . . .'

'No, you don't,' said Salt decisively.

'No?' said her friend. 'You're going to tell me that you two—'

'He was going to rape me, Carrie,' said Salt.

'Rubbish,' said Carrie without a moment's thought. 'You come on to him, watch him, and then go his warehouse and you're telling me *he* tries to rape *you*? I don't believe you. Not for a minute.'

'I don't want to believe it either,' said Salt, 'but it's true.'

'I've been going out with Ben for months. He's not a saint, but he's not that kind of man. I can guess exactly what happened. You came on to him and he turned you down and before he can tell me about it, you've come here to get yourself off the hook.

'And, by the way, how did you escape my rapist boyfriend? You fought him off, I suppose? So where are the bruises, Jane?'

'Look,' she said, and pointed back down the street to her Volvo in the distance.

'What about it?' said Carrie.

'That's Frank in the car. He turned up just in time. We'd spoken on the phone and he just knew something was going on, and yes, he did want to see me, but he got there just in time. You *have* to believe me.'

'Have you taken your things from the cottage?' Carrie asked, and turned away.

'Carrie?' called Jane to her former friend's departing back.

'Fuck off,' she shouted. A woman looked up, a nail file in her hand as she rubbed away at her scratch card.

'Just fuck off. I don't ever want to see you again.'

TWENTY-EIGHT

Jane Salt knew there was no chance whatsoever of bringing a charge against her would-be assailant, but she also knew that she absolutely had to tell the local police about it: sexual predators rarely attacked women only once. Their behaviour was invariably ingrained and recidivist. If some other woman was assaulted by Ben Williams in the future and she'd done nothing to report her own claims about him, she would feel ashamed as well as responsible.

Geographically, this might have been merely two hundred miles from London, but in every other respect, the little market town could have been on another planet, and rather than being seen as some irksome interruption and fobbed off with a junior officer, down at the police station the two out-of-town cops were treated with courtesy.

Kavanagh and Salt showed the man their warrant cards and the front desk PC immediately called up to his boss and in only a few minutes the station DI came down to reception to meet them.

Studious looking Michael Scrivens escorted the officers up to his first-floor office where he listened to Salt's story. 'Give me a minute while I check Williams's record,' he said, pushing his spectacles up onto his forehead. He leaned over the screen and accessed the police national computer as the two officers sat there.

'Yes, it's as you say,' he confirmed as he scrolled down the information. 'And you're right, of course,' he added, logging off, 'there's nothing we can do on the basis of what you've just told me, Ms Salt.'

'Jane, please,' she said.

'Jane. All we can do right now is have an informal "word", just to let him know that we know what happened, and that we're on his case, but there's no way we can charge him with anything. The CPS would laugh us out.'

'I knew it,' she said, 'but thanks anyway.'

'What about your friend, though, the woman you say he's dating? Do you not think that she might be in danger?' the DI asked reasonably.

'Carrie?' said Salt. 'It's become difficult. We're speaking off the record?'

'Of course,' said the local DI.

'Like I say, firstly, she's a friend, or at least she was until an hour ago when I told her what had happened. She stuck by him, said she knew he wouldn't do such a thing and, anyway, if anything at all had happened, it was my fault for giving off the "wrong" signals.'

'Blimey,' he said. 'What happened to sisterly?'

'She's not going to take advice about him from me, and it's obviously the end of our friendship,' she said.

'Sure,' he said. 'She must know she's also breaking every rule in the book, though?' he offered. 'You know, the probation officer/client relationship?'

'I know, and she knows, but she's a grown-up and it's up to her what she does,' said Salt frustrated and deflated.

Scrivens called for some coffee to be sent up and offered Salt the use of the adjacent office to write up her account of what had happened 'for the record'. The room was available to them, he explained, as his own senior officer was on leave at present.

'Stress?' asked Kavanagh. Most police absenteeism in the city was attributed to this very real malaise, rather than physical assaults, and Kavanagh imagined the figure wouldn't be a lot different up here in the sticks.

'Not exactly,' said Scrivens. 'He crashed his Mazda coming into work the other day and he's off for at least a couple of weeks with his neck in plaster.'

'I see,' said Kavanagh. 'You take your life in your hands these days every time you get behind the wheel. Every other civilian out there's nuts, I reckon.'

'Yes,' agreed Scrivens. 'Except on this occasion it was John who drove into the back of some other poor sod!'

'Oh, dear,' said Kavanagh.

'He was texting his ex-wife at the time, too,' added Scrivens drily.

'Ouch,' said Kavanagh. 'I bet he's popular.'

'Just a bit,' agreed Scrivens with a sigh. 'I'll let you two get on with it for half an hour,' he said. 'OK? Anything you need, give me a call,' and he left the room.

Whilst Salt wrote up her report, Kavanagh logged into HOLMES, the ponderously-named Home Office Large Major Enquiry System. The cross-referencing database was devised following the bungling of the Yorkshire Ripper case back in the Seventies, when all sorts of links that should have identified serial killer Peter Sutcliffe were repeatedly overlooked.

There appeared to be little significant progress being made on the Somali boy's drive-by murder – no surprise given the nature, location and context of the killing where silence was the name of the game and people rarely spoke to the police about anything, and certainly not a gang-related shooting.

After he'd logged off, Kavanagh called DI Skinner down at the station in London and got the story behind the cold facts on the screen.

'How's it going?' asked Salt twenty minutes later as she tapped the final keys on the computer on her side of the room and finished her report.

'Skinner says they've got one witness, and she's just about holding up, but she's very flaky and could cut and run at any time,' he said.

'It's the usual: if the girl gets fed up playing computer games in the hotel room, or if our lot looking after her start getting under her skin, the whole thing'll collapse. But for now, it looks like they're just about still on.'

Scrivens sent out for some sandwiches, crisps and a carton of juice from the local supermarket and had them brought up.

'So, where are you two staying now?' he asked.

'We've got a bed and breakfast off Water Street,' said Salt.

'And are you planning on sticking around for a bit?' he said.

'We're off tomorrow, maybe the next day at a push,' said Salt. 'But there's just something I wanted to check before we go,' she added.

'Yes?' he said. 'What's that? Anything I can help with?'

'It's a bit of a flyer,' said Salt. 'But a day or two ago, Carrie told me about an old man's property being torched.'

Scrivens smiled. 'Billy Hughes's place? It's common knowledge.'

'And you know who did it?' she asked.

'We think we know,' he said, 'but it's like your bit of unpleasantness with Williams here today. How do you make it stand up? Locally, everyone knows it was a local operator called Gareth Thomas.

'He owns tons of commercial property round here as well as flats and warehouses. He started in the building trade years ago, but now he runs car dealerships and all sorts. He began with nothing, and the man's done well, but there's plenty of folk wonder just how he achieved it.'

'I see,' said Kavanagh.

'But as far as the fire at Billy's place was concerned, Jane, there's not a shred of evidence, and believe me, we've looked for it.'

'Do you mind if I go down there and have a look around for myself, unofficially of course?' said Salt.

'Help yourself,' said Scrivens. 'And good luck, but there's nothing to find. We checked every angle and Thomas is clean. He had an alibi for the night in question. We could never have made it stick. But have a word with Ted Sillence if you like, too. He's the chief fire officer.' He jotted the man's number down on a card and handed it to Salt.

'So, what's all this arson business about?' asked Kavanagh half an hour later as he and Salt drove out of town to the site of the burned-down buildings.

'When we were out for a walk, when I was first up here, we could see the place in the distance and Carrie told me she was sure that Thomas was responsible,' she said.

'Yes?' said Kavanagh. 'Why so?'

'He wanted a better view from his own property,' she said.

'I bet,' said the inspector. 'Pull the other one, as they used to say.'

'I'm serious,' said Salt. 'You'll see when we get down there. He buys a mansion that's in a bit of a state and, when he's done it up, the whole thing's perfect except for a bit of an eyesore of an old property right across the lane from the place.'

'Yes, go on,' he urged.

'I know, it sounds mad,' she agreed, 'but Carrie said that

when his offers to buy the old man out were rejected, he simply had the place burned down.'

'Just to improve the view?' added Kavanagh, not a little sceptical.

'I know, it's crazy,' she agreed.

'Just a bit,' said Kavanagh, acquiescent. He turned up the CD in the car and put his hand on her knee as she drove.

'Mr Amenable, eh?' she said smiling. 'I like this new DI, but don't agree with everything I say, because if you do, then I won't believe anything and I'll know you're just faking.'

'Me? Faking?' he said. 'Would I?'

TWENTY-NINE

The balaclava-wearing man parked in a lay-by two hundred yards away and walked up the suburban road, the only sound an owl hooting from somewhere in the trees, and the rustling of copper beech leaves as they skitted down the pavement in the breeze.

At the back of the house, he found one of the sitting-room windows open a crack. Pulling on surgical gloves, he stood on a patio chair and teased a length of picture wire down and around the handle of the solid uPVC window and drew it slowly open.

A few minutes later and he stood in darkness in the room breathing hard. After a good two minutes more of standing there and sensing the layout of the place, he clicked his head torch on and opened the man's desk drawers. Pens and paper, bills and computer cables and printer-ink cartridges. He ignored the bureau and corner wall cupboard with its writing awards and fine wine glasses.

Out in the hall, he stepped on a creaking floorboard and stood rigid, his foot immobile on the maple plank as his heart thumped rapidly. But there was no movement, no sound from any of the bedrooms above him. He eventually eased his foot away and moved on through the house, shading the light from his torch with a cupped hand around the beam.

In the kitchen were the signs of the man's last few tasks before going to bed: a whisky glass and an ashtray with three filter stubs in it. There was a black bin bag tucked away beneath the kitchen table. He reached down to open it, but just as he got his hand around the thing, he heard a bedroom door open. He immediately clicked off the head torch and stood there, frozen, and listened as Betts made a wheezy progress along the landing at the top of the stairs.

The man breathed rasping breaths into the stifling wool of the balaclava as he stood there, motionless, the plastic

bag clutched in his hand, and waited. The writer must be standing at the lavatory bowl, he reckoned. Eventually, he heard
the dribble of the slow start of Betts's urinating. The man
broke wind and then depressed the flush button. Under the
cover of the noise of the cistern refilling, the hooded man
took a step around the kitchen wall and into the open-
plan dining room.

He waited there in the darkness, just a little light shed from
the open bathroom door filtering down the stairs and into the
room.

But Betts didn't return to his bedroom. Instead, he descended
the stairs very slowly and deliberately. From the hall, he stepped
into the kitchen and switched on the light.

He leaned at the sink and looked at his reflection in the
black, kitchen window glass. He took up his filmy whisky
glass, swilled it out and filled it with tap water. He drank
half a glass as he stood there and then put the tumbler back
on the draining board. He looked around the room and
turned to go. He switched off the kitchen light, but had no
sooner done so than he put it back on and went back to
the sink unit. He picked up the glass again, took another
sip and, with the preternatural sense that there was something not quite right, took the three or four steps into the
dining room.

'What the . . .?' he began to say, even as his instincts told
him to turn and try to get away. But the intruder lunged at
him and pushed him heavily to the floor.

The man clambered on top of Betts and, straddling his
chest, knees either side of the slight figure, now grasped the
writer's pallid neck. Betts instinctively reached up. He
brushed the man's balaclava to one side of his face as massive
hands met around his throat. One side of a face looked down
at Betts whose life was now ebbing away. He squeezed hard
for a very long time. At last, Betts's mouth opened fully and
his swollen tongue hung out. Only his dead eyes registered the
fear and awful pain that he had felt as his life was throttled
out of him.

At last, his killer got to his feet, his woollen mask soaking
wet with sweat. He stepped over the man's body, went to
the kitchen, picked up the black bin bag and turned off the

light. He then went back to the desk drawers and bureau and collected several items from around the house.

Five minutes later, he pulled the front door very quietly shut, and left.

THIRTY

Brian Dalton, editor of the *Oswestry Gazette* for the last twenty-odd years, had long since given up any hope of being headhunted to come down to London to edit the *Daily Mirror* or the *Express*, or even relocate to Manchester and take on the running of that city's *Evening News*. And, OK, it was a long time since the paper had had anything resembling a scoop, but he still felt the reporter's thrill at finding a *real* story, even if it was only a very *small* real story, and he hadn't entirely lost his nose for one of these.

When Julian Betts, his esteemed colleague in the business, failed to call him back – as he had reluctantly agreed to do – Dalton telephoned him again, but there was no answer. He left a message, a jovial, speaking-to-one-another-as-equals-in-this-business-of-ours message, reminding the former food writer and now Sunday broadsheet columnist, of his undertaking to be in touch.

But a day later, the man still hadn't phoned, and Dalton called him once more. He tried again after lunch. Still nothing. You can only leave so many messages before you're in the awkward area of being intrusive, as opposed to merely assiduous.

Truth to tell, the paper virtually ran itself these days. The junior reporters tried to get the names of the schoolteachers and fund-raisers and goalscorers right (and just as often failed), and the photographer drove around to her assignments each week, calling at swimming galas and darts presentations and salsa evenings. The advertising girls made their phone calls and tried to sell the space to fill the pages, sales without which none of the 'news' would be appearing at all.

Dalton decided to get into his old Nissan and drive up and see Betts himself to see whether, in spite of his not responding to the telephone calls and emails he had sent, he could prevail upon the man to share more fully his story of the old lunch bag that had been found at his home. It wasn't *that* much of a story, admittedly, but then again, it wasn't that much of a newspaper, either.

And if there was one thing that Dalton had learned during his time as editor, it was that there might be financial meltdown in Tokyo, London and New York, and yes, governments did come and go, but people in this market town – and others like it too, he imagined – were much more interested in a story with a bit of local interest than any of these supposedly more serious events. And that was why, notwithstanding his having rather glossed over the fact when he had spoken to Betts earlier in the week, certain of the fact that whatever the outcome of their meeting he would have *some* kind of story to write up, there were now sandwich boards outside every newsagent's in the town declaiming in anticipation of that week's edition: LUNCH BAG IN ATTIC MYSTERY.

At the house on Low Brook Road things were customarily quiet. Dalton pulled onto the drive of number 33 and parked behind Betts's Audi.

Out of mere politeness, he sat in his car for a few moments, allowing Betts, should he so wish, to step out of the house to meet him. It looked like there'd been rather more than a bit of chaotic planting going on in the garden, with several saplings lying about near to their dug holes. There were also a good number of bedding plants randomly scattered around the place. The man was clearly no horticulturist, thought Dalton, a city type who'd no idea how to systematically approach his gardening hobby.

The editor eventually tapped at the front door, but there was no answer. He walked around the side of the house to the back lawn and stood discreetly at the open sitting-room window. 'Julian?' he called. 'Excuse me, Julian. It's Brian. From the *Gazette*.' Nothing.

He called again but, sensing that there was something not quite right about the window being open and the complete domestic silence, he put his face to the window and called again, a little louder, 'Hello, Julian. It's Brian, Brian Dalton. Hello . . .?'

Eventually, following his instincts, he pulled the curtain aside and peered in. He immediately saw Betts's leg straddling the open space between the kitchen and the dining room. Had he fallen? Had a heart attack or stroke? Was he still breathing?

Dalton stood on the nearby patio chair as the thing creaked and rocked beneath him, and climbed very awkwardly onto the window sill before clambering down into the room.

Betts looked asleep. Dalton had seen more death than most people, given the nature of his daily work, and no one slept like this, legs splayed apart and arms akimbo.

He knelt down and touched Betts's neck. His skin was cold. He'd been here some time. The pathetic man's ankles were very pale, his chest hairless, but his throat was welted and red with bruising and his eyes open. Dalton got to his feet. He felt ashamed to be glancing around the room, looking for the bag that he suspected must be here somewhere. A moment later he dialled 999 on his cell phone.

THIRTY-ONE

Salt and Kavanagh parked on the track adjacent to the site of the burned-out farm buildings but, as DI Scrivens had suggested, there was very little to see. Nothing material, anyway. There were piles of bricks, the glazed tiles from a 1960s' fireplace and a scorched Rayburn cooker that someone had smashed with a sledgehammer in what looked like a final act of destruction but had, in fact, probably been the only way to get the ancient thing out of the ruin of the house once demolition had begun.

'What do you reckon?' asked Kavanagh, deferring to Salt, given her involvement with the suspected arson attack.

'No idea,' she answered.

Kavanagh teased from the ground a piece of charred wood with the heel of his shoe and the residual smell of smoke in the thing was released into the still air.

Some gardeners were working in the grounds of the black-and-white timbered mansion on the hill that overlooked the place a hundred yards away.

'That's your man's place, then?' said Kavanagh, indicating the huge building with its ornate spiral chimneys and dozens of multipane windows glinting in the sun.

'That's it,' said Salt.

Kavanagh strolled over to a big pile of charred timbers that had been stacked in the corner of what had been the garden, whilst Salt wandered around the few courses of bricks, all that now remained of the former barn.

A few minutes later, she called from the little wicket gate, 'Let's get away, Frank. Perhaps get some lunch, and then this afternoon I'll have a word with the fire officer.'

'Sure,' he said, joining her. 'And then?'

'Back to London, I guess,' she said. 'But you know, I really hate the thought of some local bully getting away with this, don't you?'

'Of course,' he said, 'but it's too late now. The man's got

what he wanted, and no one's going to be able to do anything about that.'

'Maybe,' she said.

After lunch, whilst Salt was down at the fire station, Kavanagh took advantage of a quiet half an hour back at the bed and breakfast to grab a few minutes' sleep and take the weight off his ankle. However he hadn't been asleep long when his phone rang.

'Yes?'

'Frank, it's Michael. Michael Scrivens down at the station.'

'Hi, Michael,' said Kavanagh. 'What can I do for you?'

'We've had something come up. Something serious.'

'Yes? What's that?' said the London inspector as he swung his legs down from the bed.

'We've got a murder, Frank.'

'Really?' said Kavanagh, surprised.

'I'm afraid so,' said Scrivens, almost as if he was somehow responsible for the outrage himself.

'Who is it?' asked Kavanagh.

'He's a journalist. A bloke called Betts. He only moved up here from London a few months ago.'

'I see,' said Kavanagh. 'Is there anything I can do?'

'I was wondering whether you might pop down, Frank – unofficially, of course – it's just that I've got John off with his neck in plaster, and until I can get the troops reinforced, what with Betts being a Londoner and all . . .'

'Give me ten minutes,' said Kavanagh. 'I'll be there.'

THIRTY-TWO

'It's Julian Betts, you say?' said Kavanagh as the two men stood in the rear car park of the police station and the crime-scene vehicles came and went.

'Why? Do you know him?' asked Scrivens.

'Well, not personally,' said Kavanagh, 'but I know the column that he writes. It's only very recently that I learned that he lived here. Before that I'd never realized he was writing about this town. He doesn't identify it, just writes about the goings on. It's a bit of a piss-take really, you know? But nothing too harsh.'

'I'd never even heard of him,' said Scrivens. 'Which paper does he write for?'

'*Sunday Times*,' said Kavanagh, 'but there was a mention of a couple of his most recent pieces in your local paper the other day.'

'Yes?' said Scrivens. 'I never see it. And on Sundays, I get the *Express*,' added the younger copper. 'And if there's time, I might read a bit of the wife's *News of the World*.'

'Betts was having a bit of a pop at the local eco-bunch,' said Kavanagh. 'You know? Some campaign to keep the supermarkets out of the town?' added the inspector.

''Course I know,' said Scrivens. 'We've had a march through the town, and one of the reasons I don't read the local rag is because it's full of letters from nutters who've nothing better to do.'

'How nutty are they?' asked Kavanagh. 'These campaigners?'

'How do you mean?' said Scrivens.

'Well, you remember those antivivisectionists a few years ago? I was involved on the intelligence side of that and they were *seriously* dangerous. They firebombed things and attacked the cars and property of researchers, lab technicians and suppliers, anyone at all connected with the business. They were fully prepared to kill. There wasn't any doubt about that.'

'I don't think our lot are going to be killing anyone just to stop Tesco building a supermarket here,' said Scrivens.

'I doubt it,' agreed Kavanagh. 'But it only takes one, you know.'

'Let's get up to Betts's house to see how Forensics are going. Do you fancy coming along, Frank?'

'Sure,' said Kavanagh. 'Who found him?' he asked as the men walked over to Scrivens's car.

'Brian Dalton, the local paper's editor. Good bloke. I've known him since I was promoted up here. There's nothing and no one he doesn't know in this neck of the woods. He's been here donkey's.'

'Right,' said Kavanagh. 'Let's see what Forensics have got.'

There was a lot of activity on the formerly quiet road. The local press and TV had been quick off the mark, their correspondents already speaking to cameras and jotting gleanings in their notepads. And now the national stations were starting to roll up, too, not in three-year-old Fords, but in smart, silver Mercedes vans. While the technicians oriented the roof-mounted satellite dishes, the presenters, familiar to any TV news viewer, strolled around the area like lords of the dance with a couple of phones, one in each hand, and picked the brains of local colleagues who were honoured to share their information with these media stars.

At the same time, press reporters, mostly girls of about twenty-five, followed one another up and down the road and randomly knocked on doors for any additional morsels of the story that they would soon be phoning through to their subs for the evening editions.

The only reason that any of them were here at all, of course, was on account of Betts's minor celebrity, the fact that he'd once been a well-known food writer, and was now a features columnist for a top Sunday broadsheet. Without this, his brutal demise would have been merely another neighbourhood murder that would, on a quiet day, have just about rated a brief item on the region's TV news programme.

But there was one other thing, too, that had drawn the media to this prosperous suburban road in a Shropshire market town. It wouldn't be referred to directly, of course, but the man's lifestyle would be alluded to merely as 'colourful' or 'unconventional'. But only the very dimmest of viewers would not know that the euphemism was the universally-accepted synonym for the deceased man being gay. And if a gay writer was murdered in his home, then the story immediately had a cachet that it would otherwise lack. No matter that the man had quite possibly been living the life of a celibate mendicant, his sexual orientation meant that the story attracted to itself a mildly salacious element that a heterosexual killing would always lack.

And so now, at last, in death, the moderately successful erstwhile food writer had found the lasting fame and glancing notoriety that had eluded him throughout his long career.

In London, Tom Penney, Betts's editor, was preparing a front page tribute to their journalist of thirty years' standing and was arranging to reprint a couple of his columns from the archives, as well as his most recently filed contribution on his new – supposedly placid – life in the suburbs.

Up in Shropshire, too, his demise seemed to be having a strangely galvanizing effect on his immediate neighbours, an effect out of all proportion to what his presence in the community had hitherto been.

Neighbours who had barely spoken a word to one another in twenty years of living in close proximity were suddenly on the street sharing their views with one another as well as any reporter who cared to speak to them. Even Betts's formerly taciturn next-door neighbours seemed now to be perfectly at ease as they spoke about the 'charming man' in a TV interview in their front garden amongst the hydrangeas.

It was universally claimed that Betts would be very much missed – even by those people who had wilfully avoided him entirely until that very day.

The main feature of all the print and broadcast news interviews was the repeated expressions of shock and horror at what had taken place. But oddly, there seemed little actual shock and no horror whatsoever to be seen in any of the interviewees. Was it the fact that having seen this kind of thing in a thousand movies and TV shows, as well as myriad times on the TV news, everyone was now entirely divorced – at least in public – from the actual emotions of which they were speaking?

Only one woman, a widow two or three years older than

the late writer, and who lived on the opposite side of the road and a little further up the hill, declined to speak to the press. Betts had often seen her leave home, usually at about two in the afternoon, and she always wore exactly the same coat, a long, dark blue pleated skirt and black, laced 'sensible' shoes.

She had never spoken to the man in the few months that he had been there and she, he had felt sure, had no idea that he had frequently watched her walk down the road. But, simply out of courtesy and respect for the deceased man, when a girl from the *Mail* in a belted camel coat, black tights and high heels knocked at her door and asked her what she knew of the man, she apologized, but said that she had nothing to say.

'Did you know Mr Betts, though?' pursued the callow youngster.

'No,' said the woman. 'Not at all. We'd never spoken.'

'And, are you shocked by his death?' she persisted.

'Of course,' said the woman.

'Can I quote you?' asked the reporter.

'I'd really rather you didn't,' she said and added, 'would you excuse me now, please?' and quietly closed the door as the girl jotted in her notepad.

The weather forecast had predicted more dry weather, and the widow had fully intended to hoe around her borders and possibly even do a little digging in of new bedding plants but, with a man lying dead, murdered in his own home only fifty yards away, it seemed to her wholly inappropriate now and she remained indoors for the rest of the day.

THIRTY-THREE

Kavanagh and Scrivens got suited up in the Major Incident truck as detective constables began house-to-house enquiries and garnered CCTV security camera footage from the several houses that had domestic systems fitted.

Clad in their blue slippers and white over-suits the two detective inspectors entered the house. It was a hive of carefully choreographed activity of the sort familiar to every viewer of cop shows from *The Bill* to *Crimewatch*. The forensics investigators were pasting, taping and finger-print dusting window glass and surfaces, and collecting the fibres, hair and particles of dust and dirt that had been deposited on carpets and floorboards from the soles of shoes.

The pathologist was still in attendance as she awaited the return of Scrivens, who had initially visited the murder scene as soon as Dalton's 999 call had come in, and immediately ensured that the crime scene was quarantined, the road closed, and the surrounding area sealed off.

'A burglary that's gone wrong?' said Scrivens to Kavanagh, awaiting his confirmation as they stood a few feet away from the man's corpse.

'I suppose so,' said Kavanagh. 'It certainly looks that way.'

The man's laptop was gone. The house was bereft of jewellery, and there was no sight of either his watch or his wallet. Anything of value that was portable and readily disposable appeared to have been stolen, and the drawers to his bureau, his writing desk and bedside tables all showed the signs of having been riffled through.

'You got any local villains with this kind of form?' asked the London inspector.

'You're joking,' said Scrivens. 'The worst we get round here's Saturday night fights and smashed windows, but that's about it. There's the odd garden shed broken into and a mower nicked to feed some junkie's habit, but they don't do house break-ins, not really, or at least, very rarely.'

'Lucky you,' said Kavanagh.

'They know there's no point,' said Scrivens. 'They know that we know who they are, and anyway, where are they going to flog the stuff? On ebay? Our people check those sites the whole time. We know all the second-hand shops and the antique dealers round here, and they know we know them. It's just not a goer. Just occasionally, we might get some out-of-town scallies come down from Liverpool or Manchester or across from Telford way, but that's very unusual.'

'So, what do you reckon?' asked Kavanagh reasonably.

'My guess would be that it'll be one of the blokes from away he's had working here during the last few months. The neighbours say there's been tradesmen in and out of the place non-stop: chippies, sparks, plumbers, gardeners, roofers, all sorts. They'll not have needed to be Mystic Meg to know the bloke's a bit tasty, just the way he spoke and all, as well as the nice bits and pieces he'll have had knocking around the place. One of these blokes will have come back himself or he'll have blabbed it to a mate down the pub, and some other geezer's come round for the easy pickings.'

'Yes,' said Kavanagh. 'I guess you could be right.'

'I don't suppose anybody intended to kill him,' went on the local DI, 'but Betts has been disturbed, he's woken up or something, and it's cost the poor man his life.'

'Especially if he recognized him?' offered Kavanagh. 'If it was someone who'd done work in the house?'

'Yes,' agreed Scrivens. 'I reckon.'

'But they left his car behind?' said Kavanagh, gesturing to £15,000 worth of newish Audi on the drive. 'What's that all about?'

'Means they didn't fancy the odds of getting shot of it without it being traced,' replied Scrivens confidently.

'Or that it wasn't a "they",' suggested Kavanagh. 'And that whoever it was arrived on his own: he came in a car and he had to leave in the same car?'

'Could be,' agreed Scrivens.

Kavanagh picked up a leaflet from the dining table in his

gloved hand. 'Keep It Local, eh?' he said, and passed it to Scrivens. 'Unfortunate acronym, I'd say.'

'KIL? Sure is,' said Scrivens. 'Anyway, I guess we're done here for the time being. Let's leave them to it.'

'OK,' said Kavanagh.

As they got to the front door, Kavanagh said to the officer on duty there. 'Incidentally, did any of your people find a bag . . .?'

'What bag's that then, sir?' asked the PC.

'An old lunch bag. Bit of a relic, I believe.'

'No idea, sir. Not that I'm aware of.'

'Thanks,' said the inspector.

'What's this lunch bag, then?' asked Scrivens as the two men walked down the drive.

'You really *don't* read your local paper?' said Kavanagh.

'Never,' he said. 'Too depressing: full of stuff about drunk kids beating one another up! Why? You say you do?'

'I did this week,' said Kavanagh. 'I'd got a few minutes on my hands whilst Jane was sorting out things with her mate Carrie, and I picked one up.'

'So, go on?' he said.

'It wasn't much of a story, they'd made a lot of nothing, really,' he said. 'Just a few paragraphs about a couple of blokes working on the roof here and how they found an old lunch bag that had been hidden away in the eaves. It had probably been there since the house was built. They ran it as a local interest thing, you know. And it's on the sandwich boards outside the shops, you must have seen them?'

'Oh, I wondered what that was all about,' said Scrivens, little interested and getting into the car.

'Bit odd,' continued Kavanagh, putting on his seat belt. 'I think they'd got the story from Betts himself. The story's written up, and then the man's burgled and gets himself killed.'

'I'll put someone onto it if you like, Frank, if we're not too tied up infiltrating the Keep It Local mob,' he joked. 'This is Oswestry, Frank, not an underpass in Paris. We don't do conspiracies here.'

''Course not,' agreed Kavanagh.

'Whoever did this isn't interested in an old bag, I can tell you that,' said Scrivens as they drove away. 'It's his Apple Mac and his Rolex that these guys have had away.'

'Sure,' said Kavanagh. 'Just a thought.'

That night, as darkness fell, the reporters and TV crews all gone home or holed up in the hotel bars, Betts's widow neighbour slipped on her coat, laced her shoes and walked down the deserted road. She crossed and stood for a moment outside the writer's house. Lights were on throughout the house and there was the diesel throb of a single police car parked on the drive, a uniformed officer sitting in it.

Against the low front wall the woman knelt down and placed a rose from her own back garden amongst the floral tributes there.

THIRTY-FOUR

'**B**rian Dalton,' said the ruddy-faced man in the country-check shirt and yellow knitted tie as he extended his hand.

'Pleased to meet you,' said Kavanagh, 'and thanks for finding the time to see me.'

Dalton opened his hands in a gesture that conveyed to his guest that it wasn't quite the *New York Times* he was engaged in getting out onto the streets of the town each week.

'No problem,' he said, offering Kavanagh a chair opposite his own at his very big, old-fashioned desk. 'What can I do for you, Inspector?'

'I'm up here from London with a colleague. Not really business, we were just having a little break,' he said, circumventing his own personal travails of the last few days.

'Yes,' said Dalton warily, almost as if he thought this might be some kind of sting. 'What was it you wanted to know then?'

'It's about the Julian Betts murder,' said Kavanagh.

'Yes? Very tragic,' said the editor.

'You found him, I believe?' said the inspector.

'I did, yes,' he said. 'And how unpleasant that was, too,' he said reflectively. 'I've seen quite a few deceased people in my time, but the poor man did look pathetic, lying there with his pyjamas all askew. A very undignified way to die, somehow.'

'Of course,' agreed Kavanagh. He'd not only seen Julian Betts himself in exactly this position, but he had also seen many corpses during his career, and the thing that had struck him repeatedly was exactly this: how entirely stripped of dignity were most people in their ultimate demise. 'Anyway, what I wanted to ask you about was the old lunch bag that you wrote about in the paper recently.'

'Yes? It was just a couple of paragraphs. Something to engage the older readers, really. It wouldn't mean anything to any of the youngsters. What is it you wanted to know?'

'How did you come to hear about the thing in the first place?' asked Kavanagh.

'A council employee down at the tip told a mate of his, and he happened to mention it to his missus, who told one of our subs at his pub quiz night, and then he told me. I was short of a filler, and so I stuck it in on page . . . seven, I think it was.'

'Nine,' Kavanagh corrected him.

'Was it?' he said. 'Nine, then. I gave Betts a ring to ask him about it, but, to be honest, I think he was a bit protective of what he was thinking of as his story. He said he'd call me back, but he never did, which is the very reason I went up there. And that's when I found him.'

'I see,' said Kavanagh.

'Do you think the bag's got something to do with his being killed, Inspector?' said the rubicund newspaper man as he scented the possibility of his little story lifting off.

'No,' said Kavanagh. 'I doubt it, it's just a bit odd, that's all, and I thought I could check it out while your local DI, Michael Scrivens, is following through on the main avenues of enquiry.'

'Well, I'm sorry I can't tell you more,' said Dalton, 'but that's all I know about it.'

'Thanks,' said Kavanagh, and glanced at his pad. 'DI Scrivens says you know pretty well everyone in the town?'

'Well, that's a bit of an exaggeration, but go on?'

'Is there anyone still around who might remember those houses being built, I wondered?'

'It's a long time ago,' said Dalton and picked up the phone.

Good, thought Kavanagh, someone who gets right on with things, that's what I like. 'Kath, bring us up a nice pot of tea, would you?' said the editor, and replaced the receiver.

'So, how old is the housing estate?' asked the policeman.

'I'm not exactly sure,' he said. 'I was a youngster when it was going up. Mid- to late-Sixties, I think? But the council will tell you, no doubt.'

'And you don't happen to know who built it, I suppose?' asked Kavanagh.

'Of course I do,' said Dalton. 'It was Phil Penley. He was

the biggest builder around here for a long time. His son took over the business about twenty years ago. But it was his dad, old Phil, who built the estate up there.'

'Is Mr Penley still alive?' asked Kavanagh tentatively.

'I think so,' said Dalton. 'But he must be in his eighties now, if he's a day. He and his wife had a very plush bungalow until a few years ago, and then she passed away. Phil's in a nursing home now I think. Least he was, the last I heard.'

DC Jane Salt had had a pleasant, but entirely fruitless time with Ted Sillence, the chief fire officer. He'd explained to her that their investigations had left them in no doubt that the blaze out at Billy Hughes's smallholding had been started deliberately, but that they'd looked in vain for evidence of the identity of the actual fire-raiser. 'We had our own investigators in there, then we handed it over to the police forensic science service and they brought in their experts.

'We know the accelerant was petrol, the fire dog trained on detecting it left them in no doubt at all about that and,' he concluded with considerable understatement, 'it's what we record officially as a fire of "doubtful origin".'

'I see,' said Salt. 'And the old man was lucky to survive?'

'As well as the inferno,' he added, 'there'd almost certainly have been something like an explosion when it went off, which is probably what saved Mr Hughes's life. If that hadn't woken him, the smoke would have killed him before the fire had destroyed the building. Yes, he was very lucky indeed.

'Off the record, we all know who did it – or at least who was responsible for the fire – but there was no evidence against him and he was bombproof.'

'So, you've nothing new on your arsonist?' asked Kavanagh as he and Salt sat in a little booth in the pub nearest to their bed and breakfast that evening. 'And I've got a columnist who's been killed in what DI Scrivens seems convinced is just a burglary gone wrong.'

'And you?' said Salt. 'What does Inspector Frank Kavanagh of the Yard think?'

'I'm not really sure what I think, Jane. But I'm due to see

the old chap who built the estate, see if he can throw light on anything.'

'Throw light on what?' she asked. 'And over forty years on? How old is he going to be now?'

'He's in his late eighties,' said Kavanagh, grimacing. 'I know. But it's all I've got and so it seems worth a shout. I've spoken to his son, and who knows, maybe the old boy's got a good memory?' added the inspector optimistically.

'Maybe,' said Salt. 'When are you seeing him?'

'Should be the day after tomorrow. He's just had his replacement hip replaced, and so he won't be back at the care home where he's resident until then. Do you fancy coming along?'

'Yes, sure,' she said. 'I think I'd better book us another night at the B and B.'

'Maybe two,' he agreed.

'Life in a market town, eh?' she said. 'We started with a burned-down house, and now we've got a murder. So, what's next?'

'I tell you what, Jane, if that bag they found in the loft isn't involved in Julian Betts's death in some way, I'm Mr Tambourine Man.'

'"*Play a song for me*",' she said as she picked up his glass. 'Same again?'

'Cheers,' he said as she got up. 'Hey?'

'What?'

'I'm glad you're back,' he said. 'Really.'

THIRTY-FIVE

Young Lauren Thomas had all of her father's will, but it wasn't his business 'acumen' that she had inherited, simply his determination to succeed.

Like many sixteen-year-olds, the girl had much better things to do than take any interest in her parents and their tedious doings. Frankly, like most girls of her age, she found them embarrassing, didn't like to be seen out with them and very rarely spoke more than the absolute minimum to them.

Occasionally, under some duress, she'd sit down and eat a meal with her mother and father, and to her absolutely excruciating embarrassment she had, on two recent occasions now, heard what must have been them making love, once when she'd returned from horse-riding lessons early one Sunday afternoon, and another time when she'd got up during the night to go downstairs for a drink of milk.

The idea that her parents even *had* sex was distressing enough, to actually hear them doing it, mortifyingly so, and she'd been close to tears as she sat back on her bed, her ears covered against the abomination. Unfortunately, though, when it came to her imagination, she had nothing whatsoever to protect herself from the unbearable notion.

The next morning as they sat at the breakfast table she stared down morosely at her fruit and yoghurt, left most of it uneaten and then departed silently for the sanctuary of her school, brimming with resentment at her parents' inappropriate behaviour.

Some kids might do their homework or studying whilst curled up on their beds, in front of the TV or with their music on the stereo or iPod, and happily interrupt themselves every few minutes to check their Facebook page and send or receive a text or email. But Lauren resisted these distractions for most of the time, and when she settled down to do an hour's work for her history or English literature mock A level exams, she really *did* do an hour's work.

Yes, OK, she was also a young girl with all of the thoughts

that a girl of sixteen has about a seventeen-year-old boyfriend. She and Danny would often make love in her bedroom when her parents were out and, just a few times, when the young-sters' feelings had got the better of them, even as her parents were actually downstairs watching TV.

Daniel had been afraid they might pop up to check that Lauren and he weren't doing precisely what they were doing, but the girl assured him that her room was sacrosanct and they would never dream of entering it unannounced. No matter, Danny kept his black skintight jeans and Slipknot T-shirt very close at hand and wondered just how quickly he might be able to struggle back into his clothes should his girlfriend's father – a formidably-built man and a person with something of a reputation for no-nonsense dealing in the town – enter his daughter's bedroom.

But Lauren wasn't with Danny this morning: it was half-term and she was sitting at the bespoke desk that her father had had made for her along one wall of her bedroom, one of several first-floor rooms that fronted the house. She had been trying to work for half an hour now, but the noise outside her window was making it increasingly impossible. She eventually flounced downstairs, irate.

Her father was standing beside a lorry which had a hoist on its flat back, the thing revving up as it lifted each of the several huge stone sculptures from the truck and onto the ground in their heavy wooden crates.

'Dad,' she said, entirely ignoring her father's new and very expensive purchases. 'I've got an exam coming up. Don't you care? Do you want me to fail?'

'Settle down,' he said, not even looking at her but watching closely as the sculpture swung down from the truck, suspended on its ropes. 'We'll only be an hour or two more getting these off.'

'"An hour or two",' she replied petulantly. 'I've got to go out this afternoon. I'm meeting people. It's *now* I've got to do my revising. Don't you care about my results?'

'Lauren, calm down,' he said firmly, as the man operating the hoist looked away, embarrassed to hear the youngster speaking to her father in this way.

'Can't you do this some other time?' she demanded.

'Oh, yes,' her father said, finally losing patience with the girl. 'These have come from Romania by boat and by lorry up from the port and you'd like us to hang around unloading them just so that you can do a bit of revising? I think you've had a bit too much time and money spent on you, young lady . . .'

'Do you?' she said. 'You wait till I fail and I won't even be able to go to university.' She turned and stalked away.

'Carry on,' said her father, addressing the man who had the control box in his hand. 'I won't be long,' he added as he walked after his daughter.

'Lauren. Lauren, come here,' he said angrily.

She ignored him and walked away towards the side of the house.

'I said come here, and I mean it. You stop there or I'll cancel your riding lessons.' He pulled his Blackberry from his pocket.

He never bluffed, ever, and she knew that he meant it. She stood there, not turning, but looking straight ahead.

He stood by her side and put his phone away inside the breast pocket of his body-warmer. 'You might be a bit stressed, but this is important to me, and the whole thing'll only take an hour. And anyway, if the noise is too much just go and work in one of the other rooms. God knows we've got enough of 'em.'

'Yes? And what about all my books and my computer that are in my room?' she said, as if this represented some wholly insurmountable difficulty.

'Just move them, and stop being so bloody unreasonable,' he said, beginning now to run out of patience with his daughter.

'You don't know what it's like,' she said vaguely.

'Don't I?' he said, and moved round to stand in front of her. She steadfastly looked at the ground.

'Look, Lauren, you take a lot of things for granted.'

'Yes, so you're always telling me,' she sneered.

'You do,' he retorted. 'You've got all this, and you take it for granted. I've got kids work for me, not much older than you, and they'd give their right arm for what you have.'

'Yes, I bet,' she said. 'All you ever think about is running your businesses.'

'Is that right?' he replied.

'Yes,' she shouted back at her father. 'Your work's every-thing to you, but what do you ever do for *us*?'

'What do I do for you?' he snarled. 'Everything I do is for you. Everything. I sort things out that you've no idea about.'

'What?' she sneered, eyes fixed firmly on the ground.

'Look –' he gestured to the rolling fields in front of them – 'what do you see?'

She refused to look up. 'I know what's there. I live here,' she said.

'I'll tell you what you see. The *fucking* sky and nothing but green fields and trees.'

She was shocked. Her father often swore, but not at her, and certainly not the F-word that many of her friends used in every other sentence they spoke.

'You see all that? Do you know *why* you can see it?'

What was he on about now? Where was all this going? It certainly wasn't the usual lecture she got when they had this kind of falling out.

'What are you *talking* about?' she said.

'Nothing,' he said. 'Just think about it.'

'Go on,' she said. 'We've got a view, yes? So what?'

'We've got a view, that's right,' he said nodding his head. 'At least we have now.'

'What are you saying to me?' she asked, looking up and confronting him as she perceived the meaning behind his words. 'You're not saying that you . . .? That it was you that . . .?'

'I didn't say anything,' he asserted, retrenching.

'*You* did that?' she said quietly. 'To that old man, just so we could . . .?'

'Of course I didn't,' he said, afraid now of what he might have implied. 'All I'm saying is, I take care of everything that needs to be done around here, and you need to take care of yourself. Right? I'm trying to teach you a lesson here. Not about exams, but about life: you have to be determined if you're going to get what you want.'

'I'm disgusted,' she said with deep feeling. 'I can't believe this,' and she stalked away.

'I haven't said anything, Lauren,' he shouted after her. 'And don't you ever dare say I have. Do you understand me?'

She ignored him and walked determinedly on.

'Fuck,' he said to her departing back. 'Fuck.'

THIRTY-SIX

'How's it going, Scriv?' asked Kavanagh brightly, the very invoking of a nickname vouchsafing the two men's growing friendship.

'Slow,' said DI Scrivens. 'We've tracked down most of the local tradesmen, but a couple of the ones who came from further away are proving a bit more difficult to get hold of.'

'But nothing on the local blokes?' said Kavanagh.

'They're all sound,' said Scrivens. 'Alibis for the night in question, family blokes, regular guys, that sort of thing. There's no one in the frame from round here. There's a Scouser who did the wiring, though. His girlfriend's from the town and that's why he was down here and got the job, word-of-mouth recommendation, but they've since moved to Portugal. We're trying to get hold of them at some little log cabin holiday resort in a village near Oporto.'

'Sounds promising,' said Kavanagh.

'Maybe,' agreed Scrivens. 'The only other half decent lead we've got is about some hobo who's been sleeping rough not a million miles from Betts's place on Low Brook Road. A few people have seen him around. He's a bit of an alky, which doesn't usually fit with burglary blags, but we need to speak to him, obviously.'

'Right,' said Kavanagh. 'Where's he bedded down?'

'He was in some woodland on the edge of town that belongs to our local big wheel, you know, the bloke who we had in the frame for the arson business, Gareth Thomas?'

'You say he "was" sleeping there?' asked Kavanagh.

'He seems to have scarpered. But we'll find him. He won't have gone far.'

'And have you spoken to this Thomas geezer yet about his unwanted guest?' asked Kavanagh.

'He's away on business, but he's due back the day after tomorrow.'

'It's worth a punt, I guess, and anyway, I'd like to get a look at him if he reckons he's getting away with arson. Do you mind if I come along when you speak to him?' asked the London cop.

'Of course,' said Scrivens. 'Be pleased. We're meeting down at his place on the industrial estate, the big one.'

'Right,' said Kavanagh. 'Anything else? What about the foot soldiers on house-to-house?'

'Nothing much, just a tickle, maybe.'

'Yes? What's that?' asked Kavanagh.

'Betts's next-door neighbours say a few days before his murder – they're a quiet couple and keep themselves to themselves, so the wife says—'

'Quiet couple? It's probably them that killed him, then,' interrupted Kavanagh.

'Could be,' said Scrivens. 'Anyway, they say Betts came round to them very upset because someone had wrecked his garden.'

'Really?' asked Kavanagh, intrigued.

'Yes. Somebody had thrown the plants about, pulled up his little trees and been pogo-ing in the flower beds. They'd made a right mess of the place.'

'Sounds odd,' said Kavanagh. 'You reckon it might be connected?'

'It's a chance. Could have been just kids messing about, but it's not very likely, not up there. Down on the estate on the other side of town, maybe, but you don't get that kind of thing up on Meadow Rise.'

'I suppose he might've pissed off the anti-supermarket development lot,' suggested Kavanagh.

'Yes?' asked Scrivens.

'Sure. Betts did that piece in his column about your Keep It Local lot just being a bunch of NIMBYs.'

'NIMBYs?' said Scrivens.

'Not in My Back Yarders,' explained Kavanagh.

'Right,' said Scrivens. 'But to be honest, Frank – off the record – I know of some of them and they're not vandals. They're the ones who used to be in CND and who want cycle lanes and all that kind of thing. Also, between me and you, I think they've got a point: if a big supermarket does set up on the edge of town, the town will die.'

'Yes?' said Kavanagh. 'No scrapping kids for your lot to deal with Friday nights!'

'Guaranteed,' said Scrivens. 'Seriously, people get bought off with the idea of a multiplex cinema and a drive-in burger joint. Up in these parts, that sounds like the promised land.'

'So, what are we going to do, Mr Greenpeace?' asked Kavanagh.

'They're not wrong 'uns,' he said. 'I'd guarantee it, but we'll need to check 'em out and see exactly what's what.'

'Who's the main person? Do you know them?'

'Yes, I know of her,' said the DI. 'Her name's Carol. Carol Reddy, she's an ex-school teacher, a magistrate and club secretary of the local tennis club. I'll make the arrangements for us to see her. And what about yourself?' he asked. 'Any good on the old sandwich bag trail?'

'You can mock,' said Kavanagh.

'I am,' he said. 'Have you tried the Oxfam shop? I think they take in a lot of old stuff,' he added.

Kavanagh ignored the man's sarcasm. 'I'm due to see someone called Philip Penley, the old chap who built the housing estate, as soon as he's well enough for a chat after a hip replacement he's had, see if he's got anything useful to say.'

'How did you get on to him?' asked Scrivens.

'Your mate Brian Dalton at the *Gazette* put me on to him and I've spoken to his son, Rob. He's going to let me know when his dad's up for it.'

'Good luck,' said Scrivens. 'Anyway, Sherlock, I've got to get on now, I've got a real murder enquiry under way.'

'Piss off, Watson,' said Kavanagh. 'Give me a bell when you've fixed a date with the Keep It Local woman.'

'Sure,' said Scrivens. 'Will do.'

Back at the B and B in the lane at the top of the town, Kavanagh's heart sank as he saw the note in Salt's handwriting propped up on the pillow of their bed. They'd been fine, hadn't they? Why this? He opened the little sheet of paper.

'Sorry, Frank. I've had to go to London. Call me as soon as you can. Jane x.'

He stood at the bedside and fumbled the buttons on his phone, barely breathing as he did so.

'Hi, Frank. You OK?' Salt asked brightly.

'I'm alright,' he said. 'What is it, Jane? What's happened?'

'It's Dad, he shouldn't even be driving any more. You know that. He was reversing out of the garage, Mum was guiding him out, and he's only driven right over her foot.'

'Jesus,' said Kavanagh. 'Sorry. I mean, I'm so sorry. Is she alright?'

'She's broken at least one bone, maybe two. She's in the hospital now. I have to get down to be with her. Dad won't be able to cope on his own.'

'Of course,' he said, relieved to hear the news, and ashamed of his relief.

'I tried to call you,' said Salt, 'but my phone was flat. I got a cab and took the first train. It's been on charge here in the carriage.'

'Sure,' he said. 'I understand. You take care, Jane.'

'Of course,' she said. 'Are you alright, Frank? You sound quiet. Is everything alright on the case?'

'Yes, I'm fine' he murmured. 'And everything's going OK. Give your mum my best, and your dad, and you take care.'

'Sure,' she said.

'When will you be back? Do you have any idea?' he asked.

'A day or two, I guess. I'll have to see how things go,' she said.

'Yes. Come back safe,' he said. ''Bye.'

''Bye, Frank.'

THIRTY-SEVEN

KIL pressure group chair, Carol Reddy, offered the policemen water. Just water. Kavanagh accepted merely out of politeness and the woman returned from the kitchen a moment later and handed him a glass of tepid tap water. As the policemen had walked through the hall of the woman's Victorian semi-detached house they'd passed her kit bag on the floor. She was still wearing her shorts and a pink tennis top. 'It's about the campaign, Mrs Reddy,' began Scrivens.

'Yes?' she said. 'Keep It Local?'

'Exactly,' said Scrivens.

'What about it?' she asked, and took a long drink of what looked like very diluted blackcurrant juice from the bottle beside her chair.

'It's a bit . . . tangential,' said Kavanagh, 'but it's one of the avenues of enquiry that we are following.'

The woman glanced his way and raised an eyebrow, apparently approving of his use of the word.

'Tangential?' she repeated, and put the bottle back down on the floor beside her. She had nice legs. They were very brown and Kavanagh reckoned she probably played outdoors a good deal given that it was still only early summer. Her short hair was dyed blonde. She was in her mid-sixties but wasn't carrying an ounce of extra weight. Something about her demeanour and the way she carried herself suggested to Kavanagh that she probably played a decent game. He'd been wrong before; he'd often looked on as a new member turned up at the club where he occasionally played with one of those huge kitbags that takes half-a-dozen rackets, only to float some limp first serve over the net and then sky a lob right into the field next door.

'I wonder, could you tell us a little bit about your group?' he asked.

'Well, it's hardly mine,' she corrected him, 'but yes, of course I can. What would you like to know, Inspector?'

'You oppose supermarkets, I believe,' Kavanagh said.

'No,' she said. 'Not really. At least, not supermarkets *per se*. What we do oppose is an edge-of-town supermarket on the site that has been earmarked as the most likely location for it.'

'I see,' said the inspector. 'But you'd be happy to see it sited somewhere else?'

'We're democrats, Inspector, and have no wish to dictate where the town's people should shop. Our only concern is that the store, if there is to be one, does not destroy the town centre and our local community and shops. Without them, the place would die.'

'I see,' he said.

'There's plenty of evidence of this happening elsewhere, wherever a supermarket sets up very close to the town, the place soon withers and it eventually dies. It's a self-fulfilling cycle.'

'And what are your alternative ideas?' asked Scrivens.

'Well, personally, I'd rather supply all of my needs from local shops. I'm old enough to remember the smallest town, even villages sometimes, having haberdashers and iron-mongers and several provisions stores and a couple of bakers. I don't think we can expect to return to those days. I know people like supermarkets, but to site this one further away from the town centre would be the best compromise, and then we'd still have our own butchers and greengrocers and all. We don't think that's too much to ask. Do you?'

'Sounds reasonable to me,' agreed Kavanagh. 'So it's just the one site that your group objects to?'

'Yes,' she agreed.

'And this alternative . . .?' he asked.

'Another site was identified by the planners. It's four miles from the town − far enough away to suit both parties, we think − and it would be ideal.'

'Right,' said Scrivens, thinking that they were getting rather more in the way of planning application information than they actually needed, perhaps.

The woman must have sensed his feelings. 'Anyway, unless I can sign you up as members,' she said briskly, 'something which I'd be delighted to do, we'd better move on. I have to shower, and I'm sure you're not here just to talk about the campaign?'

'No, you're right,' said Scrivens. 'I'm afraid we're not, or at least not directly. You'll know there was a murder in the town recently, of course?'

'Yes, I do,' she said. 'Julian Betts, the writer. I always read his column.'

'Really?' said Scrivens.

'Yes,' she said. 'I disagree with just about everything he appeared to believe in, but he wrote so well and amusingly that I always read him.'

'I think in one of his recent pieces he said something about the Keep It Local group?' said Kavanagh.

'Yes,' she replied. 'He did. He was quite rude about us in that underhand way that he has. Or had. And of course he then went on to sing the praises of supermarkets.'

'I don't know whether you know this, Mrs Reddy,' said Scrivens, 'but shortly before he died, and only a little time after that column appeared, his garden was . . . desecrated.'

'Really?' said the woman. She exchanged a quick glance with Kavanagh. 'I think the inspector means it was vandalized,' added Kavanagh.

'No. I had no idea,' she said.

'He didn't report it – at least not officially – he just told his neighbours. Not surprisingly, he was very upset.'

'Of course,' she said. 'That's awful. And do you think that whoever it was who . . . vandalized his garden then went on to murder him?'

'It's impossible to say,' said Kavanagh. 'I very much doubt it, but there could be a link, and until it's established that whoever did it had nothing to do with the killing, it remains something that we have to investigate.'

'But you're not suggesting that our people could have been involved?'

'Well, we're not suggesting anything,' said Scrivens, 'but do you have any members who might sympathize with the idea of "direct action" of any sort?'

'Of course not,' she asserted. 'We're not that kind of group.'

'You sound very sure,' said Kavanagh. 'It wouldn't be unheard of, after all.'

'Keep It Local is made up of people from a very wide cross section of the community: there are students through to pensioners, and all sorts of professions are represented, right across the board,' she added.

'Yes?' said Scrivens. 'But you can't know them all, surely?'

'It's true that we've grown bigger as time has gone on. When we began, we all knew one another, and we even squeezed into this room for our first couple of meetings. Those days have passed, it's true, and of course there is now a much wider range of people involved.'

'Go on,' said Kavanagh.

She reflected for a moment, took another drink from her bottle of blackcurrant juice. 'You could be right, I suppose, and perhaps a few of the younger members might prefer us to be a little more "proactive". But we need them very much. They're the lifeblood of the campaign, otherwise we'd just be seen as a lot of old folk who are resistant to any kind of change.'

'I see,' said Scrivens. 'And you think they'd like to . . . what, exactly?'

'I don't know. But perhaps some of them are not entirely content with marches and petitions.'

'Is that the extent of your campaigning activities, then?' he asked.

'Just about,' she said. 'That, and of course we regularly write letters to the newspaper. We've worked out a very effective system of getting them published: we take it in turns to write to the editor.'

'Really?' said Kavanagh.

'In that way they don't have any excuse for not publishing our views,' she said, clearly proud of their campaigning wiles.

'So, you are the chair?' said Scrivens. 'And you set the organization up originally?'

'Yes,' she said. 'As soon as I heard that the supermarket people had bought the land – secretly, of course, by using an agent – I called a meeting and within a month we had a committee, a constitution, a bank account and over five hundred members who opposed the plans.'

'I see,' he said, 'and who is on the committee?' he asked as he got out his pad.

'You'd like their names?' she asked.

'Yes, please,' he said. 'A membership list would be useful, too.'

'Of course,' she agreed. 'Are you sure you wouldn't like a drink, Inspector?' she asked Scrivens again.

'Thank you, I'm fine,' he said.

'Excuse me,' she said, and went to the hall and came back pulling on a sweatshirt. 'Mustn't stiffen up,' she said. 'I've just played three sets of doubles.'

'How did you get on?' asked Kavanagh.

'Won, two - one,' she said. 'Do you play?'

'Just a bit,' he said. 'And not very well, especially now.' He lifted his trouser leg a few inches to show the woman his ankle strapping. 'Five-a-side,' he said. 'Stupid, I guess, but it's history now. It'll be only tennis in future.'

'It's such a good game,' she asserted. 'No matter what level you play. Almost every time I serve – and half of them don't go in – do you know what I think about?'

'Venus Williams?' suggested Kavanagh.

'No, not Venus or Serena Williams. I think about Hitler.'

'Really?' said the inspector, surprised. 'Why on earth do you think of Adolf Hitler?'

'I always think that tennis for most of us is more Jacques Tati than Roger Federer. I'm convinced that if Hitler's parents had given him a tennis racket on his tenth birthday, he would never have been able to take himself so seriously and European history might have been very different.'

'It's an interesting notion,' said Kavanagh, a little sceptical.

'Anyway, perhaps when your ankle is stronger, I'll take you down to the club for a knock,' she offered.

'Thanks,' said Kavanagh. 'If we ever get through this I might just take you up on that.'

'So, you were saying, Inspector Scrivens?'

'The committee?'

'Yes?'

'Who, exactly, is on it?'

'Just myself, the vice chair, the treasurer and a publicity person. But the day-to-day business is done by myself and Valery.'

'And who's she?' asked Kavanagh, opening his pad.

'Valery's a man,' said Reddy. 'Valery Poole.'

'Really?' said Kavanagh. 'And what is Mr Poole's background?'

'He's recently returned to the UK from Zimbabwe. His family's farm was seized by Mugabe's people and they lost just about everything.'

'I see,' said Kavanagh. 'And he chose to get involved with this . . . local issue?' he asked, intrigued.

'I think he feels just as strongly about the growing power of the supermarkets as we all do?' she suggested. 'Maybe there is a tenuous connection? After all, it is a sort of tyranny.'

'But, compared with the situation in Zimbabwe, it must seem a relatively minor matter?' ventured the DI. 'The last time I heard they'd devalued the currency again and inflation was running at about a thousand percent.'

'It takes all sorts, I suppose,' she agreed. 'Things are very bad there, but that's no reason not to fight against lesser wrongs here,' she gamely suggested.

Scrivens knew his market town and the people who lived there well. 'Valery is quite an unusual name for this part of the world,' he gently ventured. 'I'm wondering just how he was received by the other campaigners in your group?'

'I won't be breaking any confidences if I tell you that, like yourselves, not everyone was convinced that his motives for getting involved were quite as straightforward as they might have appeared.'

'Please, go on?' said Scrivens.

'There was a feeling amongst some of the group that Valery might even be some sort of mole.'

'Mole? Why would he be that?' asked Kavanagh.

'A few of the younger ones seemed to think that he might be a spy of some sort. For the supermarket company. Or even the developer, perhaps. It's all nonsense, of course, just resentment at his accent and his background, probably. I'm quite sure he's simply a person who wants to do the right thing, just the same as the rest of us.

'Anyway, he seems to be fully accepted now. He's even become quite close to another one of the members, a nice-looking young girl called Chloe. She's quite a bit younger than he is,' she said, with a knowing look.

'I see,' said Scrivens. 'And the membership?' he said. 'I wonder if you could let us have a list of names, with people's numbers and home details etc?'

'Of course,' she said. 'I'll run one off for you now.' She went through to the sitting room from where they soon heard the sound of a printer running off several pages.

'What do you reckon?' asked Scrivens as he and Kavanagh walked towards their car.

'Well, she's as straight as can be, but *Valery* . . .' He gave the name three syllables. 'My Mum once told me never to trust a woman who wore nail varnish on her toes, or a man called Vyvian.'

'But he's not *called* Vyvian,' said Scrivens.

'No, he's not. But I don't think Mum knew you could even *call* a bloke Valery,' he said. 'I think we ought to have a proper look at his background and then maybe have a word with him.'

'Go on?' said Scrivens.

'Look, if his CV is felt not to be quite kosher by some of this lot, and he wants to establish his credibility within the KIL group, what better way to go about it than doing a bit of gardening in Betts's plot after the man's written abusively about them?'

'Only one better way I can think of,' added Scrivens.

'Yes? What's that?' asked Kavanagh.

'Bedding down with a tasty youngster with the same aims as his own,' said the local man.

THIRTY-EIGHT

Valery Poole might have been run out of Zimbabwe, his family's farm appropriated by Mugabe's 'war veterans' but the policemen's immediate impressions suggested that he hadn't been too compromised by this unfortunate turn of events. His big, steel-and-glass-fronted flat was in a newly-built block in a tree-lined road that was otherwise occupied by red-brick detached houses that had been there since the late nineteenth century.

He opened the door to the policemen in his dressing gown and invited them into the semi-darkened sitting room. He had that relaxed bearing that seems to come as standard issue to the privately educated. His mouth had a slightly sardonic turn about it that suggested that he might not need to take things quite so seriously as some other people.

There were the muffled sounds of another person moving about in the bedroom next door. Poole drew open the heavy curtains, sat at the dining table and gestured the two men towards the big sofa.

'What can I do for you?' he asked, lighting a cigarette.

'Are you not having to go to work today?' asked Scrivens, stating the obvious at ten o'clock on a weekday morning.

'I'm involved with planning a couple of projects just now,' said the man vaguely.

'Yes? What sort of area are you in?' enquired Kavanagh, equally nebulously.

'This and that,' he offered. 'I've not long returned from Africa,' he added. 'I'm exploring several avenues.'

'I see,' said Kavanagh, clearly not doing so at all. The man appeared able to sustain a nice lifestyle without any visible means of support, and he clearly also had that trait of uttering words, the actual meaning of which tended to be elusive.

A girl with tousled pink hair, a nose ring and wearing a long T-shirt over cotton shorts came in to the room. 'Hello,' she said, without looking directly at the men and sauntered through to the kitchen.

'Was there something important?' Poole asked the officers.

'Yes. It's about the Keep It Local group,' said Kavanagh.

'Yes,' said the man.

'You've become quite heavily involved, I believe?' enquired Scrivens.

'Yes, quite a bit,' he said. 'I attend meetings and do a bit of leafleting,' he offered.

'You are actually the vice chair, I think?' said Kavanagh.

'Yes, I am,' he said, and stubbed out his cigarette, most of it unsmoked. 'Like all committee stuff, it's a pretty thankless task,' he added.

'I'm sure,' agreed the inspector.

'Anyway, what is it I can help you with?' he asked.

'We've recently spoken to Carol Reddy,' said Scrivens.

'Chairperson Reddy,' he said with a smile. 'Good woman. Very committed to the cause.'

'We spoke to her about the murder of the local writer, Julian Betts,' said Scrivens, with a deal more seriousness.

'Yes?' he said. 'But what's that to do with me?'

'Well, just before he was killed, Mr Betts's property was vandalized.'

'Really?' said the man.

'Yes, his newly-planted garden was destroyed,' said Kavanagh.

'I'm sorry to hear it,' said Poole. 'But how does that concern me?'

'It happened very shortly after he wrote about the Keep It Local group in his Sunday newspaper column.'

'Yes?' said the man.

'Yes,' said Scrivens. 'His article wasn't very complimentary about KIL. Betts suggested there was a deal of self-servingness, and that your people are little more than middle-class NIMBYs.'

'Did you happen to see the piece?' asked Kavanagh.

There was a moment's hesitation.

'Well?' asked the officer.

'I think I might have seen it,' said Poole.

'You don't remember?' pursued Kavanagh. 'It's no crime reading a newspaper article, surely?' he added pointedly.

'I don't recall, exactly,' offered Poole, taking out another cigarette.

'The thing is, Valery, Carol Reddy explained to us that the group isn't opposed to *all* supermarkets, just this development, its being so close to the town centre and all.'

'That's absolutely right,' he said.

'Do you want a coffee, Valery?' called the girl from the kitchen. She didn't extend the offer to the policemen.

'No, I'm alright, Chloe,' he called back. 'Please, go on, Inspector.'

'We understand that if the favoured development doesn't go ahead, it's likely an alternative might be considered?' pursued Scrivens.

'I believe so,' he replied.

'And exactly who is it who owns that other parcel of land?' asked Kavanagh directly.

The girl came through from the kitchen carrying a small tray with coffee and a bowl of cereal on it. 'Are you sure you don't want any, Valery?' she asked.

'No, I'm alright,' he said. 'Chloe, could you just give us a few minutes?' he added, and she took her breakfast through to the bedroom and closed the door.

'I don't know,' he said. 'Why do you ask?'

'I believe I'm right in saying there was a feeling that you didn't quite fit in with some of the locals who are involved with the campaign?' said Scrivens.

'What do you mean?' asked Poole, shifting a little in his chair and lighting his cigarette.

'Some people couldn't quite see what your interest was. Your involvement seemed a bit more than might have been expected. Given your . . . position.'

'Really?' he said.

'Did you feel a need to establish your bona fides, perhaps?' probed Kavanagh.

'Why would I need to do that?' he asked.

'Why, indeed?' said Kavanagh, but the man remained silent. 'You know very well who owns the alternative parcel of land,' asserted the inspector.

Poole rolled the lighted end of his cigarette around the ashtray but didn't look up.

'Our financial people are pretty astute these days,' said Scrivens. 'They're not just button counters. It took them an hour and half a dozen clicks of the mouse to establish your connection with the offshore company that the land is registered with.

'It might have been beyond the do-gooders in the local crew to identify your financial interest, but our people are not thrown off the money trail quite so easily,' he added.

'Are you alright, Valery?' came the girl's voice from the bedroom. 'I'm just going to have a shower.'

'Yes, I'm fine,' he called back. 'Go ahead, we'll be a few minutes yet.'

'Betts?' said Scrivens.

'I don't know anything about the man,' he said.

'No?' said Kavanagh. 'But his garden?'

'What about it?'

'What size shoes do you wear, Mr Poole?' asked Scrivens.

'Sorry?' said the man.

'Your shoes? What size are they?'

'Eight. Eight-and-a-half. Why?'

'So how come there were size twelve wellington boot foot-marks all over Betts's garden?' said the local DI.

'I've no idea what you're talking about,' said the man.

'Look, Valery,' spelled out Kavanagh. 'We've got a man who's been brutally killed. You are a possible suspect, and if you were involved in the vandalism, I think it might serve you very well to admit to it before you are answering questions about a much more serious crime.'

'My family does own the land, it's true, and of course I should have declared an interest, but that's all.'

The girl could be heard singing in the shower from the adjoining bedroom. Whatever Valery Poole had been involved with, she clearly had other things on her mind.

'We'd like to show you something,' said Scrivens.

'Yes?'

He opened his laptop bag, took out a small DVD player and brought it over to the table where Poole was sitting. 'Would you like to have a look?' he said, and turned the screen towards the man.

'What's this?' he said as the screen filled. The shaky images were clearly from a pretty antiquated security system, but there was no doubt about the identity of the man standing at the counter in the agricultural merchants.

'It was our first port of call once we'd got the impressions from the footwear in the garden. We visited every agricultural and horticultural outlet in the area. We have the date and the time, as well as the till roll copy. You bought a pair of Hunter wellingtons, size twelve,' said Scrivens conclusively.

Poole added quietly, 'And then I wore three pairs of chunky socks inside them.'

Kavanagh barely contained a derisive snigger.

'Not very original ploy, I suppose,' added the man.

'No, not very,' agreed Scrivens.

'I had no idea the man was going to be killed so soon after. I had nothing to do with that. You do believe me?'

'Where are the wellingtons now?' asked Scrivens.

'At the bottom of the canal,' he said. 'I tied them together, put them in a bag and weighed it with stones and then dropped it in the canal.'

'And his killing?' asked Scrivens again.

'I swear, I know nothing at all about that,' he said. 'Nothing whatsoever.'

'You're sure?' said Kavanagh.

'I was mortified when I heard what had happened to him. Honestly.'

'So, why the gardening?' he asked.

'You were right about what you said,' he began. 'Some of the members of the group obviously didn't believe in me. If I was ever going to have any influence over future decisions about the siting of the supermarket, I needed to convince them of my real commitment to the cause.

'And I need the development to go to my site. I've no money, really. I'm living on credit cards and loans, one servicing another, but time's running out. And incidentally, as it happens, I believe in the plan too: it *is* the right place for it to be. It's called serendipity,' he said.

'So, in your need to impress, one of the ways was to attack Betts?' asked Scrivens.

'I didn't attack *him*. After his newspaper article, I went and messed up his plot and just quietly let one or two people –'

and here he nodded to the closed bedroom door, the shower running, the girl singing – 'know what I had done, and I knew it would get around and others would see my commitment.'

'And you're quite sure it didn't go any further?'

'Of course not. I didn't even know the man. But between ourselves, I've always liked his column.' He managed a fleeting smile.

'We'd better get down to the station,' said Scrivens. 'We can take a formal statement down there and then we'll have to see about the charges that should be brought.'

The girl came through from the bedroom, drying her hair with a towel. 'Are you alright, Valery?' she asked.

'Yes, I'm fine,' he said. 'I just have to go down the road for a while. I'm "helping the police with their enquiries",' he added. 'I shouldn't be too long, but you'd better let yourself out when you're done. OK?'

THIRTY-NINE

People tend to keep their appointments with police officers, at least they do if they're sensible; if they're in any way involved with a crime – feeling guilty, or just trying to save their skins – they cooperate in an attempt to deflect any notion of their wrongdoing. And if they're not involved, and their consciences are clear, they're invariably curious to know just what it is that the police want from them.

Bear in mind, too, that most people are only too happy to share knowledge of their neighbours', acquaintances' and even friends' misdemeanours with people in authority, for not only can they then claim that they are doing their civic duty, but few people like to see miscreants prosper, whether they are fiddling their housing benefit or are smash-and-grab robbers. It's human nature, after all.

It was odd therefore, that at ten twenty the following morning, Scrivens and Kavanagh were still sitting in the outer office at Gareth Thomas's warehouse awaiting the arrival of the owner of the business.

'Could you telephone Mr Thomas's home, please?' Scrivens asked the secretary. 'Tell him we are very busy just now and we can't wait for him here much longer.'

'Of course,' she said and called her boss as Scrivens stood beside her desk and listened.

'Hello, Jennifer. It's Sue down at the office . . .' She didn't complete the sentence. 'Oh, dear, I'm so sorry,' she said, shocked. 'I don't know what to say. It's just that the police are here waiting to speak to Gary. Yes, of course. I'll put him on now.' She handed the receiver to a bemused-looking DI Scrivens.

'Detective Inspector Scrivens here, Mrs Thomas,' said the policeman. 'What seems to be the problem?' There was a pause as he listened to the woman for a few moments. 'Are you sure? And when did this happen? I see. Mrs Thomas, don't do anything at all, and most importantly, don't touch anything in the house, we'll be with you directly,' he said and handed the telephone receiver back to the secretary.

'Gone missing?' said Kavanagh, as Scrivens drove through the little town, the blue lights in the radiator grille of his BMW flashing, the siren blaring in the unmarked police car.

'So her mother says,' replied Scrivens. 'She says she went to her daughter's room this morning to wake her up for an exam, and she'd gone. They've been phoning around her mates. They've spoken to her boyfriend, but no joy. They were just about to call us down at the warehouse when I got through to them.'

'How do you feel about coincidences, Michael?' asked Kavanagh innocently, looking across at his colleague.

'I don't like them,' said Scrivens. 'And I tell you something else, Frank, the next time you fancy a few days away, will you go to Brighton or Hastings, and leave us in peace up here in the sticks?'

FORTY

'We'd just like to ask you a few questions first,' said Scrivens, as the girl's parents stood with the policemen in the huge kitchen of their home, The Heights. 'This is a colleague from London, Detective Inspector Kavanagh.'

Jennifer Thomas extended her hand, and then Kavanagh shook hands very briefly with her husband, knowing it was he who had burned down his neighbour's house and very nearly killed the elderly occupant there.

'When's the last time you actually saw your daughter?' asked Scrivens.

'Last night, when I went up to her room,' her mother said.

'What time would that have been?' he asked.

'Early,' she replied. 'She's got her English literature mock A level exam today and so she was up there all evening, revising. I just called in to say goodnight. It was about ten o'clock, I think.'

'And you, Mr Thomas?'

'What?' he said.

'Did you go up and say goodnight to your daughter?'

'No,' he said.

'Is that . . . usual?'

'Sometimes I do, sometimes I don't,' he said unhelpfully.

'But not last night?'

'No.' There was an uncomfortable silence.

'Was there something you wanted to say?' asked Kavanagh.

'What are we doing standing around here? What are you actually doing about finding Lauren?' said her father abruptly.

'We'll be doing everything we can very shortly,' replied Scrivens. 'We'll be speaking to her friends and trying to find out if there's anything that might have led to her going away. But it's in the nature of this sort of incident that we have to start our enquiries close to home. Is there anything you are aware of that might have led to Lauren wanting to leave?'

'"Close to home". What's that supposed to mean?' railed Gareth Thomas.

'Statistics show that—' began Scrivens.

'Statistics!' her father sneered. 'If you're going to do anything, you'd be better off out there looking for her.'

'Gary,' said his wife. 'Be patient. I'm sure they know what they're doing.'

'Yes?' he said scathingly.

'The thing is, Mrs Thomas,' said Kavanagh, addressing the woman and ignoring her intemperate husband, 'youngsters these days, they often have a life other than the one their parents know about. You know, there's drink and drugs and boyfriends and all sorts of things happening that they keep to themselves—'

'Not Lauren,' interrupted Mrs Thomas.

'Well, perhaps not,' acquiesced the inspector. 'And then there's all the Internet stuff – Facebook and Bebo and all that. We'll have to check it all, because teenagers are sometimes getting up to things that their parents have no idea about, and frankly, they'd probably rather not know.'

'Lauren's not into drink and drugs,' said her father decisively. 'And she's got a steady boyfriend. She's got everything she could ever want right here.'

'Yes, of course she has,' said Scrivens, glancing around the kitchen with its range cooker, American refrigerator the size of a small car, granite worktops, Italian marble floor tiles and recessed lighting. 'But kids don't think like that. That's why they're kids, I guess,' he added.

'What do you know about her boyfriend?' asked Kavanagh.

'Daniel's the son of a doctor,' said the girl's mother. 'He's the first person I called this morning, but he says he doesn't know anything. He says the last time they spoke was on the phone last night. He's got an exam himself later today.'

'Is he the same age as your daughter?' asked Scrivens, jotting the details in his notepad.

'He's a year older than Lauren,' she said.

'And they've been going out long?' he asked.

'About six months,' she said. 'We don't see a lot of him. He comes in here, says hello and they go off up to her room.'

'Sure,' said Scrivens. He had a teenage daughter himself

and knew exactly what that meant. As a parent, what can you do? Kids would get it on wherever they were, and whenever they could. Their hormones were unstoppable. He would never forget having it off with his first girlfriend as they lay down in a field of snow somewhere. They were fourteen and it was bitterly cold, but their need to have one another was greater than anything else that night, and on lots of subsequent nights, too.

'I'm sorry to have to ask these things, but have there been any problems at home recently?' asked the local cop.

'No,' said Thomas flatly.

'None?' enquired the DI, more than a little sceptical about the man's claim. 'Teenagers, parents. I know myself, it can often get stressful. No problems at all?' he pursued.

'Nothing to speak of,' said her mother. 'Mostly, we get on very well. Lauren's a good girl, and she's very considerate. Like any teenager, she's a bit quiet sometimes, you know, but everything's alright, I think. Gary?'

'I've just said, everything's alright,' he said again, declining to elaborate.

'You're in business, I believe,' said Kavanagh, changing tack.

'Yes,' said Thomas.

'Any enemies?' asked the cop.

'Hundreds,' said the man.

'Really?' said the DI, surprised by the candour of his admission.

'If you do well, if you make some money, there's always people who resent you. I've got plenty of those kind of enemies. It's just jealousy.'

'Is there anyone who would think of trying to harm you, or those close to you?' asked Scrivens.

'Who knows?' he said. 'People get pissed off. It's business. Ask anyone, but no one who's going to do something like this.'

'Like what?' enquired Kavanagh.

'I don't know,' said Thomas. 'What you're suggesting.'

'I wasn't suggesting anything,' said the policeman.

'And you don't think she's gone off with someone she knows?' asked Scrivens. 'Maybe even someone she's met on the Internet, perhaps?'

'Don't be so stupid,' said her father. 'She's got her exams. She'd got one today. And she's been working hard, believe me. She's not just going to throw all that away.'

'I think we'd better have a look at her room now, see what she's taken with her. Perhaps it'll give us some idea of her intentions.' said Scrivens.

'Of course,' said Lauren's mother.

Mr Thomas stayed in the kitchen as she led them up to the girl's room at the front of the house.

As estate agents know very well, people's bedrooms really should remain private. Just seeing that telltale box of tissues on the bedside table speaks volumes, and the volumes spoken, whilst they might be fitting for the midnight hour, tend to look inappropriate at eleven in the morning or two in the afternoon.

The girl's diary was there, barely concealed in her underwear drawer, along with a couple of notes from her boyfriend and a packet of contraceptives. The girl's mother looked embarrassed, and felt as if she should apologize. The policemen said nothing, just took the little sheaf of letters and several personal emails that she'd taken the trouble to print off.

Kavanagh tucked the girl's laptop computer under his arm. 'I'm sorry, Mrs Thomas,' he said, 'We'll have to check it, obviously.'

'Of course,' said her mother.

'Does she have a passport?' said Scrivens.

'Yes,' said her mother, 'but she keeps it herself. I've no idea where it is.'

'And how about debit and credit cards?' he asked.

'She has an allowance and her own bank cards. Her father sees to all of that,' she said.

'Good,' said Scrivens. 'It'll help us trace her when she uses them.'

'What about her clothes, Mrs Thomas?' asked Kavanagh. 'Would you mind having a look through her wardrobe and drawers to see what she's taken? And the same with cases and bags if you don't mind. It'll give us an idea as to whether she was planning to be away for some time. We'll need a photograph, too, something recent that's a good likeness if possible.'

'Of course,' she said and started to riffle through the clothes hanging in the girl's wardrobe, pausing to touch the occasional dress, something which had particular meaning to her, or evoked a special recollection of her daughter.

'Here's her passport,' said Scrivens, as he checked the bedside cabinet. 'At least she isn't planning on leaving the country,' he added, trying to lift the gloomy atmosphere and the sense of foreboding.

'I can't see that she's taken much with her, if anything,' said her mother. 'Perhaps some underwear? It's difficult to say,' she added as she closed the wardrobe doors. She began to sob. 'It means someone's taken her, doesn't it?'

'We can't by any means be sure of that,' said Scrivens. 'Really, Mrs Thomas, it's very early yet, and Lauren being abducted is the least likely thing to have happened.'

Back downstairs, the woman's husband was standing at the kitchen window and looking out across the fields to the mauve hills of Wales in the distance.

'Mr Thomas,' said DI Scrivens, interrupting the man's rather untimely reverie, 'before we get going, we had an appointment to speak to you this morning. It was about a man who's been sleeping rough on your land.'

'Yes?' said Thomas.

'You've obviously heard about the murder in town? A writer called Julian Betts was killed.'

'Of course,' said Thomas.

'We need to speak to anyone who's been in the area, check out that they're not involved, or whether they've seen anything,' added Kavanagh.

'Yes?' said Thomas.

'Did you speak to the man who's been on your land? His name's Terry Morgan,' said Scrivens.

'I know of him,' said Thomas. 'But I didn't speak to him.'

'How's that?' asked Scrivens directly.

'How do you mean?' said the man.

'Well, my sergeant tells me a couple of your men were working on repairing the wall down there—'

'The kids are always smashing into it,' he interrupted. 'It's a full-time job. The insurance won't even cover it anymore.'

'I see,' said Scrivens. 'And?'

'And what?'

'Apparently your men told you about Morgan sleeping there?'

'They didn't know who it was, they just said someone was sleeping rough behind the wall. One of the lads saw his stuff there. Booze bottles and bin bags, that kind of thing. I thought it might be Morgan cos he's alcoholic and I'd heard he was back in town.'

'How come?' said the cop.

'He's local. People know him and that wherever he'd been, he'd come back.'

'So your blokes didn't move him on?' said Kavanagh. 'And you didn't either?'

'No.'

'Why not?'

There was a silence.

'Mr Thomas?'

'I used to know him a bit, a long time ago. When we were both young. Everyone knew him. Nobody knew anybody else round here that was playing professional football. He was the only one who made it.'

'I see,' said the cop. 'So, you were mates?'

'Not really,' he said, unsure as to whether the police knew about that more tangible, distant connection between the two men. How thorough were they in their 'enquiries', and what might they have found out so far?

'We worked together for a little bit when we were kids.'

'Yes?' said the detective. 'Worked at what?'

'Bit of this and that. We were both in the building game.'

'I see,' said the cop. 'But you didn't speak with your old workmate?'

'I went down there to find him, but he wasn't there.'

'No?'

'No.'

'And you didn't bother going back?'

'I didn't get round to it. He wasn't doing any harm, was he? At least not then. He's just a drunk . . .'

'Very decent of you,' said Kavanagh. 'A lot of people wouldn't be so understanding about other people's . . . what shall we say? Shortcomings.'

'Do you think he's had something to do with Lauren's disappearance?' asked Mrs Thomas.

'Well, obviously anything's possible,' said the policeman guardedly, 'but there's very little evidence of that sort of behaviour from men with a drink problem. I'm sure it's not unheard of, but it would be unusual.'

'We do need to know where he is, though,' said Scrivens. 'He's gone missing at the same time as your daughter, and we have to consider the possibility that there could be a connection.

'And there's also the possibility that he might have seen or heard something around the time of the murder of Julian Betts,' added Kavanagh, 'so we need to speak to him on that account, too.'

'Anyway, I think we're about done here,' said the local DI. 'We'll get things moving straight away. It would be best if you and your husband stayed here at home for the time being, just in case.'

'In case of what?' asked the girl's mother.

'Anything,' said Scrivens. 'She might phone, anything at all. But I think it would be best for you to be here. I'll have a liaison officer come over and stay with you, too.'

Kavanagh and Scrivens walked across the lawn in front of The Heights, down into the meadow, and eventually into the birch and sycamore scrub woodland that was Terry Morgan's former hideaway.

A PC had already been stationed there to keep the place off limits until it had been thoroughly examined by the forensics team. It was clear even from the most cursory glance from outside the crime-scene boundary tape that although Morgan might have relocated, he'd left plenty of evidence of his stay behind the wall – a couple of dozen empty wine bottles and as many strong cider ones lay in a heap there – but the man himself was gone, as was his sleeping bag and tarpaulin.

They left the police constable sheltering under a tree at the site as a light drizzle started to fall.

Back at the police station, the well-practised procedures for instigating a nationwide search for the missing young-ster, as well as a local one for the disappeared alcoholic, were immediately put into motion.

FORTY-ONE

The thing about Terry Morgan was that he was never going to be a hard man to find. Until very recently, his well-worn route had taken him from his tarpaulin cover and damp sleeping bag in the bit of woodland that he had made his home on Thomas's estate, up to any one of the cheap booze outlets on the high street a mile away.

And the fact was Terry had been arrested so many times on drunk and disorderly charges, as well as a good few for petty theft – mostly bottles of booze from late-night supermarket shelves – that he'd developed a natural antipathy to the police. Just as soon as they were in evidence that morning, driving up and down the road near his shelter, and even more pressingly, as soon as a few of them were detailed to mount line-abreast foot patrols along the adjacent footpath, Morgan had wasted no time in making off in the opposite direction – across country – to avoid any dealings with them.

He had no regrets; his new sleeping place was, if anything, rather better than the shelter that he'd made, hidden away in a bit of Gareth Thomas's woodland. The newly-refurbished cricket pavilion on a leafy road on the outskirts of the north side of the town had a dry balcony, and if the wind didn't get up in the east and blow the rain in, he reckoned he'd be both warm and dry bedded down on his cardboard 'mattress' there.

That evening, whilst he was sitting on one of the timber struts out of sight behind the big scoreboard, drinking from a bottle of wine and smoking a roll-up, a few teenagers turned up and loitered about the pavilion for an hour. They were unaware of him, but he'd heard them discussing the possibilities of breaking into the building: there was no CCTV, but the steel security shutters on the windows and over the door that they began to examine would prove a formidable obstacle. Eventually, they'd thought better of it and left, and Morgan had spent the night alone with his gloomy booze-sodden thoughts.

He had no money, no home, no family or particular friend. But he did have one thing that very few other people have: he had a secret, the mere utterance of which – a few injudicious words spoken – could spin back the clock and the years and destroy several lives.

As it happened, even in his befuddled state – assuming that he might have been able to frame the thought at all, a notion long since perished by drink – he had no intention of revealing the secret to anyone, and he would have said that he fully intended to take it with him to his grave. However, his co-conspirator from all those years ago had no idea that he had retained, in spite of everything that he had lost, this one vestige of probity, and Gareth Thomas was not in any way cognizant of the shreds of Terry Morgan's scruples.

For himself, Thomas's world was in grave danger of falling apart. Out of the blue, some Londoner who had nothing to do with anything in these parts had stumbled upon the old lunch bag of Joe Tate and the stupid find had now surfaced in the local paper.

How long would it be before the police would link that bag with Tate's disappearance all those years ago? And then, who knows what might happen? Wouldn't the police feel obliged to reopen the case?

Didn't they have all sorts of techniques these days to ascertain any number of things? *Crimewatch* was always blowing its smug trumpet about how some rapist from twenty years ago had been tracked down, and the police even caught murderers who were living new lives in foreign countries, using forensic science techniques that were unheard of only a few years previously.

Could they really detect 'hot spots'? Places where the earth had been disturbed and, possibly, a body buried, no matter how long ago? Or was that just TV? *CSI* something or other, a load of fiction, stuff and nonsense, that didn't really exist? Thomas certainly *did* know that DNA was used in solving all sorts of cold-case crimes. Could there have been something in that bag from several decades ago that would somehow, even now, link it to the missing foreman? He'd read about these things, how some kid on a charge for a little driving offence or assault gets himself put on the DNA database, and the next thing is, his dad or his uncle gets roped in for a murder that they thought they'd got away with from decades ago.

Yes, once the cops got involved, anything could happen. They'd start to question whether Tate really did go missing on account of his having drowned or some-such, or whether, in fact, he'd been the victim of foul play.

And what if they started to set about trying to trace the people who were working with him on that fateful day? They'd start with himself and Terry Morgan. Who else? Terry Morgan? Alcoholic Terry who didn't know what day it was and who would no doubt sell his mother for a bottle of cider. Was this drunk likely to keep his mouth shut?

Thomas was no Alan Sugar or Richard Branson, but he had been very successful in business, and one of the reasons for that success was that he had always been remarkably adept at turning the most unpropitious of circumstances to his own advantage.

He knew very well that his daughter had no more been abducted than he had. She was punishing him for his admission of behaviour of which she didn't approve. Fair enough. She'd been nicely brought up, as a day girl in the best private school in town. She had nice friends, a decent boyfriend and read books that he, Thomas, could not have begun to understand. Unfortunately, of course, this kind of thing had almost certainly given her ideas above her station, ideas that didn't allow her to countenance the sort of rough-and-ready behaviour that her father had embraced naturally more or less all of his life.

Yes, there was the remotest of chances that he was wrong, but what was the likelihood of that? When's the last time any youngster in these parts had been taken away against her will? Never. Never at all. No, Lauren Thomas had done a runner. The wilful child had got on her high horse once her father had foolishly intimated to her his little bit of coercion of the old neighbour and the destruction of the rundown farm buildings. She'd taken the moral high ground and decided to disappear simply to punish him for his wrongdoing.

But she would, he felt sure, be back just as soon as she started to miss her en-suite shower room and the comfort of sleeping in freshly-laundered sheets each night, to say nothing of her boyfriend, and even her mum and dad.

In the meantime, though, his daughter's contrary behaviour might just be made to serve his own purposes, for there are some people who can never act quickly enough when it comes to others' transgressions, especially when those transgressions appear to involve the suspected abduction of a teenage girl.

Yes, Gareth Thomas had a good deal on his mind.

FORTY-TWO

Morgan's detaining at the hands of the police wasn't very high drama.

As he listed along the high street on his way to the supermarket, before even Bargain Booze had opened its doors for business, a local constable on patrol with a community police officer stood in his path and said politely. 'Excuse me, sir, is your name Terry Morgan?'

'So what?' said Morgan. The policeman placed his hand lightly on the man's arm.

'We'd like you to pop down to the station, Terry. It's just routine. We've been looking to ask you a couple of questions, that's all.'

'Why?' he asked.

'It's about a missing girl, and perhaps some other matters,' offered the community policewoman.

'Missing girl? What you on about?' he said. 'I need to get a drink.'

'You'll have to do that later,' said the male cop, his hand just a little firmer on the man's arm, and the three of them moved discreetly into a vacant shop doorway as the constable called for a car to take them down to the police station.

This was about as sober as an alcoholic got, Kavanagh imagined. The man was running on alcohol and, as such, wasn't susceptible to the parameters and behaviours of any kind of social drinker, no matter how much they'd drunk. He was neither the eighteen-year-old binger on a Saturday night, whether the throwing-up on the street sort, or the one who wants to fight and shout and swear, nor the happy drunk who is your friend until he eventually simply falls asleep, exhausted by his own wearying bonhomie.

Morgan was beyond any of this, way beyond it. He simply needed to be kept topped up with spirits to function at all, and he hadn't yet, today, taken on board that morning's fuel.

He was contrary and palpably put out but, better this, the cops reckoned, than incomprehensible.

'Terry, we need to ask you a few questions,' began DI Michael Scrivens.

The man's head rocked down towards his chest, and when he managed to look up, it was through eyes that were barely open at all.

'Terry, you listen to me. We're recording this interview and I have to give you the following information . . .' The cop trotted out the mandatory PACE caution.

'Look, if you can help me with these questions, then there's no reason all being well,' he added as a vital caveat, 'why you can't soon be on your way. OK?'

'Can I get a drink?' said Morgan.

'You can have a cup of tea,' offered Scrivens.

'Can I get a drink?' the man said again, this time more aggressively.

'I can arrange some tea or coffee, but you can't have alcohol in here. It's against the rules. Later, maybe, when you're on your way?'

The inspector began again. 'A girl's gone missing. A youngster, do you hear me? I think a long time ago you knew the girl's father, Gareth Thomas. Her name's Lauren. We're concerned for her welfare, we don't know what's happened to her, and her parents are worried sick.'

'Why me?' he asked. 'What's it to me?'

'She lives in the big house outside town, and we know you've been sleeping in the grounds of the estate there. Yes?'

'Yes,' he agreed. 'I haven't seen any girl.'

'No?' said Kavanagh. 'Are you sure, Terry? You've got to think and you've got to help us. It's important for you, as well as for us. Do you understand what I'm saying? The place where you were getting your head down, the girl often walks up and down that way. To school, to meet her mates, that kind of thing. It's possible some people might think you could be involved with her disappearance?'

Morgan forced a little laugh at the suggestion. Kavanagh glanced at Scrivens. He went on: 'It might seem silly to you, Terry, but not everybody would understand that, that's why you've got to help us, to help yourself. You understand?'

'She went up and down that road,' said Kavanagh again, labouring the point in an attempt to get through to the man. 'On her way to school, on her way back, to meet her friends in town. Do you remember seeing her at all?'

He nodded his head from side to side. 'Can I get a drink of tea?'

'Sure,' said Scrivens, ''course you can.' He went to the door and asked the constable there to bring tea for the three of them.

'Did you ever see her?' he repeated. 'You must have . . .?'

'I did see a girl one day,' he began, not looking up. 'She was . . .'

'Yes? Go on,' urged Kavanagh. 'Go on, Terry, she was what?'

'Walking up the road, in and out she was going. Maybe she'd had a drink?'

'Yes?' encouraged Scrivens.

'A car stopped by her.'

'Really?' said Kavanagh. 'Go on.'

'Yes, he stopped and he . . . I dunno, then he drove off, and someone else picked her up.'

'When was this?' asked Kavanagh.

The man smiled. The smile said, You *are* joking.

'Fair enough,' said the inspector. 'The car, Terry, if we showed you some pictures, would you recognize it, do you think?'

'No,' he said.

'What colour was it?' asked Scrivens.

He moved his shoulders in the approximation of a shrug.

'Please,' said Scrivens, 'try and think, Terry. It's important. Was it blue? Silver? Red? Black?'

The man nodded his head, and murmured, 'Dunno.'

'We could narrow it down,' said Scrivens brightly. 'Was it a big car, a four by four, maybe? Or a pickup? An estate car, perhaps?'

'I'm telling you,' he said wearily but firmly, 'I don't know.'

The constable brought in a tray of tea.

'What about the car that came and picked her up, then?' asked Scrivens.

'I don't know. I'm not playing I-spy am I? They're just

cars. I don't know what they are.' He cupped his hand around
the polystyrene cup of tea.

'Where are you sleeping now?' asked Kavanagh.

'You going to move me?' he asked mockingly, looking up.

'No, there's no need. But I'm thinking ahead, for you.
When you get out of here, keep a low profile. Keep out of
the way. People get ideas into their heads, Terry, you know?
You could even stay here. It might be best for you?'

'Drink,' he said, by way of an answer to the invitation.

'So, where are you sleeping, Terry?' asked the inspector
again.

'At the cricket pitch,' he said. 'Can I go now?'

'Not long. Just one more thing,' said Scrivens.

'What?' said the man.

'Someone was killed the other night on the posh housing
estate. I know it's not exactly near to where you were sleeping,'
said the DI, 'but you being out there, in the open, I wondered,
you didn't see or hear anything unusual, I suppose?'

Apparently unmoved by the idea of a killing, Morgan simply
looked up again and asked with a shrug of the shoulders, 'What's
unusual?'

'Anything, Terry. The man was killed in cold blood, up at
his house on Meadow Rise.'

Morgan nodded his head. He put his cup down on the table
with a shaking hand. 'Can I go now?' he said once more.

Kavanagh looked at Scrivens as much as to say, why not?

'Yes, you can go,' said Scrivens, 'but first, I'm going to
show you a few pictures of cars before you get on your way.
OK? Just see if you recognize either of the ones that stopped
for Lauren Thomas that day. It might jog your memory, and
it'll only take twenty minutes to flip through them.'

'I don't know cars any more,' he said, and then, with a nod
to a distant, barely remembered past, added, 'I used to have a
Capri. A Ford Capri. And after that, a Jag. That was when I
was a player. Leather seats, in racing green,' he mumbled, 'went
like a rocket. I had a girl, too. My little Katie . . .'

Whether it was his increasingly pressing need for a drink,
or a genuine desire to help the police in their search for the
missing teenager, by the time that Morgan walked out of the
police station an hour later, the cops believed themselves to

be looking for what he had told them was a dark red Vauxhall, possibly an Astra. It also seemed very likely that her father's distinctive black Range Rover was the vehicle that had picked her up that day. And at least that was something which could be easily verified.

'So, what do you reckon?' said Scrivens to Kavanagh as an image of a Vauxhall Astra flickered on the screen in front of them.

'It could be complete bollocks,' said Kavanagh, 'or he just might have identified a would-be abductor's car.'

'Do you believe what he's told us, then?' asked Scrivens.

'Why would he make a story up about seeing her almost get into a car? There's no reason for him to say that, is there?'

'Unless he's involved?' suggested Scrivens reasonably.

'We both know there's no chance of that,' said Kavanagh. 'It's just not his style.'

'I agree,' said Scrivens. 'But he's addled with booze and so there's probably no logic in anything that he's saying,' he posited.

'Exactly,' said Kavanagh. 'The poor bloke's a soak and that's why I don't think he's got the wherewithal to make a story like that up. But I reckon he *has* still got the remains of what was once a memory, enough at least, when pushed a bit, to recall that car.'

'You could be right,' agreed Scrivens. 'Or he could just have seen it as being the quickest way out of here and back to a bottle.'

'Maybe,' agreed Kavanagh. 'But worst case scenario, if we assume that he's telling us the truth and that the car's local, there aren't going to be that many red Vauxhall Astras knocking about.'

'Sure,' said Scrivens. 'Let's get onto DVLA and get the addresses and we can start hunting them down. Give the lads something to do, anyway. There's not much else on right now,' he said.

'Incidentally, any joy on that Scouser electrician who'd worked on Betts's house before he nipped off to Portugal?' asked Kavanagh.

'Yes, we've traced him, and there's a British Embassy

consul or attaché or something on his way out to see him with a detailed list of questions from us.'

'Right, I'll join the boys and start checking out the cars,' said the London inspector.

When, late that same afternoon, a junior reporter on the *Gazette* made her daily telephone call to the police station, they gave her – as, in the interests of good media relations they were more or less obliged to do – the bare minimum of a statement about the questioning and subsequent release of Terry Morgan. 'In connection with continuing enquiries into the disappearance of school girl, Lauren Thomas, a man who has recently returned to the area and who has former connections with the town, was earlier today assisting police with their enquiries. He has since been released without charge.'

In a town of this size, they might as well have printed Morgan's name and an accompanying photograph of him.

FORTY-THREE

'Frank?'

'Scriv?' replied Kavanagh. 'What you got?

'Where are you?' asked the detective inspector.

'I'm with Nick, we're on our way to check out an Astra in some unpronounceable Welsh place.' He passed the cell phone to constable Nicky Holden who was at the wheel of the police car.

'Llanrhaeadr ym Mochnant,' said Holden as the men drove along the B4396 towards the Welsh beauty spot, and then handed back the phone to Kavanagh.

'We've found the girl,' said the local DI, unable to disguise a certain professional pleasure in being able to make the announcement to his more experienced colleague.

'Is she OK?' said Kavanagh immediately.

'She's fine,' said DI Scrivens. 'She's not here yet, and apparently she's not saying a lot, but she's fine.'

'Where was she found?' asked Kavanagh as he revolved his finger and gestured to the PC to turn the car round and head back to town.

'Cumbria. Bit of a story,' said Scrivens. 'Her mother's on her way up there now to pick her up.'

'What was she doing there?' asked Kavanagh.

'She says she got the train to Chester, and from there took one to Penrith.'

'Yes?' said Kavanagh.

'Seems so,' said Scrivens. 'She's probably just being a bit ballsy, but she told the local sergeant she liked the name. A PC spotted her wandering about in the town. He thought she looked a bit suspicious, and at first he didn't connect her with our missing girl alert. He followed her in to Top Shop where she tried nicking a few bits of underwear. She'd nothing with her except a shoulder bag, apparently. So they took her into the manager's office to have a word. Her story was all over the place and that's when they rumbled who she was.'

'So where had she spent the night?' asked Kavanagh.

'Travelodge. Paid for with the last bit of cash she'd got, so it didn't come through to us on tracking the use of her cards.'

'And now?' he asked.

'She's in the custody suite at the station having a bite to eat and waiting for her mum. She's pretty sulky, but the main thing is that she's OK.'

'You bet,' said DI Kavanagh. 'We're on our way back, Scriv. Be with you shortly.'

'So, what's the story?' asked Kavanagh as he and Scrivens sat in the DI's office right next to the incident room on the first floor.

'Like I said, she's staying tight-lipped, but her boyfriend, Daniel – the doctor's son – had already called and told us that she'd texted him about where she was. He was worried about her up there on her own and so he called us. We'd got her text message, anyway, on the intercept we'd set up, but the boy wasn't to know that, and before we could put things in motion, the local PC nabbed her trying to nick the clothes.'

'And does the lad know why she'd gone?'

'He won't say much. He's afraid of what her reaction's going to be if she finds out he's been in touch with us. All he'll say is that she and her old man had a big fall out about something. But he won't say what.'

'Do we think her old man really knew that was the reason she'd gone?' asked Kavanagh. 'It must have been something pretty serious if he knew, and yet he was prepared to let us think – as well as his missus, presumably – that the girl might have been abducted?'

'Absolutely,' agreed Scrivens.

'I reckon we need to speak to the boyfriend before she gets down here, see if we can get him to open up a bit,' said the London DI.

'He's on his way over now,' said Scrivens. 'And the girl and her mother should be down here within a couple of hours.'

The incident room was a scene of industrious quiet activity as other desks and officers dealt with the methodical, ongoing enquiries into Julian Betts's murder, with witness statements, sightings, timings and background information all being painstakingly collated on HOLMES.

'Any good with the Scouse electrician yet?' asked Kavanagh as the two senior officers checked on progress there.

'Yes and no,' said Scrivens. 'The attaché's spoken to him over in Portugal and faxed his answers back to us. He's no robber, and he's got a cast-iron alibi for the night Betts was murdered.'

'Go on?' said Kavanagh.

'He was with his girlfriend and loads of their mates having a night out before they went off to live in the sun. She'd got a job as a holiday rep at a caravan park, and he planned on getting work as an electrician for the expats living over there.'

'And?' asked Kavanagh.

'He's landed on his feet: the caravan park owner's given him three months' work as a sparks and odd-job bloke on the same site as his woman.'

'And there's folk who'll vouch for him?' asked the London DI. 'For the night of the killing?'

'At least a dozen of them were partying that night. Apparently he's a nice lad. He even offered the bloke from the consulate a bit of a deal on a log cabin if he fancied a holiday there later in the year.'

'What you got, son?' asked Scrivens as a young PC strode into the room and approached him and Kavanagh with an air that exceeded by some margin his lowly rank.

'I've got the Vauxhall Astra we're looking for, guv,' the young man said, unable to conceal a smile.

'Blimey,' said Scrivens. 'That didn't take long. Go on?'

'It belongs to a bloke called Broadbent.'

'Yes?' said Scrivens.

'Simon Broadbent,' repeated the PC.

'And what was Mr Broadbent doing trying to entice young girls into his car then?' he asked.

'I've no idea, sir,' said the youth. 'All I've done is brought him in for questioning. He's downstairs in custody.'

'And you're sure it's his car that was seen with the girl?'

'Yes. He's admitted it. It was just another one I was following through on from my list. I gave him the routine questions: where were you on such and such? Have you had any occasion to be

on that road out of town in recent times? Did you see this girl
at all? And I showed him the photo. He stood there at his front
door and the sweat was dripping off him. Whatever he's been
up to, he's terrified, that's for sure.'

'Well, good work, son. We've actually located the girl in
the last couple of hours,' said Scrivens, 'and she'll be on her
way down here shortly, but let's see what your man Mr
Broadbent's been up to with her.'

'Where's the car?' asked Kavanagh as they headed for the
door.

'It's still on the road, outside his house.'

'Where's that?' asked Scrivens.

'It's a rented place. A two-up, two-down in Belvedere
Street.'

'Get yourself a cuppa,' said Scrivens, 'you've done well.'

The young man turned and left the room looking very
pleased with himself.

'Hey up, lads,' announced Scrivens to the crowded room.
'On the missing girl, it looks like we've got the Vauxhall, too.
I'll keep you up to speed as soon as we know more. We're
going to speak to the owner now before speaking to Lauren
Thomas herself. Keep going on Betts. I'll be back up here
later.'

'Right, Frank,' he said, 'let's see what Simon Broadbent's
got to say for himself.' The DI headed down the stairs at a
smart pace, Kavanagh limping behind and holding the stair
rail with one hand as he followed him.

FORTY-FOUR

The young PC was right. The man *was* terrified. Scrivens had dealt with a few hard-faced criminals in his time, and it was unusual for Kavanagh to try and interview anyone these days who didn't go the No Comment route for hours, sometimes days, before he was able to tease open a crack or manage to induce some answers with a sweetener of some sort.

But Simon Broadbent wasn't one of these. Apart from anything else, the man looked unwell. His cheeks were hollow and his eyes were set deep in dark sockets that suggested he hadn't slept well for a very long time.

'So, Mr Broadbent, what exactly were you doing with Lauren Thomas?' asked Scrivens directly, very aware of the lack of time available to them.

'I don't know,' he said.

'What do you mean, you "don't know"? You were seen trying to get her into your car,' said Scrivens. 'You agree you stopped and approached her?'

'Yes,' he murmured.

'So, why would you do that?'

'I was lost . . .?' he offered, phrasing it as a question, so ludicrous did he know his answer to be.

'Simon, look, you live a mile away from where we know you stopped for the girl. That's not going to wash, is it? If you've got some problems, you'd better open up, tell the truth, and we'll do our best to help you.'

'Problems?' he repeated.

'You know, with young girls,' said Kavanagh.

'Of course not,' he said.

'You've no criminal record?' said Scrivens.

'No,' he said.

'Have you ever changed your name or been arrested for any offence?' the DI asked.

'No, never,' said Broadbent.

'Are you sure? Lying to us will go badly for you,' added Kavanagh.

'I've never been in trouble with the police,' he said. 'Ever.'

'So, what were you doing with Lauren Thomas if you weren't trying to get her into the car with you?'

'I . . .' he began and faltered.

'Yes, go on,' encouraged Kavanagh. 'You . . .?'

'I was going to try and get my revenge on her father.'

'Why? What's her father got to do with you?' asked Kavanagh.

'He's ruined me,' said the man, 'that's what.'

'What do you mean, he's "ruined you"?' asked Scrivens, running out of patience.

'He's taken me for everything I've got. I lost my house and everything I owned trying to fight him. I was going to get even by taking his daughter. It was mad, I know that. And anyway, what was I going to do with her?' he said hopelessly.

'What *were* you going to do with her?' asked Scrivens, registering his deep concern.

'Nothing. I wasn't going to do anything like that.'

'Like what?' said Kavanagh.

'Anything. My own son is only twelve. I'd never hurt any child.'

'So, what is it that Gareth Thomas did to you?' asked Scrivens.

'I built my business up over the last twenty years, built it up from nothing. Graphics and printing. You know the industrial estate on the Welshpool Road outside Morda?' he said.

'Yes,' said Scrivens. 'Of course.' He glanced at Kavanagh who had known the place briefly only days previously as the scene of Salt's near rape.

'I leased all of that land, as well as the old Ministry of Defence buildings there. I had my offices and workshop and studio there, and I got change of use for the other buildings on the site so they were all let out to small operations like my own.

'I was doing really well from my own work, and also the rents on the other units. We'd moved to a bigger house and I'd got eight people working for me. I invested in new,

state-of-the-art German printing presses and took out some
hefty loans, but they were being serviced alright because the
business was doing well and everything was going OK.'

'And?' said Kavanagh.

'Thomas got involved in buying the adjacent land for a
new car dealership that he was negotiating for. It's not far
from the site of the proposed supermarket development, and
he must have thought that with thousands of customers
coming through there every day, it would be a window on
his car lot, and he'd have loads of potential buyers.

'In the course of his lawyers drawing up the purchase
deeds, they found that the access lane to my site was in his
gift: due to some ancient anomaly, the right of way to my
units was now over his land.

'I wasn't worried. I thought it was just a technicality, something we'd be able to smooth out between us. Why would
he want to make things difficult for me? I'd never even met
him, never had any dealings with him whatsoever. My legal
people tried to negotiate with him. I offered everything that
I could afford, but it was soon clear he didn't want that: he
wanted to put me out of business.

'Overnight, it became impossible. He put a gate across
the lane and no one could get on or off my premises. My
tenants had to get special permission to even leave and get
their stuff out. From a good business one month, I was facing
bankruptcy the next. I couldn't even sell the lease on the
site. Anyone else would have been in the same position as
I was.

'In the end, he got the whole set up for next to nothing. He
took over the property and the buildings and immediately put
in new tenants.'

'And yourself?' asked Scrivens. 'What happened?'

'I had to sell the house to pay the legal bills and settle
my loans for machinery I could no longer use. It was all too
much for my wife. She couldn't stand the strain of living
with me and she eventually left and took our boy with her.

'Now, I'm on antidepressants and living in a rented terraced
house in town. And do you know what I do for a living?'
he asked rhetorically. 'I deliver leaflets for local businesses:
flyers for the Indian restaurant and the roller blind company,

places like that. Good, eh?' he said bitterly. 'The very things
I would once have been making a good living at printing.'

'And what about the girl?' ventured Kavanagh. 'What were
you thinking you were doing with her? You say you'd never
met him. How did you even know he had a girl?'

'Everyone knows of Gareth Thomas round here. They
know his big house on the road out of town, and when his
daughter was younger she was always in the paper winning
cups and things for horse riding.

'I just drove up there a couple of times past their house
. . . what I did . . . what I was going to do, it was insane,
and it was unforgivable, but he'd pushed me to the edge
and I wanted to make him suffer for what he'd done to
me.'

'But you didn't go ahead with it? Why didn't you actually take her?' asked Scrivens.

'I've told you. I didn't even know what I was going to do
with her, but before I could . . .'

'Yes?' said Kavanagh.

'Before I had the opportunity to get her into the car,
Thomas came down the hill in that Range Rover of his, and
I drove away. It was the best thing that could have happened
to me. Really, I swear it. I haven't been near her since. I
know I'd no right to involve anyone else in what he did to
me, and certainly not his daughter.'

There was silence, with just the hum of the recorder and
the red light glowing.

'Is there anything else you want to tell us?' asked Scrivens.
'Anything at all?'

'No,' he said. 'Except, I am wondering how you even know
that I'd stopped for her that day? I made sure there was no
one around. Did she report me?'

'No, she didn't report you,' said Scrivens. 'Someone
witnessed you stopping near her, and when she went missing
that witness was interviewed and gave us a description of
your car.

'We've actually traced the girl now, and she's alright.
When we speak to her later, we'll check your account of
events, and if it all adds up, we'll see how we proceed with
you. For the time being, you'll have to wait back down in

the cells. I'll get the sergeant to get you a cup of tea or something. OK?'

'Thanks,' he said. 'I'm sorry for what I've done. Really, I am.'

'And so Gareth Thomas owns the little industrial estate?' said Kavanagh as soon as Broadbent had been escorted from the room.

'So?' said Scrivens.

'And he rents a unit to ex-con, Williams, the flower seller?'

'Well, that's no crime,' said Scrivens.

'No, it's no crime,' agreed Kavanagh. 'But since when was Thomas all heart?'

'You're such a hard man, Frank,' said Scrivens.

'Rehabilitation of offenders?' said Kavanagh.

'Yes, I bet,' replied the local DI.

'Anyway, let's leave Williams on the back-burner for a while,' said Kavanagh. 'And I know we've got a murder enquiry underway, but I think we need to have a chat with Lauren Thomas's boyfriend before she gets back to town.'

'Why?' asked Scrivens. 'What's the hurry? The girl's safe and well now.'

'If we don't do it now, and she gets to her boyfriend, he'll probably clam up and it'll be too late.'

'But what are we hoping to find?' asked Scrivens. 'What's he got to tell us that's so important?'

'Look, Michael, I wouldn't say this if she were here, but Salt's a good cop, and if she reckons that Gareth Thomas was responsible for the arson that nearly killed that old guy, I'll back her that she's probably right.'

'So?' said Scrivens.

'Thomas is a dodgy geezer. He's a local bully who's got lucky.'

'So far,' agreed Scrivens.

'We've evidence of malice and coercion, plenty of hearsay and a ton of innuendo, but nothing that'll stand up. Daniel's only a lad, and if we lean on him a bit we just might get him to open up about whatever it was that his girlfriend really had a row with her father about.'

'And what do you think it was?'

'I don't know. But if she's prepared to leave home on the

day she's got an exam, and put her mother through all that deception, it's not going to be nothing, that's for sure.'

'OK,' agreed Scrivens. 'I'm not sure it's worth the candle, but an hour's not going to make a lot of difference. Let's talk to the boy pronto.'

FORTY-FIVE

'So, are you going to tell us what this is all about, Daniel?' asked Scrivens of the pale, long-haired boy. His T-shirt said 'Slipknot' and, although his pallor didn't suggest an outdoor type, Scrivens wondered whether he might be in the Boy Scouts or some-such outdoor group.

'I can't tell you anything else,' he said. 'It's up to Lauren what she tells you, not me. I've already said too much.'

'And what if Lauren won't tell us? What if she has her own reasons?'

'I'm not going to say anything else,' he said. He held a guitar plectrum in his right hand and ran it over the knuckles of his left. 'You can't make me.'

'No, we can't,' agreed Kavanagh. 'But we've had every police force in the country out looking for your girlfriend, Daniel. It's cost thousands of pounds. And, OK, she's been found safely, partly thanks to you – although we had a trace on the text message she sent to you anyway – but we need to find out what happened between her and her father that led to her running away.'

'That's up to you,' he said. 'I'm not telling you anything else. I only contacted you because she was on her own and I was afraid she might be in danger.'

'You did well, and you were right to,' said Scrivens.

'Lauren missed her mock A level English exam?' said Kavanagh. 'And after all that work she'd done,' he added.

'Yes,' said the boy a little wistfully.

'You sat one of yours the same day?'

'Biology,' he said.

'When's your next one, Danny?'

'The day after tomorrow.'

'What is it?'

'Maths.'

'And you've done a lot of work for it?'

'Of course.'

'You're going to study medicine, I believe?'

'Yes.'

'It's in the family?'

'My dad's a GP. I'm sure you know that. My mum's a practice nurse. I want to do paediatrics.'

'Your mum's downstairs; she's here for you now. She's off work from the surgery, and you should be at home revising. Why don't we get this sorted, and then you can both get on properly with your work again?'

The boy said nothing.

'Your university place must depend upon your grades?'

''Course,' he agreed.

'In a few years' time,' continued Kavanagh, 'if you're not working in medicine, this might all look a bit silly, especially if you don't take up your place at . . . where are you supposed to be going?'

'Durham,' he said, 'depending on my grades.'

'Think about it, Danny. You're an intelligent lad. Anyone can see that. Put it all in the thinking pot, eh, and just give us some idea about what it was that happened between Lauren and her father.'

The boy moved his head from side to side, and continued to flick the plectrum repeatedly over the back of his fingers.

Kavanagh had a sense that he might be weakening in his resolve. He tried another tack. 'You play?' he asked.

'A bit,' said the boy.

'In a band?' said the cop.

'Sort of,' he said.

'Who do you like?' asked the DI.

The boy smiled indulgently at the man who was more than three times his age. 'I don't think you'll know them,' he said more politely than he needed to.

'Sure,' agreed Kavanagh. 'I don't suppose I would. So, what do you think? It's your call. You might not make it in a rock and roll band, but you could be a good doctor, you know?'

The boy sighed deeply and nodded his head again, but he was clearly thinking about his choices. 'If I tell you what I know, is there any way we can keep Lauren from knowing that it was me who told you?' he asked.

'I can't guarantee it, but we can do our best. And to be

honest, once the story's out, I think the emphasis will be elsewhere,' he said vaguely.

'She'll kill me,' said the boy. 'And I'll lose her, that's for sure.'

'I doubt it,' said Kavanagh, 'just so long as she understands that what you've done is for the best, and all that you did was to try and keep her safe.'

'She and her father had a bad row,' he began. Neither Kavanagh nor Scrivens initially realized that he'd actually begun to impart the information. He didn't change the tone of his voice or look up at either of the policemen, as if he wouldn't be able to maintain the effort of will involved if he broke the spell of the moment in any way.

'She told me it just sprang out of nothing. Something about some noise in the grounds while a bloke was unloading statues or something for around their house and she was upstairs trying to revise. She came downstairs and that's when she had this row with her dad. It got very heated and then . . .'

'Yes?' urged Kavanagh. 'Go on. What?'

'He virtually told her, not in so many words, that he'd been involved in something . . .'

'Yes?' said Scrivens.

'I hate doing this. I feel like I'm betraying her, and I know I'm going to regret it,' he said. 'I just know I am.'

'Go on, Daniel,' said Kavanagh. 'It really is for the best.'

'There was a fire at a property across the road from them. A lot of people thought it was her dad who was responsible. He has got a bit of a reputation, but he's always been alright with me.'

'Yes?' said Kavanagh.

'He virtually told her that it was him who'd been responsible for it.'

'Yes?' said Scrivens. 'And why did he tell her this?'

'I dunno. Making some point about having to do stuff to get whatever it is you want in life, I think she said,' said the boy.

'I see,' said Kavanagh.

The boy shifted his position on the grey plastic seat. 'She phoned me that night and said she was leaving. Said she was going to teach him a lesson. I'm sure she wanted me to say

I'd come with her, but I couldn't, even though I didn't want her to go on her own. I've done so much work for my A levels, and I've got my place at Durham and everything. I just couldn't throw all that away . . . but I still felt shit . . .'

'Right,' said Scrivens, 'go on.'

'When she did go, I was worried sick for her. I think she was frightened and she was lonely, too. That's all I know. When she texted me, that's when I phoned you lot. And that's it, really.'

'Thanks, Danny,' said Scrivens. 'We'll speak to her, of course, when she gets down here, and we'll keep you out of it if we possibly can.'

'That isn't going to happen though, is it?' he said. 'I know I've just lost her.'

'I hope not,' said Kavanagh. 'You don't deserve to, son.'

'Yes, I bet I don't,' he said. 'But who gets what they deserve?'

'Hi, Frank.' His phone rang as he was walking back to Scrivens' office after having escorted Daniel and his mother back downstairs to the exit of the station.

'Jane. How's things? Where are you?'

'I'm still at Mum and Dad's.'

'And how's your mum?'

'She's not too bad. She came out of hospital this morning and they've got a carer coming in twice a day. Dad says he'll be OK with that and they can manage.'

'So, you're coming back up?'

'I've got a mid-morning train tomorrow.'

'Great. I'll meet you. What time?'

'Gets in at 10.45.'

'I'll be there and I'll bring you up to speed. Take care.'

'See you at quarter to. 'Bye.'

'Bye.' Kavanagh smiled, quietly relieved and reassured that Jane was coming back to him.

FORTY-SIX

Terry Morgan might have been well advised to have accepted the cops' earlier suggestion that he remain within the safety of the confines of the police station for a day or two, at least until rumours in the town of his involvement in a teenage girl's abduction had died down.

But taking advice from the police wasn't in his reckoning, and he hadn't.

Kavanagh and Scrivens stood side by side and recoiled at the sight before them. The man was barely recognizable as the person with whom they had spoken only days before. What was left of his smashed and bloodied head was swollen to very nearly twice its former size, his clothes were covered in caked, dried blood, and even the cricket pavilion balcony timbers were stained ochre.

'Jesus,' said Kavanagh with deep feeling.

Scrivens breathed hard through his nose and looked away once more. Morgan had suffered a savage beating of the sort that very occasionally happens in dank city underpasses to hapless tramps and winos. But here, in a Shropshire market town? The place wasn't crime free, but the terrible injuries that had been inflicted on the emaciated alcoholic were not the kind of thing any Shropshire police officer might have been expected to see during an entire career.

'OK,' Scrivens eventually said to the pathologist who stood a few feet away, 'when you've done here, and the photographer's finished, let's get him into the coroner's van and down to the mortuary.'

A helicopter, hired by a TV news channel, an excitable reporter doubtless sitting in the passenger seat and filing his or her live report, throbbed in over the cricket field from the east. 'And get the screen up around here, quick,' he said to the waiting forensics people.

*   *   *

Morgan, talented footballer in his distant youth, and shambling
drunk for the thirty-odd years following that golden period,
had died a most awful death. Vigilantes, presumably, had
decided that, rather than await the soft punishment that would,
doubtless, be meted out to the man – assuming he wouldn't
be in a position to hire some slimy lawyer who might just get
him off completely – they'd short-circuit the entire system and
deal with matters themselves in a more visceral and summary
fashion.

For who would argue that, with a would-be abductor gone,
and teenage girls safe from the attentions of at least one broken-
down paedophile, the world would not be a better place?

Only a few hours before news of the girl being found safe
and well, and her imminent return to her parents' home had
been made public, therefore, the hysteria that accompanies
such outrages had, apparently, exploded in this bout of terrible
violence.

'Who knew he was here?' asked Kavanagh as the pathologist began her work and the protective screen was manoeuvred
into place and erected around the balcony of the pavilion.

'Who knows?' said Scrivens. 'He won't exactly have kept
his whereabouts secret. We told him to be discreet, but I
don't suppose he was. Anyone could have known, and round
here, word travels.'

Even though both men knew that the greater the horror,
the more terrible and depraved the crime, the less likely it
was that it would involve more than one person, it appeared
that several people must have been responsible for this attack.
The fact that Brady had found a woman in Hindley who was
prepared to take part in his killings, and that avuncular Fred
West had found a wife who, even if she had not taken part
in his brutal crimes was, nevertheless, prepared to stand beside
him whilst he did those things, had made those barbarities
almost unique: the most heinous crimes were invariably
perpetrated by lone individuals.

'Andrea,' said Scrivens, turning to the pathologist, 'what
I need to know is whether there was more than one person
involved in this. Is it how it looks?'

'Give me a few hours and I should have some initial
answers for you,' said the doctor.

'Thanks. OK, Frank. There's nothing more we can do here, let's get back to the station,' he said.

'Sure,' said Kavanagh. 'Shall I get on with tracking down any next of kin?'

'Please,' said Scrivens. 'Let's get on with it and find the bastards who did this to the poor bugger.'

FORTY-SEVEN

'Good morning,' said the DI to the builder in his check shirt and jeans. 'I'm Detective Inspector Kavanagh, up from London. Your local inspector, DI Scrivens, is away dealing with another part of the enquiry.'

It was almost true. Kavanagh was out here at an old people's home in the countryside. Scrivens was in the incident room back at the station dealing with the mountain of data that every single hour of every day brought forth. The information from dozens of sources was being collated in an exhaustive attempt to recreate the choreography of events on the nights of both Julian Betts's murder, and now that of the horrific killing of Terry Morgan, too.

And what would, until recently, have been simply piles of paper, but were now memory sticks and hard drives which hadn't, unfortunately, led to any diminution of actual material; in reality more like the contrary.

But although Scrivens abhorred as much as the next officer what was still called 'paperwork', he was, in fact, more than content to spend a few hours on it whilst his out-of-town colleagues went about pursuing their fanciful notions, no matter how improbable were the lines of enquiry that Kavanagh and Jane Salt seemed still determined to pursue.

'Yes?' said Rob, Philip Penley's son. 'What's this other "line of enquiry", then?' and the two men shook hands.

'I'd be happy to tell you, but it's more than my job's worth,' said Kavanagh. 'Sorry. And this is DC Jane Salt,' he said, as the builder took her hand in his.

'So, how's your father keeping?' asked the detective inspector. The question masked his real agenda. What he would have wished to say was: your father's in his late eighties now, how's his memory? Has he, in other words, succumbed to dementia or some other mind-degenerating malaise?

'Dad's OK,' said Penley. 'He's got terrible arthritis, and he's had his replacement hip replaced only a couple of days' ago, like I told you on the phone. His chest's buggered through smoking too many of these –' Penley ground his boot down on his cigarette butt on the drive outside the care home – 'but I tell you, he's still got all his marbles. He might not remember what he had for breakfast, or what he watched on TV last night, but you ask him who won the league in 1985 and he'd still make the quiz team!'

'That's great,' said Kavanagh. 'Let's hope he can remember a bit about the houses he built up on the estate at the top of the town way back when.'

'Sure,' said his son. 'Ask him anything you like, but just don't mention the Beatles, that's all,' said Penley as he rang the doorbell for the warden.

'The Beatles?' queried Salt. 'Why not? What's the matter with them?'

'He's been a fan for over forty years and he knows every song word perfect. Get him going and he'll start singing "Penny Lane" or "Get Back" and you'll never shut him up! The staff have threatened to have him moved out!'

'Could be worse,' said Kavanagh.

'Not much. You haven't heard his voice,' said his son quietly, 'believe me.'

'Mr Penley,' said Kavanagh, the three men and Jane Salt now sitting in the conservatory at the old people's home. 'It's good of you to see us.'

'Pleasure,' he said. 'There's bugger all happens here. Breakfast. Sleep. Lunch. Sleep. Tea. Sleep. *Coronation Street*. Sleep. Bedtime . . .'

'Sleep?' offered Kavanagh.

'No,' said the man, indignant. 'Can't sleep then. I lie awake half the night just waiting for the dawn. Why can't I sleep at night like I sleep at two o'clock in the afternoon?'

'Dad, like I told you last night, Inspector Kavanagh, and this lady, Ms Salt, they're from the police.'

'Last night?' he said. 'You didn't say anything to me about the police.'

'Well, I did, Dad, when I came to see you, but it's slipped your mind, maybe?'

'I know you didn't,' he said, testily. 'I'd remember if you had.'

'Fair enough, Dad. Anyway, they're here now and they want to ask you about something from years ago. I said you might be able to help.'

'Yes?' he said, and with some difficulty eased himself forward in his wheelchair.

'Thanks, Mr Penley,' said Kavanagh. 'We appreciate it. It is a long time ago, but I believe you built the houses on the estate at the top of town. The one called Meadow Rise?'

'Yes, we did,' he said. 'Why?'

'Well, just recently, a man moved into one of those houses, one on Low Brook Road, and he was having some work done in the roof, and the men found an old sandwich bag tucked away deep in the eaves.'

'Yes?' said Penley. 'Why? What was it doing there?'

'Exactly,' said Salt. 'We've no idea. We were hoping you might be able to give us a clue. Why would someone leave a thing like that hidden up there?'

'No idea,' said the man, again adjusting himself in his chair and wincing. 'Frigging arthritis,' he said. 'Excuse me French, love. Bone on bone. It's bloody terrible. And now this hip, too.'

'I'm sure,' said Salt. 'Is there anything at all we can do?' she offered.

'Can you operate?' he said, and the policewoman smiled at the elderly man's enduring capacity for grim humour.

'Do you remember putting them up, Dad?' his son asked.

'Those houses? 'Course I do. They're built on the hill and we had to have a bulldozer in for weeks to level a lot of ground before we could even start, and even so, all the gardens slope away. I thought we'd never sell the buggers, but it's a nice spot up there, and they went alright. At the end of the day, people didn't mind terracing the gardens and all.'

'But you don't know nothing about that bag, then, Dad?' his son pursued.

'No,' said the man flatly. 'Everybody brought their lunch bags in them days. I suppose they still do?'

'Yes, mostly,' agreed his son. 'And a van comes round to some of the sites with sandwiches for the lads who are too lazy in the morning to make their own.'

'There was one thing happened up there,' said Philip Penley, ignoring his son, but recollecting events. 'You know about it?'

'What's that, then?' asked Kavanagh.

'One of my foremen went missing one day, and nobody ever saw him again. It was the strangest thing that ever happened in all the years I was working.'

'Yes?' said the inspector, intrigued. 'Tell me what happened, Mr Penley.'

'His name was Joe Tate, and I can see him in my mind's eye as if he was standing there now. Big bloke, fit and tanned, out in all weathers and a good worker. He was a real loss to me. Bit of a lad, he was, liked a drink and had a reputation with the women.

'One Saturday, after doing the morning on overtime, he went missing, and we never saw him again.'

'Really?' said Salt. 'He was never found?'

'Never,' said Penley. 'He must have gone for a drink or something and got into a bit of bother somehow, but whatever happened to him, nobody ever saw him again.' Using his hands on the arms, he adjusted himself once more in the wheelchair. 'Some lads said he must have got some girl into trouble and didn't fancy sticking around for the nipper, and so he just buggered off. America or Canada, some said. But whatever it was, it must've been serious cos he didn't even come back for his wages. I kept 'em in an envelope in the safe for him for years. But he never came back for 'em.'

'And what do *you* think happened to him?' asked Kavanagh.

'No idea. I know he was a good bloke when he was at work, and I had to get someone else to run that job to the finish. But I never saw him again,' he repeated thoughtfully, almost to himself.

'Was there anyone working with him that day?' asked Salt.

'Just two lads. It was overtime. A couple of youngsters labouring for him.'

'You don't remember who, I suppose?' asked Kavanagh.

''Course I do,' he said. 'Gareth Thomas is the biggest builder in these parts now.' Kavanagh and Salt exchanged glances. 'Still is, isn't he, Rob?' continued his father.

'He certainly is,' said his son.

'And what about the other man?' asked Salt.

'Oh, he went to the bad, poor lad,' said the old man. 'Played professional football up north for a while, and then he got on the booze and that was him gone. I never heard what happened to him again.'

'And what was his name?' asked Kavanagh, needlessly.

'Terry. Terry Morgan,' said Penley. 'Made quite a name for himself for a bit, but football, it's even worse than the building trade,' he added emphatically.

'And when was this?' asked Kavanagh. 'Do you have any idea of the actual date, and I can check out what's known about it?'

'It was June 1969,' he asserted without hesitation.

'June 1969?' repeated Kavanagh, a little sceptical. 'That's very precise. How are you so sure, Mr Penley?'

The old builder began to utter a wheezing, tuneless, '"Christ, you know it ain't easy . . ."'

'The Beatles, eh,' said Salt, and nodding towards the man's son in acknowledgement of his previous warning.

'It's not The Beatles,' said Penley firmly. 'It's John Lennon. It was top of the hit parade for three weeks,' he added. '"Standing on the dock at Southampton",' he began again.

'It's a good song, Dad, but how about you sing it later, in the bath, maybe?' said his son.

'Good bloke, Lennon,' said Penley. 'Not sure about that bird he was with. That Japanese woman. And then some friggin' nutcase comes and shoots him.'

'Yes,' said Kavanagh thoughtfully. 'I'm afraid they did.'

'So what's this bag all about, then?' Penley asked.

'It was found in the house, at number 33. It didn't seem important, but then the man who was living there was killed, and the bag's disappeared. It's just a bit of a coincidence, so I reckon we need to find it.'

'Well, I haven't got it,' he jested, and winced again at his arthritic pain. 'I'm gonna have to lie down,' he said. 'I'm about ready for a kip. Didn't sleep two hours together last night,' he added.

'Thanks for your time, Mr Penley,' said Salt. 'It's been good to meet you.'

'Pleasure,' he said, and started to hum once more the

'Ballad of John and Yoko' as his son helped him slowly along the corridor to his room.

Outside, in the well-tended gardens, the two police officers stood together with the man's son. 'I can't thank you enough, Rob,' said Kavanagh.

'No problem,' said the builder. 'I'd best get back, though. We've got a big job on for the council. New leisure centre and we're running a couple of weeks behind on account of the bad weather after Christmas. There's big penalties if we don't hand over on time.'

'Sure,' said Kavanagh.

'Where do you go from here?' asked the builder.

'Well, that bag's critical. If we had it, given what your dad's just said, we might be able to establish whether it had ever belonged to the bloke who went missing. And if it did, it raises a whole lot of questions about whether he went to America, or anywhere else for that matter. At least of his own accord. And there's also a question as to whether it can have had anything to do with Julian Betts's death.'

'But without it?' said Penley.

'Without it, we're stuck,' said the policeman. 'And heaven only knows where it is now.'

'Who'd be a copper, eh?' said the man. 'I'll see you around,' he said and climbed up into his battered Toyota HiLux pickup truck.

'Thanks a lot,' said Salt. 'You've been a great help.'

FORTY-EIGHT

'So, how'd do you get on with the Thomas girl?' Kavanagh asked Scrivens back in the incident room. 'Clammed up completely,' said the local DI. 'I tried everything. Told her in the end that we knew about the arson. "I don't know what you're talking about", she says, cool as anything. Whatever she does know, she's had a change of heart.'

'Blood? Water?' said Kavanagh.

'I guess so, push comes to shove and she's sticking by her old man, no matter what she knows he's done. There was nothing more I could do. I threatened her with bringing a charge of wasting police time, but she wasn't bothered. I've had to let her go with a warning.'

'So, what exactly have we got?' said Kavanagh, and immediately began a summary himself. 'Julian Betts is dead, killed during the course of what's made to look like a bungled burglary. And that old bag, assuming it was still in his house, is gone.'

'OK, fair enough, I grant you, it could be playing a part given what the old builder's told you,' said Scrivens only a little reluctantly.

Kavanagh didn't crow, merely continued his resume. 'We know that Terry Morgan was one of the two lads working with the foreman who went missing all those years ago,' he continued.

'Which leaves only . . .' said the local DI.

'Exactly,' said Kavanagh. 'Gary Thomas. And we know that he's such a decent sort that he muscles Simon Broadbent out of his business and off the industrial estate so that he can install his own tenants there.'

'One of whom,' said Scrivens, picking up the refrain, 'is ex-con and all round nice guy, Ben Williams the flower seller . . . Thomas has been around long enough to know that it's a fair chance that it won't be a month of Sundays before Ben

Williams is up to his old dope-dealing ways, and once he's got something on him, he can recruit him to do any dirty work that comes up. As it happens, it's a bit of arson on a recalcitrant neighbour who's proving reluctant to move house.'

'He has a row with his daughter,' said Kavanagh, 'during which somehow she finds out what he did, and she does a runner to punish him. But this is a man so calculating that, because he's got Terry Morgan in his sights, and who's a real threat to him, he doesn't let on what he suspects has really happened to her in case she shops him. Instead, he's happy to let us think she's been abducted . . .'

'And his missus, too,' added Scrivens. 'And whether he's planned it or not, when word starts getting around the town that his daughter's missing – presumed abducted – and that alcoholic Terry Morgan's been interviewed by us in connection with her disappearance, he's well chuffed. Two and two, and the poor alcoholic's days are numbered.'

'All he has to do is make it look like some bunch of rednecks came and attacked him,' agreed Kavanagh. 'And with Terry Morgan dead, Gareth Thomas is the only living witness to what happened all those years ago.'

'But how do we go about proving any of it?' said Scrivens. 'And, just as importantly, what happened to the foreman's body? Where is it?'

'Where, indeed?' said Kavanagh.

'Anyway, how did you get on with tracing Morgan's next of kin?' Scrivens asked.

'I've got a bit, but I don't know how much use it'll be. Morgan was married. His wife's a Scotswoman called Abigail Ross and they had a child together. Morgan said something about his little girl when we had him in the station the other day when he was rambling a bit.

'But he and his missus hadn't seen one another since the 1970s. They were married for a year or so, but after his injury he got on the booze and he never managed to get off it. She gave him a couple of chances but he couldn't break the habit, and he never saw her again, nor his daughter.'

'I see,' said Scrivens. 'So, are they going to take care of the arrangements, when Morgan's body's eventually released?'

'It won't be the wife, I'm afraid. She's got the illness that nobody wants, and she's not got very long to live. She's in a hospice up there. I've spoken to the daughter and she's going to look after the funeral arrangements for her dad, even though she did not know him.'

'Perhaps they'll be buried together?' added Scrivens. '"United in death." Isn't that what the headstones say?'

'I think it is,' agreed Kavanagh, and each man paused for a moment's reflection about a dying woman that neither of them even knew and her estranged husband's terrible end.

Kavanagh eventually broke the silence.

'Have we got anything back from the pathologist yet?'

'No. Not yet, but she's promised to come through to me just as soon as she's got the preliminaries,' said Scrivens. 'Shall we get out of here for a bit and nip downstairs for a coffee?' he suggested. 'You look like you could use one.'

'Sure,' said Kavanagh, and the two men headed for the temporary catering truck that was parked out in the station yard.

As they stood under the awning with their drinks, Scrivens asked, 'How are things shaping up in the city? What's happening with your drive-by shooting of the Somali lad?'

'I was on to Skinner an hour ago. He's a good bloke, but the whole thing's falling apart around him,' said Kavanagh. 'The witness has got cold feet. Somehow the bad guys got through to her and threatened her younger brothers if she goes anywhere near a witness box.'

'Terrific,' said Scrivens.

'Yes. New identity, new flat in the Midlands and a bit of a facial as well as money in the bank, but he doesn't think she'll go near it now.'

'Can you blame her?' asked Scrivens.

''Course not,' said Kavanagh. 'With her kid brothers under threat? And she'd have to leave her family, her friends. They might not be the Waltons, but they're all she's got, same as any of us. I don't blame her at all. What it does mean, though, is that an innocent kid's been killed and it looks like no one's going to be going down for it. His killer's no doubt a top bloke on some poxy estate, too. It sucks, but it's just how it is.'

'Right,' said Scrivens. 'Bad crack,' he commented as he chucked half his cup of instant coffee on the tarmac. 'So, where do we go from here? I'm thinking before we call on Gareth Thomas we ought to visit the flower-man, put a bit of a squeeze on him and see what pops out, eh?'

'Sure,' said Kavanagh.

'Are you OK with that, Frank? Or would you rather I took someone else along?'

'I'm good. Let's just keep Jane out of it,' said Kavanagh.

FORTY-NINE

'Hello, Ben,' said Scrivens.

'Do I know you?' said the flower seller, barely looking up as he continued to trim the ends on a bunch of carnations at his table-mounted guillotine.

'Not yet,' said Scrivens.

Williams put the flowers down and took a few steps towards the DI. He sniffed at his chest. 'Do I smell copper,' he said.

'Nothing wrong with your nose, then,' said the detective.

'Nothing wrong with any of me,' retorted Williams as he returned to his workbench. He severed a couple of inches from the blue-green stems of another bunch of flowers. 'So, you want some?' he mocked as he dropped the flowers into the cardboard box at his feet.

'I don't think so. Not today,' said the policeman.

'What *do* you want?' asked Williams. 'I'm busy.'

'We've come for a word,' said Kavanagh. The London DI kept his distance, remained leaning against the open warehouse doors. Even with a strapped ankle, he'd have been prepared to hobble over and smash his fist into the man's face as he thought about how close the florist had come to sexually violating Jane Salt.

'Didn't I see you before?' said Williams, sneering at the policeman standing in the bright sunlight. 'You came by –' Kavanagh clenched his fist behind his back and felt his knuckles tighten – 'looking for that "friend" of yours. Nice looking woman,' he leered dangerously. 'Yes?' The man carried the box of flowers and stacked it with several others on a pallet. 'So, what do you want?' he said again. 'I'm busy. Got to get these delivered.'

'How long you been renting this, then?' gestured Scrivens to the shed.

'Few months.'

'Who do you rent from?'

'What's it to you?' he asked.

'I'll do the questions, you do the answers,' said Scrivens.

This time there was no smart retort. 'Gary Thomas. Everybody here does.'

'The man owns a lot,' said Kavanagh.

'Yes?' said Williams, looking at the London cop as he weighed him up anew. 'Lucky, eh?'

'Did he know your background when he took you on?' asked Scrivens.

'"Background"?' said Williams, mock affronted. 'What's that, then?'

'Did he know you'd been inside?' asked Kavanagh.

'You know the rules, mate,' said Williams, lifting another armful of the blooms from one of the boxes beside him. 'You got to tell any employer, any landlord or business associate if you've done time when you're on probation.'

'And Thomas was OK with that? About leasing to you?' asked Kavanagh. 'He didn't mind a con renting his warehouse?'

Williams smirked at the insult. 'Gave me a chance,' he said. 'Someone's got to. Otherwise it's a revolving door, mate: in and out of nick. Know what I mean? No good to anyone, that, costs society a fortune,' he said, smiling as he enjoyed his own smug performance.

'You certainly got the answers,' said Kavanagh, taking a couple of steps further into the warehouse.

'Frank,' said Scrivens, separating the men.

'I reckon I do,' taunted the flower seller.

'Gareth Thomas got rid of the former landlord, a man called Simon Broadbent, and then he leased this unit to you,' said Kavanagh. 'Why was that, then?'

'Don't know anything about any former landlord. But he rents to me. I just said so, didn't I?'

'And what were you able to offer in exchange?' asked the inspector, closing in a little further.

'No idea what you mean, mate. Dunno what it's like where you're from, but up here, we don't do bartering any more, it's money we exchange for services. It's what we do. Works alright, too.'

'Yes?' said Kavanagh.

Scrivens intercepted. 'You know, when old Billy Hughes's place burned down, your landlord was out of town? He had

a solid alibi. Very solid. He could have almost arranged things
that way.'

'Who's Billy Hughes then?' asked Williams, sidestepping
the implication.

Scrivens ignored the facetious enquiry. 'How about yourself, Williams? Where were you that night?'

'What night was that, then?' he responded deftly.

'Quite,' said the copper, not prepared even to rehearse
another bit of pointless theatre with the man.

'I tell you what, Ben,' continued the DI. 'You might think
you're sitting pretty. For Frank, here, this has all got a bit
too personal, and that's why he's standing there and I'm
standing here, but we all know how close you got to—'

'What?' challenged the man.

'Don't push it, Ben. You know exactly what I'm saying here.
You also know the sexual harassment thing won't stand up.
We all do. But I can have you back inside in an hour. See this
. . .' He slipped on a glove and took from his inside pocket a
decent-sized bag of skunk and chucked it on the man's work-
table. 'You know what it is, right? Let's say I got a tip-off
about a flower importer with his warehouse down on this industrial estate. He's got lots of tulips coming over from those jolly
Dutchmen; customs can't check 'em all, and low and behold,
what's all this then? You get the picture, I'm sure?'

Williams said nothing. He knew how plausible it was and
how easily it could be made to stick. The idea that fit-ups were
somehow a thing of the past was a joke. He knew that, too.

'What do you want?' he said again, this time with a very
different tone.

'What was it that Gary Thomas had on you? I'm right in
saying you torched the old man's house? Yes? He must have
had something to push with?'

Silence.

'What was it he had on you?' repeated Kavanagh.

The man knew which side up his buttered toast was falling.
What he didn't know was just how long he had before it hit
the carpet. 'You keep me out of nick if I tell you what I
know?' he said. 'And it's off the record, too?'

'Let's hear what you've got to say,' said Scrivens, 'and
then we'll see about that.'

Williams weighed his options for fully half a minute.

'All I'll say is,' he began, 'if somebody had something on somebody, that person could make them do things they didn't want to do. You know what I'm saying?'

'Go on,' said Scrivens.

'When he rented me this, I thought maybe he was just a decent bloke. But Thomas isn't stupid, and he knew that there was no way I could be selling enough daffodils to make this thing pay. He wasn't bothered what I was doing down here, said it was up to me if I wanted to make a few quid on the side, but he might occasionally need a little favour.'

'And that was . . .?' began Kavanagh.

The man said nothing, just shifted his weight from foot to foot.

'The old man living there could have died,' urged Scrivens.

'Maybe there wasn't supposed to be anybody there? Maybe that's what Thomas said,' replied Williams.

'Yes? Well, maybe he did, but here's the thing, Ben,' continued Scrivens, 'your landlord, Gareth Thomas, he's taken on a bit more than he can handle recently, and some of it's major league and goes way, way back. And believe me, I'm talking about even more than setting fire to people's houses.

'Your man's about to take a fall. And it's gonna be a big one, and when that happens – and it won't be long now, I assure you – he'll have plenty on his plate and he won't be at all bothered who he takes with him. Do you hear what I'm saying?'

Williams's silence was acquiescent.

'You have a think about it, eh? You could do yourself a big favour by coming clean and making a full statement.'

The man pulled at the leaves from the flower stem in his calloused fingers.

'This is all going to end up in court, so there's no way we can keep it off the record. It's too big for that, and the whole thing's gone far too far for me to say you won't go back inside, but business is business, and pragmatic's the word. You know what that means?'

'I know what pragmatic means,' said Williams.

'But if the man in the funny wig and black gown knows you've done the right thing, he's gonna take the view that things could have been a lot worse for you. Have a good think about it,' repeated Scrivens, 'and when you're ready, we'll have you down the station with your brief.'

Williams stood there amongst his pink and yellow scentless carnations as the men turned and left.

FIFTY

'So, what exactly happened to Joe Tate?' asked Scrivens in front of the people crowded into the little room down at the police station.

Gareth Thomas, dressed in fawn combat trousers and a blue sweatshirt with the company's logo, Thomas Holdings, stitched onto it, turned to his solicitor.

The young man, wearing a suit that very nearly fitted him, and an inappropriately colourful tie, nodded his head very slightly. His client looked back at the detective and said again, 'No comment.'

'Joe Tate?' repeated Scrivens as he faced the man and his solicitor across the table, Jane Salt sitting next to him.

'The bloke who went missing?' offered Thomas.

The solicitor coughed quietly, suggesting that the 'no comment' route was the one that his client had been advised to follow.

Kavanagh shifted from foot to foot as he stood near the door and repeated with a deal of weary sarcasm, '"The bloke who went missing".'

'How should I know?' said Thomas.

'You'd know,' said Kavanagh in a measured voice, 'because you and poor, recently-deceased, Terry Morgan were the last people to see him alive that day. He never got home. But he certainly never went to America. Nor anywhere else. Did he?'

'No comment,' said Thomas.

'Tate didn't even have a passport. He'd never applied for one in his life,' added Scrivens.

'We think it's much more likely he came to harm, Gareth. In fact, we're sure of it,' said Salt.

Thomas looked at the woman. Perhaps it was her use of his name, but he appeared to feel obliged to respond to her more gently probing manner.

'I never saw him,' said Thomas. 'We left the building site

that lunchtime and I never saw him again. I told the police all of this years ago.'

'I'm sure you did,' said Kavanagh. 'But I think things were a little bit different back then.' He pushed himself up from the wall where he was leaning and came towards the table. 'I tell you what, Gary, let's play a bit of "what if", eh?'

'I don't know what you mean,' said Thomas.

'You try. Just come along with me. Cast your mind back to that Saturday morning, and I'm thinking that won't be all that difficult. What if there was some sort of falling-out? An argument, say, between you guys . . .?'

'There never was,' said the man.

'Hey, Gary, the game's "what if". Just roll with it for a bit or we'll never get anywhere.'

The man glanced once more to his solicitor who gave a resigned shrug of his shoulders.

Kavanagh continued, 'What if you three, or just two of you, maybe, had some sort of falling-out? About football? About a woman? Could have been anything at all. You know what blokes are like, some of them could have an argument with themselves. Maybe it was something that started as a joke and got out of hand?'

'I never had an argument with him,' said Thomas.

'You're doing it again,' said Kavanagh. 'Try this, then. Maybe it wasn't an argument. Maybe there was an accident? Perhaps he fell off something, or one of you two – you and Terry – maybe you gave him a shove or messed about with a ladder he was on? Played with the scaffolding? I don't know? There's no intention to hurt him, and he just falls?'

The man was silent. The red light of the recording machine glowed.

'Am I getting warm here?' asked Kavanagh.

'No,' said Thomas, 'you're not. I've no idea what you're talking about.'

'OK, let's just say it was an accident of some sort. No malice, no intent, but it's not every day you go to do a bit of Saturday morning overtime and you kill your foreman.

'So, what next? You're only kids, both of you, and Terry wasn't the brightest button in the box by all accounts, just a good footballer. A quiet lad, a kid with the world at his feet. Sorry. No pun. So, you're young lads and you panic, right? But what did you do with him then?'

'I didn't do anything with him,' said Thomas.

'Stick with me, Gary. I think you put his body somewhere – I'm not sure where – and when the local uniformed bobbies turned up a couple of days later, they had a little look around and, knowing Joe's reputation for being a bit of a lad, they soon decided he'd gone away somewhere, and that was the end of it. It's not quite Columbo; more Inspector Closeau, eh? But, fair dos, like I say, things really were different back then. What do you reckon? How am I doing now?'

'No comment,' said the man, without any prompting from his brief this time.

'Trouble is, all these years later, that writer, that gay guy, Julian Betts, he has some blokes fixing the loft, and they find the old lunch bag that you hid there. The story starts to get out a bit and you panic. I don't blame you, Gareth, I would have done, too. Anybody would. If we get hold of that bag, like I say, things have moved on, and we'll have tested it for DNA and connect it to the foreman and we'll be knocking at your mansion door, pronto.'

'No comment.'

Kavanagh ignored the man's refrain and continued. 'You realize you've got to get that bag back. So you pop along to Betts's house in the middle of the night. I don't know if you know this, but the writer had been a bit more insulting in one of his newspaper articles than was perhaps wise, given people's feelings, and a day or two before you paid him a visit, some nutcase with his own agenda had messed up his garden for him.

'Two and two. Naturally enough, we went that route for a while, thinking his death must be something to do with the Keep it Local brigade taking revenge. But that didn't detain us long. Yes, a bloke named Valery Poole, the vice chair of their set-up, was the midnight gardener but, like I say, that's a whole other story.

'Let's get back to you and the mouldy old lunch bag. I don't suppose for a minute you had any intention of killing Julian Betts. Why would you? What I *do* think is that he must have disturbed you after you'd broken in. He's just a harmless old man, isn't he – how old was he, Jane?' asked Kavanagh.

'Sixty-five?' she said.

'And not very fit,' continued the inspector. 'He's only ever eaten in decent restaurants and tapped the keys on his word-processor. Whereas you, you've always looked after yourself, I'd say, and you're a big bloke, just look at you. No contest.

'So, he disturbs you and you've no choice, you've got to keep him quiet. You restrain him or whatever, and the next thing, the man's dead. Yes?'

''Course not,' said Thomas. 'I've never been there. I've never seen the man.'

'Is that so?' said Scrivens, picking up the baton and continuing. 'We know there's a phone call came in from you to Betts's number one lunchtime not long before he was killed. How's that, then?'

The man opened both his hands, suggesting his innocent compliance and acceptance. 'The company calls lots of people. Maybe he'd got something on order with us. I can't be expected to know why we phoned him.'

'You've always been a quick thinker,' said Scrivens. 'I'll give you that.'

'This is all just conjecture,' said the solicitor, 'and whilst my client may choose to listen to you, I think I have to advise him not to comment any further.'

'We won't be long now,' said Scrivens. 'Mr Thomas has not been detained or charged with any offence. He's here voluntarily, simply helping us with our enquiries. I've just a couple more things for him to mull over, and we'll be done.'

The young solicitor looked to Thomas, who indicated his preparedness to remain.

'OK,' said Kavanagh briskly, continuing the refrain. 'And now things start to get worse and worse. This is real can-of-worms stuff: poor old Terry Morgan turns up in town on his drunken travels; down-and-out Terry, and he could be a real loose cannon. In his state, you know he could say or do anything about your murky past together. Bad timing. Terry's going to have to go the same way as the old food writer, eh?'

'I don't know what you're talking about,' said Thomas. 'This is all bollocks.'

'Yes? Anyway, on we go. You need a bit of good luck, and you get a bit. You have a row with your daughter and you lose your temper and you virtually confess to her that it was you who was responsible for the arson attack on your neighbour's house. She's well pissed off with you and does a runner to teach you a bit of a lesson.

'When we interview Terry about whether he knows owt about owt, he's in the frame for her disappearance. After that, if he gets a terrible beating – and you see to it that he most assuredly does – you know very well that we're likely to think it's the local rednecks who've done it, of which there is a goodly crew in these God-forsaken parts.

'However. Always the "however", eh? The forensics people reckon that, notwithstanding Terry Morgan's injuries, this was no mob of anti-paedophile vigilantes on a killing rampage. They're quite sure that only one person was on the cricket pavilion balcony wielding a baseball bat that night. Yes, of course, there's a ton of blood, the poor man's head's smashed to pieces, and what's left of his brains are all over the place. But on the surface of that mess of life, in all of that blood and bits of bone and tissue, there's actually only one set of footprints. And they're going to be from a pair of your boots, Gareth, I'll bet my rotten life on it,' said Kavanagh with feeling.

'I don't know what you're talking about,' Thomas offered weakly.

'You'll not have those boots sitting in the lobby of your house, that's for sure,' said Scrivens. 'They'll be tucked away safely somewhere, or have gone up in smoke more likely. But the thing is, Gareth, with forensics these days, it's a bit of an unequal struggle for people like you.'

'Meaning what?' said the man.

'Meaning you haven't got a chance,' said Kavanagh. 'With their microscopes and hi-tech bits and pieces – you ought to see that stuff; it's really quite unbelievable – I reckon we ought to show the public exactly what it is we've got and what it can do. The murder rate would drop by half in a week. You haven't got a chance against all that technology; really, you haven't. There'll be a speck of blood on your

shirt or something somewhere, and they'll find it. Or we'll
find the boots—'

'Inspector,' said the solicitor. 'You know as well as I do
that this is all hearsay and wild speculation. You're talking
about footprints and blood spatterings at a scene of crime,
but you don't have any footwear or anything else to connect
any of those things to my client.'

'No, we don't,' said Kavanagh. 'Not yet.'

'In which case,' said the young man, 'I think he has been
here long enough and we should be leaving.'

'Before you do,' said Scrivens, 'you should know that
we've had a word with your tenant, Ben Williams.'

'Yes?' said Thomas. 'So what?'

'Yes, we had a chat and he's told us that you were happy
to rent premises to him even with his record, but that once
you'd got a bit of leverage on him, you then asked him for
a favour.'

'A favour?' said Thomas.

'A favour that involved setting fire to an old man's house,'
added Jane Salt.

'Williams had got the oldest dope scam in the books going
down,' continued Scrivens. 'But it wouldn't have fooled a
rookie cop for a minute. Stuff coming up from the airport
with boxes of flowers, and the driver then leaving the doors
open on the truck for some third party to have it away so
there's no connection to Williams. Come *on*. The judges
aren't very bright,' added Kavanagh, 'but even they've heard
of that one, and once they'd rumbled him, Ben Williams
would have been going down quicker than Monica Lewinsky
on Bill Clinton.'

The young solicitor raised an eyebrow; he'd heard the
name but he wasn't entirely sure who Monica Lewinsky was,
but the analogy was one he was sure was smart and he most
assuredly knew it was filthy.

'He certainly didn't fool you, Gary,' he continued. 'You
soon found out what he was up to down there and you let
him know that he owed you one if you were going to keep
shtum.'

Thomas looked very uncomfortable and turned to his solicitor for help.

'I really think that will do for today,' said his brief, and got to his feet. Thomas looked steadily at Salt, then Scrivens, and finally Kavanagh and said, 'I haven't done anything,' and then added, by way of asserting the possibility of negotiating some future position, 'but arson's not murder.'

Kavanagh looked back at him. 'You're right, Mr Thomas, it's not,' he said. 'You're absolutely right.'

FIFTY-ONE

'Can we have a word?' asked DI Scrivens.

'What now?' said Gareth Thomas as he stood in the central aisle of the aircraft-hangar-sized warehouse down on the industrial estate, hemmed in by Kavanagh on one side and the local DI on his other.

'Guess?' said Kavanagh.

One of Thomas's employees skirted down the gangway on a fork-lift truck, driving it with the élan that made the task look more like adult play than any kind of work.

'Shall we move into the office?' suggested Scrivens.

Thomas led the way along banks of towering shelving and up a flight of iron stairs into an eyrie from which the man could observe operations in his vast warehouse.

'Maggie,' he said to the clerical worker there, 'can you give us a few minutes?'

'Of course,' she said. She put her computer on standby, gathered up her handbag and half-drunk cup of coffee, and left.

'Joe Tate?' repeated Scrivens.

'Jesus,' said the man. 'What the fuck now? I told you yesterday, my brief told you, I've nothing more to say. If you've got anything on me, charge me.'

'Well, we'll see about that, eh?' said Kavanagh.

'So, what do you want?' said Thomas. 'I've got a business to run.'

'We've got a little surprise for you,' said Scrivens.

'Surprise?' queried the man.

'I don't know whether you know this, Gareth, but when Terry was still playing professional football, he picked himself up a nice-looking young wife up in the north-west. Did you know that?'

''Course not,' offered Thomas, wary of any kind of trap being set for him. 'How would I?'

'Anyway, as far as we know, it was alright for a year or

so, but then, when he got injured and started drinking heavily, it all went bad and she moved back to her home in Scotland. Terry's career's over and he's hooked on booze. Abbie – that's his missus – she has a little girl, but the kid never knew her dad, he was just a man in a wedding photograph that was always sitting on her mother's bedside cabinet.

'But the little kid's mum did know what had happened on the building site that day. Terry had told her the truth not long after they got married.

'Yes, maybe he would have become a drunk anyway, with his football going down the pan and all. But, according to his wife, he had an even bigger problem: he had this terrible secret and a deeply-troubled conscience that he could never let go. So, he tried to share the burden with her and he told her what had happened. Not in detail, but he did tell her that it was you who had killed your workmate.'

'I didn't kill him,' said Thomas.

'He said it wasn't him,' continued Kavanagh, ignoring the man. 'OK, maybe he was just trying to save his own skin, or his feelings or whatever, but he said that it was *you* who did it. He claimed you didn't mean to, and that you both swore you'd never say anything to anyone.

'But he needed to tell her, and he made her swear she'd never say anything either. And for the best part of forty years, Gareth, she never did.'

'You believe this, a drunk ex-footballer's wife, but you don't believe me?' he protested.

'Abbie Morgan's dying, and she's well past the lying stage. There's no point anymore. She has absolutely nothing to gain, and nothing to lose. She has an inoperable tumour and she's in a hospice up there in Glasgow being cared for by her only daughter. But when she was eventually told about the death of her long-absent husband, she told that daughter the truth about her father and why he had probably never come back to them and, just possibly, why he'd gone to drink. Nearing her own death, she felt that she owed it to her to tell her the truth about her dad.

'Katie – that's the daughter's name, and she's a grown up woman with kids of her own now – she contacted us late last night with the story of what her mother had told her.

'She wondered about just keeping it to herself. Was there any point in telling anyone about what her father had done after all these years? But when she got to thinking about her dad being killed in suspicious circumstances, she decided to tell us what she knew.'

Thomas walked to the window and looked down to the warehouse floor. Neither man made any attempt to restrain him. Gareth Thomas was not the sort of man who was going to smash his way through a reinforced window and either attempt a dramatic escape or fall to his death on a concrete floor thirty feet below.

The only noise was a few shouts from the warehouse as a couple of youngsters loaded a pallet with drums of bitumen. Thomas watched as one of them jumped about on the pallet as the other got into the fork-lift truck driving seat. He rapped hard on the window and gesticulated at them to stop fooling about.

'I think you'd better tell us where Joe Tate's body is, and exactly what did happen on that Saturday morning,' said Kavanagh quietly.

'I need to phone my solicitor,' Thomas said picking up the telephone receiver on the desk.

FIFTY-TWO

On Thursday morning, at eight o'clock, for only the second time in just over forty years, a yellow earth-mover lumbered onto what had once been the rough, sloping ground of an edge-of-town meadow. Back then, marked by a solitary wooden stake with a cross-member, its boundary lines delineated by rope strung between posts, it had been designated plot number 33. And for the next several months the housing estate was built.

On this overcast Thursday, four decades later, it was not rope, but yellow and black scene-of-crime tape that was strung around the garden as the excavation began.

The neighbours behaved with due propriety, the heady excitement of the media intrusion of only a few days ago – doorstep TV interviews and brief newspaper celebrity – had passed. Now, once more, people withdrew behind their blinds and curtains or stood discreetly out of sight at upstairs windows and watched, wholly unobserved as the policemen and women began their gruesome work.

Where once, long ago, the big metal blade had uprooted tree roots and boulders and stones, red earth and clumps of meadow grass, today, as it rumbled over the still partly vandalized garden, it crushed in its wake hydrangea, rose and lilac bushes.

At eight fifteen, two boys cycled down the road, stopped for a few moments to take in the highly unusual scene, and then continued on to school, doing extravagant 'wheelies' as they went.

Thomas was able to pinpoint the spot exactly. The soak-away trench was precisely where he said it would be.

A mini JCB followed the heavy bulldozer onto the garden and began to excavate the first few feet of earth. The forensic team watched for an hour and then called a halt to the digging. Clad in their white overalls and slippers, they erected a protective tent and, every moment of the excavation recorded on video and by a police stills' photographer, they began the painstaking task of trowelling, brushing and chipping away at the compacted earth.

By noon, seven feet down, and entombed in his rock-hard shroud of solid mud, the first clawing finger bones of the skeleton of Joe Tate were at last rediscovered.

Scrivens, Kavanagh and Salt entered the tent to examine the sombre find.

Twenty-five years earlier, in Lindow in Cheshire, the body of an iron-age man was discovered in a peat bog there. Frank Kavanagh had seen the man's corpse in the British Museum shortly after its discovery. This man, too, had met a violent death and the detective inspector had suffered nightmares about his fate for many weeks after his visit.

The young foreman's gaping mouth – screams and pleas stifled by the mud that had killed him that day – reminded Kavanagh of that ancestor who had died two thousand years previously, and only sixty miles north of this spot.

'Two thousand years,' he murmured to Jane Salt at his side.

'Yes?' she said.

'They count for nothing when measured against this,' he said quietly.

Several hours later, young Joe Tate's corpse was finally disinterred.